PARIS NOIR

PARIS NOIR

EDITED BY AURÉLIEN MASSON

Translated by David Ball, Nicole Ball,
Carol Cosman, and Marjolijn de Jager

AKASHIC BOOKS
NEW YORK

Published by Akashic Books
©2008 Akashic Books

Series concept by Tim McLoughlin and Johnny Temple
Paris map by Sohrab Habibion

ISBN-13: 978-1-933354-63-7
Library of Congress Control Number: 2008925935
All rights reserved

First printing

Akashic Books
PO Box 1456
New York, NY 10009
info@akashicbooks.com
www.akashicbooks.com

Also in the Akashic Noir Series:

Forthcoming:

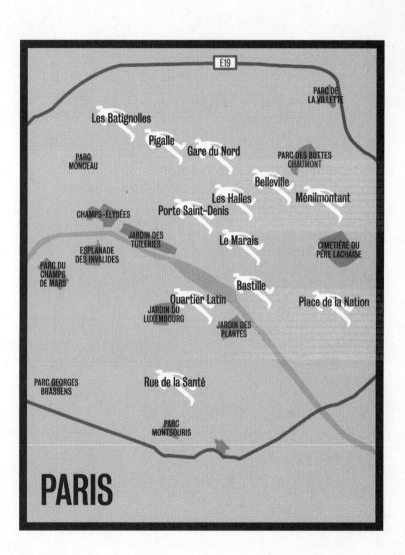

PARIS

TABLE OF CONTENTS

PART III: SOCIETY OF THE SPECTACLE

INTRODUCTION
ENTER THE DREAM

G ood to finally hear from you but don't forget to send me an introduction.

This e-mail from Akashic Books publisher Johnny Temple has been blinking on my computer screen for the last two days. But when I chose to work in book publishing, it was precisely to avoid having to write anything; I want to stay in the background, the way a bass player stands in the dark and smiles as he watches the guitarist launch into a wild solo.

I kept going around and around without a clue, like a mouse on its wheel, until I finally decided to visit Momo, the old guy who sells used books in my neighborhood. If Paris is still and always will be a "noir" city, it's in part because of Momo and his toiling colleagues, the dozens of small, independent bookstore owners who sell old pulp fiction from the '50s through the '70s. Amateurs meet every weekend and swap their own finds for new treasures. Momo's the one who trained me as a kid by handing me Goodis, Thompson, Chandler. So you can just see him going soft all over at the idea of the Série Noire making it to the American scene. We, the French, are good at importing things . . . but exporting is another story.

We're having a smoke outside the well-lit café, Momo and me. It's been eight months now that smokers walk around the sidewalks in circles like penitents. My first time in New York, I got a kick out of watching the ballet of smoked-out people moving in and out of bars. *Never in France*, I said to myself. But we French end up doing everything exactly as the Americans do, a few years later at best. So the time is right to include Paris in the Akashic Books Noir Series. Momo thinks, and rightly so, that I'm short of brilliant ideas, so there he goes drawing a historical picture of Paris, the city of crime. He tells me about the working classes, exceptionally dangerous, who peopled the belly of Paris in the nineteenth century, until the bourgeoisie kicked them out with big avenues and urban renewal under the reign of the late, unlamented Baron Haussmann.

Two beers later, Momo is on the Butte Montmartre with the gangsters of the '30s and '50s, the early days of junk deals, streetwise Parisian kids, and loud, foul-mouthed prostitutes whose slang could frighten even the bigwigs. The problem with Momo is that he loves beer and the more he's in love, the less clear his ideas are. He's now on to the filmmaker Melville, the actor Alain Delon (he's one of our specialties like unpasteurized Camembert), and sepia photographs.

But all of a sudden it dawns on me that practically nothing of this improvised lecture has registered, and I get all tense. No wonder you learn things in classrooms, not sitting on hard stools in cafés where the atmosphere is too bright (as in the famous "*Atmosphère, atmosphère, est-ce que j'ai une gueule d'atmosphère, moi?*"—Arletty's indignant response to Louis Jouvet in the film *Hôtel du Nord*).

Back in front of my insomniac computer, this is what I tell myself: The key thing to say is that Paris is a city that lives, and thus dies, every day. No point hiding behind history or war memories. What is a threat to Paris, to its noir dimension even, is potential "museumification," the possibility of the city turning into a big theme park. In Paris, after all, everything is still there. All you have to do is look around with eyes wide open. In the shadows of his big car, the chauffeur in Marc

Villard's story dreams about saving the love of his life, a prostitute stranded on the asphalt like a bird caught in an oil spill. Further up north, around the train station, Jérôme Leroy follows in the footsteps of a guy on the run with the feds at his heels, and the men in black aren't simply agents of the FBI. Concurrently, Salim Bachi lets us examine two young men of Arab descent who have a hard time fitting into a closed society; unfortunately, whether in Paris, New York, or Karachi, it's hard to resist the temptation of violence, always present, insidious, and sneaky.

And what about that Chinese guy, delightfully depicted by Chantal Pelletier? He thought he'd have a taste of the famous French cuisine . . . until he realizes that the choice dish will be himself.

Far from cliché postcard photos, we witness the revenge of the waiters along with Jean-Bernard Pouy: They go to a lot of trouble to locate an unknown jogger who has mysteriously stopped taking his daily run through the Place des Vosges and disappeared.

Everything takes place in cafés, not just Momo's beer-soaked history lessons. That's where the doomed lovers in this volume meet to secretly celebrate Christmas. Didier Daeninckx's reporter, an expert in tracking rumors on the Internet, was also seen for the last time in a café, before getting stabbed to death on rue des Degrés. But who knows, maybe those weren't actually rumors after all. And speaking of rumors, don't tell DOA that the violence of the Russians is only a rumor. Let him tell you about his precious girlfriend, a Russian model who loved diamonds too much to go unnoticed. Behind the fake jewelry and the glamour, the fashion world hides serious predators. Ask Layla, Dominique Mainard's heroine in "La Vie en Rose," if she really sees life in rosy tints. To her, life is nothing like a reality-

TV show; the budding young singer who dreamed of having top billing will end up very low on this earth. No Grammy for the young dreamer, only a body bag. Under its polished stones, Paris remains the place of daily tragedy; under the Parisian pavement, there's the Peloponnese. Like that son of Laurent Martin's coming back home after a long exile to find that you can't escape from your ghosts or from the love you have lost.

Beyond the lights, beyond the cafés and bars, Paris is sometimes like a grave. It's a city you run away from, or at least dream of running from. But on every street corner, the past jumps at your throat like a grimacing hyena. Patrick Pécherot will take you for a walk into the heart of the 17th arrondissement; in fact, the Gestapo were based in that area in the early '40s. Some would give all the money in the world to have a dead memory, but when your mind starts playing tricks on you, life quickly turns into a nightmare. Or into madness . . . Watch Hervé Prudon walk around the 14th arrondissement; if you ask him for directions, don't talk to him in English: You'll run the risk of having him answer, "No comprendo *The Stranger.*" My advice to you is to follow him without a word; take side streets, stroll with him along rue de la Santé, where you'll find a jail, a psychiatric hospital, and Samuel Beckett's last place of residence. Discover his magical Paris which exists only inside his head.

You don't inhabit your city, you dream it. All I can do now is invite you to enter the dream.

Aurélien Masson
Paris, France
August 2008

(Introduction translated by Nicole Ball)

PART I

CITY OF LIGHTS, CITY OF DARKNESS

THE CHAUFFEUR

BY MARC VILLARD

Les Halles

Translated by Nicole Ball

Vania

I wasn't too far from Les Halles, that's my fate.

Above the parking garage.

Right next to the Sunside with its tenor sax crazies. I'd pace the streets at noon along with the type of people who never work, but also Krauts smashed on beer and sluts from the Midwest.

Leather and lobotomy.

I'd walk on my shitty heels. The sexy black whore from Martinique. We worked our asses off, the pimps circled around, sold and resold the girls to each other; Alicia had even said to me, "Vania, give up the street, you deserve better."

Yeah, right.

In Fort-de-France, my mother didn't have a job so I'd send over piles of money to feed my two brothers. Incognito: She thought I was a nurse at the Hôtel Dieu hospital. I'd open my legs, I'd go, "Oh, honey, yes, yes," and the bread left for Martinique.

One fine evening, I was crying over my cup of coffee in a café on rue Montmartre when Mister K, the Halles dealer, planted himself across from me.

"You're depressed, Vania."

"I'm fucked. All my bread goes to my family."

"You're not a social worker, let 'em fend for themselves."

"I don't know what to do. Maybe I'll go back to the islands."

"I can help you."

"I can't deal anything except my ass."

"No. You'll be a mule. We load you with coke, you walk the street, my dealers come and get their stuff from your handbag."

"Ain't right for me."

"The guys don't risk a thing and the neighborhood cops know you: You're clean. Perfect for dealing."

I said yes.

The red lung of bars.

The crazy bums.

The buzzing junk.

Nothing had changed but everything was different for me. I was Mata Hari, the spy in mortal danger. The impatient street, the sweating butcher, everything was a problem. I had eyes in the back of my head.

And all the time I was at work with a john, while the guy crazy for ass grunted away between my thighs, my purse got hypnotized I'd stare at it so hard.

Mister K loaded me up at 7.

His three dealers would pick up their dose at 11, noon, and 5. Just like that, I'd double my month, buy clothes, white underwear for Sundays. The pimps knew I was on Mister K's team and left me alone.

I began heading down into the bowels of the metro to do K a favor. And once there I dove deep into the end of the night of drugs and sex.

Staggering corpses.

Crackheads.

Doberman fuckers.

The dregs of the earth were surviving in passageways abandoned by those who lived the real life. In that underworld, nothing was the way it had been before. The cops, for example. That's how I met Nico.

I had my own way of doing things under the C line.

Caches for deals.

Grungy mattresses out in the open for Peeping Toms.

The temperature could climb up to ninety-five so I'd work half naked. Then one morning this guy showed up. Curly dark hair, wrinkled suit, Hawaiian shirt. Very supple, with a springy, silent way of walking.

"Hi, Vania. I need twenty grams."

"You new here? Never saw you before."

"I'm Mister K's new little star. I show up and the market skyrockets. Come on, gimme the shit."

I hesitated. We were between two shifts and this guy turns up, all cool, like. Okay. I opened my purse, laser-beaming the place.

"Come closer and take two bags."

He clung to me, slipped his hand into my purse, and planted a Sig Sauer into my cunt.

"Don't move. You're busted, baby. Stone cold."

"You . . . you're not even a cop!"

He took his hand out of my bag and waved his card in my face.

Shit. Fuck.

Legs like cotton.

I thought of mom.

Of the smell of the slammer.

Of Mister K, of course.

Then Nico made me step back into a boiler room, confiscated my Prada purse, and threw me a mega-slap right on the cheekbone.

His body on mine.

His hands all over me.

His macaroni in a fury.

Our breath enraged.

I was pounding on him with my fists, he was ramming his gun into me. He managed to get off, but he had to suffer for it. We were looking at each other like two wild beasts in a den. I hated him.

"You raped me, you fucking son of a bitch."

"Whores can't be raped. I forgot to pay, that's all."

He took the shit out of my purse. Fifty grams in small bags. A smile like a worm.

"You busting me?"

"Don't know. I have to think."

"Hurry up, I have to change."

"Here. I got two solutions. I cuff you, you take a vacation at the Fleury-Mérogis big house and do some time there. Or I haven't seen a thing but you have to be real nice to me."

"You want to fuck me for free."

"No. I want my cut."

"On the shit?"

"Coke's over for you. Besides, it wouldn't look good for a narc-squad cop in the Saint-Denis sector to get his cut on shit. No, I want my share on the tricks."

"I have to support my family and I don't make much."

"Forget your family. I'm your family now, baby. Also, no more cheap whoring for you. Your black ass deserves better. It's your choice."

"Anything but jail."

He threw my purse back to me. I got up, my face all bloody.

"What do we do now?" I said.

"Nothing for the moment. My name's Nico Diamantis, I'll be in touch."

"Great."

I went back up to daylight. I was walking through the shady streets, heart in pieces, face smashed up. As I passed by the girls, they'd go like, "Jeez, Vania, you got beat up real bad." Right.

Mister K met me on rue des Lombards. I was so fed up I told him everything from behind my latte: the coke gone, Diamantis breathing up my ass, and the deal down the drain. He stayed calm; he's a guy from Lagos who shook hands with Fela Kuti when the Black President didn't have a clue about AIDS.

"You told me the truth, Vania. Relax, fifty grams isn't much. Do like this dirty cop says but watch your ass. I got a feeling it's not doing too well."

He slipped out into the night and I stayed there like an idiot whining over my future as a cocksucker.

Nico called me on my cell three days later.

"How'd you get my number?"

"I'm a cop, that's my job. Meet me in twenty minutes at Ciné Cité. First row of *The Three Burials of Melquiades Estrada*; move it."

He started to stroke my thighs when Tommy Lee Jones gets shot. Then he explained to me how I was to live from tomorrow on.

"I've figured the whole thing out. I'm gonna post your contact info up on the Internet. Contacts by e-mail only. After that I'll drop a card like, *Vania, all positions. Leave a message at* . . . to all the rich ones. I'll get you a second cell just for tricks; I have a pal at Orange. You give up the street, you buy yourself new clothes and wait for the john. You're like a star, see. You'll do home delivery but you'll limit pussy delivery to Paris. Not bad, eh?"

"Yeah. How much do you take?"

"I take everything and I leave you enough to live nicely."

"What? You're out of your fucking mind!"

"I had the coke bags analyzed, your fingerprints are all over them. What's that you were saying?"

Shit, shit, shit.

After that, I worked and shut up.

I bought my panties at Chantal Thomas: fifteen grams of muslin and tons of fantasies.

Sometimes I took the subway across Paris, other times when the dough came in big, I'd take a cab. Three weeks later, as I was leaving the duplex of a producer on rue de Ponthieu, I got beat up by two scumbags. The dough and my youth disappeared in five minutes.

Nico didn't like the fact that the bread had evaporated.

He got me a chauffeur.

Keller.

The six-foot, two-hundred-pound type. He looks like the killer with the pipe in *Charley Varrick*.

Keller picks me up at home, rue des Lombards, and drops me off at my client's place. While I'm performing, he waits in the car, smoking stinky cigarillos and catching neo-bop jazz on the radio. One day, before I got out of the car, I leaned over him behind his wheel.

"Hey, Keller, don't you get ideas, sitting in your Italian coach while I get screwed front and back by all these guys?"

"I try not to think about it."

I looked at his eyes. They were red and took great care to avoid turning toward me. I was such a jerk! The only guy ready to die for me. I put my hand on his forearm and pressed it for a while. Talking would have killed me.

This is all coming back to me tonight. Keller just saved me from the clutches of two Brazilian crackheads behind Beaubourg and we're catching our breath in the car.

"Don't take me back right away, Keller. Drive along the Seine for a bit."

Two a.m. We're gliding along near the Pont des Arts. The granola crowd: guitars and goat cheese. The Louvre, lopsided barges. I tap his shoulder when we hit rue du Bac.

"Stop here, I'm gonna have a smoke."

I get rid of my high heels and proceed barefoot on the bridge, sucking on a Camel. Keller, who's walking a little behind me, hasn't pulled his Davidoff pack out. The last tourist boat lights up the embankments.

Jolly Brits.

Autofocus Japs.

Nauseated broads.

Without turning toward him, I ask: "How long we been working together, Keller?"

"Six months."

"How does Nico control you?"

"I could leave."

"Why don't you then?"

He looked down at the water wriggling under our feet, black as a bad dream.

"I like the job."

We stare at each other for a whole century. I go on.

"I ride in a car, I get laid on gorgeous rugs, but I don't have much money at the end of the month. I can hardly support my family in Martinique with the money that bastard leaves me. I gotta get out of this mess, Keller."

"Turning tricks or Nico?"

"Nico first."

Finally, he lights up a cigar. I wonder what kind of first name he has.

"I know an honest cop. Well . . . I think he is."

"It'll go too far. The word of a whore against the word of a police captain, there's no way. I don't want this to be official, I don't feel up to it. I'm gonna think it over, I'll find something."

"If you need me, just say so."

"I know, Keller."

May 30 in this crazy city. Nico, flanked by his slave (Lhostis, two hundred pounds of rotten meat), honks at me on rue du Louvre. The central post office is closing, the regular folks are heading home. A couple of steps toward the black Picasso.

"Hi, Nico."

"Here's your share. You didn't work too hard this month."

"My period has been really bad."

"Right. I found you a mad scientist who wants to fuck while he watches Bambi on TV."

"Beats the Belgian guy and his snake."

"True. Hustle, Vania, I need money." Upon which, he makes a U-turn on the asphalt and disappears toward rue Montmartre.

I look inside the envelope and right there I feel like shooting that louse. Then I think of Noémie. His nice little wife.

Two kids, their hair nicely parted to the right.

Gerber baby jars.

Outings to the zoo.

The pleasant smell of cauliflower.

Sundays at Grandma's, after church.

I'm going to splatter his white paradise.

Next day. 10 a.m. Nico showed up at 2, blind drunk. He dragged me out of bed, put me naked on a chair, ass up. While he's fucking me in the ass, he yells filthy words in my ear, lacerates my back, switch languages, jabbers in Greek, shoots his come all over the place, and asks for a beer.

Okay. He just left. On duty at the precinct. So I run to the bathroom, take a shower. Black linen outfit, black shades, and a cab pronto to the Diamantis home in Neuilly, rue des Sablons.

Noémie opens the door. Nico showed me pictures: She's the freaking double of the ex-prez's wife. Anémone Giscard d'Estaing. Yuck.

"Noémie Diamantis?"

"Yes. Nico's not home."

"I know. I'm here for you."

"Can I ask who you are?'

"I'm a ho."

And I shove her back into her hallway decorated with Delft plates to die for.

"You have a really nice place, Noémie."

"But what—"

"Go take a piss, you're all red."

I sit down and take out a Camel. I love the smoke.

"I'm gonna give you the short version. Nico, your honey, improves his monthly paychecks and supports his family in Neuilly thanks to me. I fuck and suck, he gets the dough. As a bonus, he screws me in the middle of the night because you can't seem to get his Johnny up anymore, darling. I'm sick of the whole game, I need money, so tell your Nico that his wife is you, not me, and he should get off my ass. Am I making myself clear?"

A mask on Noémie's face. Chalk-white.

"Leave immediately."

One of the twins appears unexpectedly, in his Mickey Mouse pajamas and holding a broken Fisher-Price toy.

"Who is that, Mommy?"

"Nobody."

"I'm your daddy's breadwinner ho, sweetie. Okay, Noémie, I'm counting on you."

And I split, rather pleased.

Haven't heard from Nico for a whole week. Keller has a new car; we ride in a used Mercedes now. Cigar lighter and leather seats. I go visit lost souls on the Place des Victoires and rue Beaubourg. I have two clients working in advertising who survive in lofts near the Bastille. I drink Bordeaux, I eat Poilâne bread, and my butt is five pounds fatter.

Right now, we're on boulevard Sébastopol, driving toward Saint Georges. The john lives cheap in some building on rue Clauzel, fourth floor. Keller parks the car. 10 p.m.

"See you later, Keller."

"You know this guy?"

"No. Coleman, does that ring a bell?"

"No. I'll come and check."

No music in the elevator. Fourth floor. The guy who opens is standing in the dark.

"Mister Coleman?"

He pulls me inside, bangs the door shut, and I take a hit

that shatters my nose. The carpet is thick. From the corner of my eye, I adjust my vision and make out the big cop, Nico Diamantis, dressed in gym sweats. He leans over me, totally enraged, and slaps me a dozen times. I'm going to pass out.

"You showed up at MY HOUSE, you fucking whore! In my home, in front of my wife and kids, and you gave them orders! Who do you think you are, for chrissake, you're just a piece of meat with two holes. So shut your fucking mouth and remember who you are, *capish?*"

"You impotent fuck!" I stammer.

He picks me up, grabs my head, and throws me against a framed print. I crash against the glass, my face is all bloody, I can't see a thing; he catches me, rips my clothes off.

The carpet.

Blows.

His smell.

His fingers inside of me.

And then this, coming from the end of the world: Keller. I grab an ashtray, throw it at the closest window. The man's breathing like an ox, turns me over, and smashes my teeth with his brass knuckles. Something red bursts in my head.

And

I

Fall

Into

The

Black

Room.

The Others

At the sudden noise, Keller quickly raises his head. Fourth floor. Vania. He grabs his Beretta from the glove compart-

ment and, with his heart drumming, reaches the building in a
few strides. He swallows up the steps, hammers on Coleman's
door. Noise of running feet inside. Keller steps back and with
three kicks of his heel, knocks the latch free and rips open the
right panel. Everything is dark, but in the main room he trips
on a motionless pile of rags. He puts his gun away, leans above
Vania, and turns her over. Her face is nothing but a puddle of
blood. Keller, his heart violently pounding, leans lower. Listens to the young woman's heart. Then he turns away, his fists
clenched. A draft coming from the kitchen. The chauffeur
rushes there in a state of fury. The backstairs door is open.
He bends forward over the railing. Nobody. Now he goes back
to the street side, turns off the light, looks down through the
window, and sees Diamantis heading toward Saint Georges in
his nouveau-riche car. Keller comes back to Vania. Pulls his
cell out.

"Diego, it's me, Keller. You're still working at that clinic
in Poissy? . . . Okay, get a room ready and call the medics. I'm
on my way."

Then the man leans over Vania again. His eyes red, his
voice shaking. No one can hear him so he whispers against her
hair: *My angel, my love, my little girl.* He kneels down on the
acrylic carpeting, picks up the battered body, and after some
hesitation, leaves through the backstairs.

In a dingy room down in the basement of his precinct
house, Nico Diamantis throws a last slap in the face of a
local dealer.

"Dealing drugs is bad, Rachid."

"Fuck you."

The Greek raises his eyes to the sky, sweeps the legs of
the chair from under the teenager's feet, and kicks him re-

peatedly. The kid folds himself into a fetal position. Nico gets tired of him, turns away, and leaves, locking the door behind him.

Office. A thousand pounds of files. Lhostis, breathing heavily, walks toward him. Cholesterol and Marlboros. Tubular armchair.

"I checked the three neighborhood police stations like you told me. Nobody."

"The apartment?'

"I went in through the back door; she's gone."

"The morgue?"

"I called, they haven't seen a black woman in five days. You sure she was dead?"

"I'm not sure, no. I don't know. She wasn't moving and I left when I heard someone banging on the door."

"You're in deep shit."

"Thanks. You're a real help."

"What about the chauffeur, Keller?"

Now Nico is thinking. It's a painful task, he's not used to it.

"Yeah, I see. He's waiting in the car, she's not back, he knocks on the door, he knocks harder, and . . ."

"And what?"

"A hospital."

"No way. You think he's an idiot?"

"Sort of."

"A private clinic, Nico. We're gonna have to go through the whole phone book to find that stupid bitch. All this crap so you can show off in front of Noémie. I can't believe it."

"No one touches my family. Go on the Internet, it'll be faster."

While Lhostis is settling down behind his computer, Nico

looks distractedly at his files. Then thinks. Vania. The apartment. *I'm so stupid.*

He takes his jacket, goes down to the garage where the Picasso is dozing off. Two lines of coke on the dashboard. Wow, what a boost.

He rips the car out of the garage and steers for rue des Lombards. He doesn't see the Mercedes pulling out behind him.

Rue Saint Martin, Turbigo, then the underground parking garage of the Forum des Halles. He finally decided to rent a spot there year round to avoid getting depressed over the hunt for a space on the street. Third level, underground.

He makes a face.

Three
Homeless guys
Sharing
One
Muddy
Big Mac.

At the end of the second underground level, a hole between two Clios. He rushes in. Cell phone. A little kiss to Noémie then Nico thinks again: *I've got to find me a whore.* Okay. He gets out of the car, heads for the elevator. Keller, squatting behind the car to the left, dives into the cop and stabs him three times near his heart. For good measure he sticks the silencer of his Beretta into Nico's mouth and pulls the trigger two times.

Later, as he walks back to the entrance, he goes up to the guy who's been watching the poorly parked Mercedes. An illegal alien. He hands him a twenty-euro bill.

"See, it didn't take long."

* * *

An officer in uniform informs Lhostis when he arrives at the Saint-Denis precinct the next day.

"Lieutenant, Diamantis got whacked."

Lhostis freezes. So do the fatty acids.

"Shit, how?"

"Three stabs in the stomach and two bullets in the mouth. He's getting butchered at the Institute right now."

"Who found him?"

"A storekeeper from the Forum des Halles who was going to get his Clio. He was lying on the floor in the second underground level. The door of his car was still open."

"I smell a contract."

"Yeah, I agree. We're all with you to find the son of a bitch who did it."

"Okay, okay. I'm going over to the Institute, fast."

Lhostis is playing back the bad movie as he drives. Vania. Noémie. The botched killings. And now this. He's not too keen on playing the avenger. Nico, that stupid jerk. Well. Still.

Fifteen minutes later, in front of the dead meat in the morgue, he finally makes up his mind, pulls his cell out, and types in Noémie Diamantis's phone number.

At the Poissy clinic, Keller watches over the young prostitute. The upper part of her body has disappeared under layers of gauze. Magic pipes link Vania to a complicated set of digital machinery. A doctor in a white smock reminiscent of George Clooney enters the room. Spots Keller.

"Did you notify the police?"

"No. She's a prostitute."

"I know some honest cops."

"I don't. Can I sleep in this room tonight?"

"Ask the nurse. I don't know if she told you but this young woman will have to have reconstructive surgery on her face. Nothing is certain as far as the results . . ."

"I'll tell her."

"All right. I'll be back in five hours."

When Lhostis walks into the Diamantis home in Neuilly, the family is in mourning. Noémie dressed in a black Chanel suit. The kids in gray with white low socks. Noémie, furious.

"Spare me the condolences. He was cheating on me with a whore. In addition to whatever else he was hiding from me, stuff you know very well, it so happens."

"He was the father of your children."

"Thanks for the information. That's why Nico has to be avenged."

"Cops can't avenge anyone."

"Ten thousand euros might help you think about it."

Lhostis in the clouds. He's been wanting to buy a motor-boat to coast around off Marseilles for a long time now. At the moment, he's picking the color.

"Back to earth, Lhostis?"

"Five thousand now, five thousand when I deliver the man who did it."

"The woman."

"She couldn't possibly have killed him. She was very badly messed up. The chauffeur maybe."

"She's pulling the strings. Just get your ass out there and find her."

"I've checked all the hospitals in Île de France. I'm left with the clinics. It won't be long."

Noémie, bent over a small Regency desk, writes a check

and holds it out to Lhostis. The man and the woman stare at each other.

"How will you make it now with the kids and all?"

"My parents have money. It's not really a problem. Actually, yes, it is a problem since Nico always wanted to make money by himself. Which explains that prostitute. Destroy her."

Keller is in Vania's room, kneeling at her bedside. He presses the young woman's hand, and for the first time she's responsive.

She opens a swollen eye. Closes it again.

Keller, lost in a pagan prayer.

A storm is beating its knives against the windows.

Lhostis's computer has coughed up sixty-five private clinics.

Three cops in uniform helped out. Then, at 8:30 p.m., the news comes in: There is an unidentified young black woman at the intensive care unit at the Myosotis clinic in Poissy. Lhostis sends the cops home so as not to miss the France-Georgia game in the early rounds of the World Cup.

Now he's driving.

The dark ribbon of the forest of Saint-Germain stretches out before his eyes. His two combat knives are lying on the front seat.

He thinks the boat will be a fiberglass Beneteau, an excellent brand. White with blue trim and a Yamaha engine to propel the whole thing.

In Marseilles, the water is seventy degrees.

Here we are. The Myosotis clinic. Lhostis parks his Honda Civic in a nearly empty parking lot. The first floor is splashed by the light coming from the hall.

The cop puts on round glasses, a white smock complete with a stethoscope in the breast pocket, and hides a combat knife at his back, stuck inside his belt. The woman at the desk is not from Africa. She stops reading muck about stars in *Voici*.

"Doctor Granger. I'm in charge of Vania, the young woman you placed in intensive care."

"She's been transferred. She's in a private room now."

"I'm so happy. Doctor Varant told me I could come by and visit her this evening. Is that okay?"

"Certainly, doctor, but I don't have anyone to take you there. She's in room 24, on the second floor. Will you be able to find your way?"

"No problem."

The second floor is drowsy. In front of room 24, Lhostis grabs his knife, holds it tight inside his arm, opens the door.

Vania is lying in the dark. All wrapped up in bandages. Her mouth is free but her eyes are closed. The cop moves slowly forward, slipping the weapon into his hand.

Keller's Tokarev goes *plok* and its slug rips the policeman's left eye out. A splash of blood, the body sinks down. The chauffeur takes two leaps forward, catches the cop, and drags him to the sink. What he sees there under the light satisfies him. He filches Lhostis's wallet, then draws near Vania. He turns on a lamp that casts a subdued light. She's not asleep. Leaning over her, he runs his finger lightly across her lips. That mouth lets out a murmur.

"Keller . . . take me away."

The chauffeur nods, puts his gun away, and lifts the fragile body up in his arms. The rain has stopped, the scenery behind the window stands out sharply.

Keller knows an island far away, east of Sweden.

It rains all the time there and fish are a staple. For now, that will do.

THE CHINESE GUY

BY CHANTAL PELLETIER

Ménilmontant

Translated by Nicole Ball

I t's the last thing Luc said to me on his way out: "Don't be stupid, Sonia, take your pills." I nodded. I should have started my medication again but I thought I was stable and I was sick of gulping down all that shit every day. Outside, along our windows, the first hyacinths were cutting through the soil in their ceramic pots. We went out in the courtyard and I felt a surge of affection for the two cherry trees that were dying in front of the concierge's apartment and for the grass blades pushing their chlorophyll between the lopsided cobblestones. Even the faded look of the façades, I liked.

"Don't worry," I said.

He hugged me, or more exactly, I hugged him. That's how we were, us two. An inverted couple. I was taller, heavier. Luc had nothing athletic about him, and I had been a swimming champ as a teenager. Eighteen years later, I still had biceps, shoulders, and thighs to show for it. I think this is what Luc had liked: the masculine side of me. But that day, everything was over. Luc was leaving to face another opponent. We kissed on the cheek.

I watched him go. I knew I wouldn't take the time to get used to someone else again. Too much work, no more patience. As for Luc, he had started a new slalom without even bothering to train for it. So between the two of us, I was the one who smiled the most. Luc knew that by leaving he was doing a bigger favor for me than for himself. Which didn't prevent him from feeling guilty. That almost pained me.

He stepped outside the courtyard gate. I pictured him climbing into the overloaded van. He was probably feeling remorseful at that moment: He hated material problems. The inconvenience of moving was going to destabilize him for a long time.

I went back to my Greek salad dressing; I added some lemon and a pinch of ground oregano. I tasted it. Not bad. I entered the recipe, list of ingredients, and all the numbered steps into the computer. I named that banal escarole-tomato-feta-black olives salad *Greek Summer Salad*. As with everything else, a new title is enough to make an old recipe sound fresh.

Looking out the window, I saw that the cobblestones in the courtyard were less dark, the day brighter than during the previous weeks. Spring was on its way. I felt a kind of exhilaration, suddenly convinced that freedom and spring could be a beautiful wedding celebration if I wanted.

I had not decided to call Jérôme. *I'm fine, thanks!* Despite what Luc says, I'm polite, especially with my clients, and Jérôme happened to be my main one: I created most of the recipes for his magazine, *Foodgourmet.* Swamped as usual, more than usual even, he was negotiating the sale of a Chinese edition of his magazine to a publishing conglomerate in Shanghai, and given that he was capable of selling his soul cut up in little pieces to decorate key chains, he was going berserk. One billion three hundred million potential clients. Even a thousandth of that godsend would have been a fortune.

I knew right away he was asking for a favor. It took me

longer to understand what kind: For the last three days, he had been playing guide to a Chinese man. Devotedly, and for a good reason: He was the cousin of the guy he was dealing with in Shanghai! *But now, honestly, it's too much. Could you possibly take charge of this burden until 9 p.m. tonight in Orly when the cumbersome character flies off to Milan?* He gave me one of his *I'll make it up to you, the future of the company is at stake,* or, *I'm so overwhelmed by work, I'll pay you the equivalent of three recipes, you can't say no.* I said *no,* I couldn't say no.

Besides, taking a Chinese tourist around the capital wasn't worse than tinkering with recipes from photographs: If you used your imagination this could pass as a tomato, that as a Béarnaise sauce, and the whole thing as a slice of calf's head. Because that was exactly what my job had become: I looked at totally lame pictures of totally lame dishes and concocted plausible recipes from them. To tell the truth, you ended up losing your appetite, even me, and I do love to eat.

Without this new turn of events, I would have e-mailed him my autopsy of a salad and stayed home; so I printed my page without any qualms, all excited to go out and look spring straight in the eye.

I saw him right away as I was stepping into the offices of *Food-gourmet.* What a shock! My Chinese guy stood out against a lovely light and the greenery cascading down the slopes of the Parc de Belleville. In the background, misty Paris bowed down before such beauty, golden skin and turned-up lips, a true piece of China to which amber tea would have given the color of brown sugar. This is when I knew I should have taken my pills. I was losing it. And yet I wasn't really attracted to Asian men. Too smooth, not sexy at all. There was a kind of eunuch quality about them, I thought, although I had never checked the facts. I probably associated them with the servants in the imperial court of China, castrated so His Highness wouldn't have rivals under his roof. In short, I had no use for Chinese men. No, it was hoodlums who gave me my thrill: hairy hunks who fill out their shirtsleeves, display shoulders broad enough for two, thick arms and large, rugged hands, surly men who wheedle you into the underbrush with their tenor voices . . . But on that day, all of my prejudices evaporated. I would have needed heavy medication to restore my judgment which had quickly gone down the drain.

All melted, my legs like cotton, my heart sunk between my thighs and raging as if inside a nest of red ants, I had a hard time resisting the temptation to jump on him and eat him up alive, and yet I hadn't raped anyone in years.

This fellow smelled of strawberries, the kind you find in woods, not in supermarkets; it activated my saliva like crazy, a sign that I hadn't completely lost my appetite. His perfect lips flashed me an irresistible smile. The scoundrel wasn't scared: He had no idea of the risks he was running.

Jérôme came to the poor guy's rescue by grabbing my arm and whispering that he would reimburse all my expenses. I couldn't care less; I couldn't take my eyes off him. As soon as he stood up, I noticed the son of a bitch was terrifically built, not too thin but not paunchy either, strong, straight, good thighs and a nice piece of equipment that showed through his black, flowing pants. He even had shoulders and pecs under his dark blue jacket, and in his golden face, his big eyes were shining under eyelids that seemed painted with a brush. That creaseless curve was incredible! I had never seen such a thing!

He spoke a kind of kitchen English; I did too of course, so that was lucky. He was obviously pleased to stop posing as a piece of pottery in the lobby of *Foodgourmet*. I was eager to leave. I gave my Greek salad to Jérôme and grabbed the Chinese man. All he was carrying was a small bag; he traveled light, a real plus.

I made him walk across the park, just to show him that Paris had good green lungs and that the most beautiful city in the world had something else to show off besides the Eiffel Tower and the Sacré-Coeur. *Very nice!* It was indeed very nice. A group of Asian people were doing tai chi between forsythias in full bloom. They must have looked familiar to him. I explained that we were to leave his bag at my place first. What did he feel like doing after that? *As you like.* He shouldn't have said that but he had no way of knowing.

Eleven a.m. I had six or seven hours to get him in a stew. Whatever the recipe. I was ready to settle for something quick, cooked *al dente*. There, in the quiet of the park, I decided not to rush things, not to break anything. Nice and slow. Like a normal, regular woman.

At the intersection of rue des Pyrénées and rue de Ménilmontant, Paris was shamelessly exposing her underwear up to her Eiffel Tower garters; we let the lights turn green twice, the better to enjoy the strip tease. I was thinking of poor Luc, who was hurting his back as he unloaded his van. He really had no luck. I wouldn't have bet a dime on their happiness as a couple.

On the way down rue de Ménilmontant, my Chinese man was looking all around him, at the Arab grocery and butcher stores, at the bazaars. *Wonderful!* I realized that I shouldn't be counting on having poetic exchanges with him. A real advantage. He was nodding and smiling so much he seemed to be laughing all the time, with his plump mouth stretched out over China teeth militarily aligned. I felt pity for Luc—he was missing such an exciting show.

Near my place, the boarded-up buildings and the construction sites didn't exactly make for an attractive landscape,
but apparently he didn't care. As soon as we passed through
the gate into my paved courtyard, everything, the shrubbery,
the flowerpots, was suddenly more pleasant. He thought it
was *so cute!*

When he took off his jacket in the living room, I gave
in. His wild strawberry scent was unbearable. He agreed to a
cup of coffee so I made two small, very strong espressos and
I crushed five of my most potent pills inside his cup. He was
sitting on the couch, sipping his coffee without flinching. He
didn't last very long. After a *Very good, it's such a nice place*, he
fell asleep. Milan had gone down the tubes by then. I closed
the shutters, took off my dress, and delicately stripped the
product of its various cases so I could taste it. A pure delight.

When I got back from shopping at the Chinese supermarket
on rue de Belleville, he was still asleep, naked on the couch,
his hands and feet tied up, his big body well sheathed in his totally smooth, amber China skin. With just that small accident
of imperfect, slightly wrinkled flesh: his penis; a bit darker,
with a smallish hard-on between his thighs. He was a good
boy. He'd been abused for at least two hours but that hadn't
prevented him from having nice dreams. I was really lucky.

I put away my groceries, had a bite, and went back to work.
Munching on his earlobe, I could again verify that not only
did he smell of wild strawberries, he also had their taste. I was
sorry I had damaged him, though; his perfect lips were puffy
and were turning blue; I felt upset. For fifteen minutes I gave
him a hard time that left purple marks on his neck and a big
scratch on his left cheek. He was grunting in his heavy sleep,
his asshole looked sullen around a small, ugly rip. The guy was

not used to good things. I washed him with a baby wipe and put some ointment on it. I wanted him to last for a while. In that respect, I'm like any woman, I get attached fast.

At 4:00 a.m., exhausted, I rolled him over onto the wheelchair we had bought from the widower upstairs after the death of his crippled wife, when Luc had a badly broken leg. China was heavy but I managed to lay him down on the guest room bed. I had bitten his left breast so hard it had left a big bruise in the shape of a half moon. I did have good teeth.

I straightened the blanket on my little darling who was blissfully asleep; it almost felt like milk was rising inside my breasts, but I managed to get ahold of myself. I locked him up and collapsed on my bed.

Before taking a well-deserved rest, I remembered that it's never a good idea to fall in love with guys who are not your type; it always ends up badly and knocks you out for a long time. Luc, with his tiny build and sparrow voice, had been an exception to my professed fascination for hunks—an exception that had brought me bad luck.

I slept until 9 and had a dream about Luc in his wheelchair. An image which in fact represented the last stage of our love rivalry. A few weeks of recovery and I had been subjected to the whole spiel: lies, scenes. From one physical therapy session to the next, Luc had fallen in love with his physical therapist, and after that I seemed to him like a half-measure at best. He was wrong. My Chinese man, if he ever woke up, could testify to my energy to perform; I could do a beautiful job.

At 10, the breakfast tray was ready but he wasn't. He had trouble opening his eyes; they had completely shrunk in his swollen face, which was kind of yellow now. How old was he? Slightly younger than me. Thirty-two, thirty-three. But supposedly, Chinese people don't look their age. Maybe he was a fraud.

I slipped a basin under the blanket and grabbed his penis: "Pee?" I asked, in case he didn't understand.

I heard the gurgle and a wave went through my hand. Not bad. I shook his little hose before removing the basin. I think this made him feel good.

I lifted his head, brought the glass of water to his lips. He tasted it first, thought about it; he didn't trust me. I honestly couldn't resent him for that; he finally drank half of it but turned down the coffee. I could understand that. I pushed the croissant into his mouth and he ate all of it. Good: I had stuffed the carefully crushed drugs inside the dough.

He regained his spirits briefly and started to scream. I couldn't care less, no one would hear him; the widower upstairs had been in the hospital for the last three months, and the only window in the bedroom looked out onto a blind courtyard. Faced with my unruffled calm, he stopped and looked at the ceiling.

"I feel sick," he said in a blank voice.

"You'll be better soon," I replied with a shrug.

To tell the truth, if he kept on popping all the pills instead of me, chance was he wouldn't.

He closed his eyes. Not a fighter. Quite a fatalist. It's supposed to be an Oriental thing. Back in China, he was used to being mistreated perhaps. He was really calm for someone being held in confinement, I thought.

When I pulled the blanket off him and brandished the whip, he looked at me with an imploring expression, but pity is a feeling I loathe. And please, no bullshit: His dick was half stiff, and that never lies. He must have understood; he turned slightly to present his ass, or rather to protect his more fragile parts. His buns were a lot more fleshy than Luc's, who loved to be spanked, something I never refused him in fifteen years, something he couldn't complain about. The jerk should never have left, we had our little ways together, and that's not easy to lose all of a sudden, especially for someone unstable like I am, and when spring is on its way.

It's true, we were still very much in love, Luc and I. It was not like before, of course. Aside from the well-polished rituals we had established to relieve ourselves, we both kept twisting and turning to avoid any unnecessary contact with each other. Lips sealed in reaction to hurtful words, legs disentangled after sleep had unfortunately intertwined them, but we were used to it and that counts. So much dodging for some peace; marital art is a martial art, an art we had completely mastered: black belt, fourth dan. Okay even for KOs; we would crash painlessly on the tatami. The Chinese man hadn't exactly agreed to the situation so he was in pain. It's all in the head, I say! I thought he might be a bachelor and knew little about women. I hear they lack women in China.

When I had my fill of it, I felt very relaxed; I let him sleep and went to take a shower. Maybe I could keep my Chinese guy for a long time in that state—weeks, months, years even. Paris was a lot better than Milan, after all. All I had to do was feed him right and not mess him up too much. I could set up a TV and DVD player in his room to keep him entertained and then, little by little, he would learn French. That would at least be something positive.

I put on clean clothes. It was beautiful out; I watered my plants. I was happy that Luc let me live here. Our place was becoming *my* place, for years to come; that's what he had said and that was nice, he didn't have to. We had bought that first-floor apartment together fifteen years ago for pea-

nuts with a loan from the bank, and we had fixed it up ourselves, quite nicely. All I needed to do was pay the mortgage
every month. Nothing to worry about, I had the means, I
couldn't complain.

That's when I fell upon my man's backpack. As light as he
was. I found his passport. In Chinese, obviously. One hundred
dollar bills. A good-sized stack. It would be for our honeymoon. My honey bun had everything thought out.

All perked up, I sat down in front of the computer to play
with the keyboard a little. I had a message from Jérôme: *Attached are three recipes to return to me before this evening, baby.
Was everything okay yesterday? How was he?*

Great guy, I answered. *You'll have them back very soon.*

I clicked on the pictures. The first one was easy. A vegetable casserole. String beans, peas, carrots. I already had the
recipe stored in my files. All I had to do was print it out. Same
for the chocolate cake. The third one wasn't so simple. I finally
settled for veal shanks with mixed vegetables. I wrote down
the recipe card from memory; I was used to it. I sent everything via e-mail by mid-afternoon. Jérôme would be pleased.

I made myself a cup of coffee and finished some leftover
lasagna. I even treated myself to a little serving of raspberry
sherbet. The veal shank stew had obviously whetted my appetite. I thought it would be a good idea to cook such a typical
French dish for my little sweetheart. He'd like that.

So I went to rue de Belleville, near the Jourdain metro
station, to the best butcher in the arrondissement.* I bought
organic potatoes, carrots, turnips, and string beans, then I got
a great cheese assortment at a cheese store that takes quality
very seriously. My backpack was totally full when I walked
back down rue de Belleville; I made a stop at a Chinese

*Paris is divided into twenty arrondissements, which serve to delineate municipal
administrative districts within the city. The arrondissements are further subdivided
into four administrative quarters, each of which with its own police station.

grocery—it wasn't very hard to find as they're all over the neighborhood—to get three cans of Tsingtao beer and some candied ginger.

When I came back home, not a stir. I got busy in the kitchen, humming away while I cooked. I may be a little rough sometimes but I have to admit that there's nothing more sat-isfying in life than concocting fancy meals for a sleeping man. In fact, it felt as if we had already reached the pearly gates, my Chinese man and I. And that Luc who wanted me to take my pills! He was really screwed in the head!

I hadn't had so much fun cooking in a long time. Every-thing was coming back to me: the exhilaration of the move-ments, the elation that smells and flavors give you. I had lots of fun cutting the vegetables into identical little cubes. I was using a ceramic knife Luc had brought back from Japan for me. Light as a feather and sharp as a razor blade. Asia sure was showering me with presents!

While the meat and vegetables were cooking, I stirred up a mixture of chocolate, butter, and ground almonds which I poured on the pieces of candied ginger scattered on tin foil, and I put the concoction in the fridge. Ginger is an aphrodi-siac, it's a well known fact; same for the sage I had stuck inside the meat. The evening was promising.

I set the table with special care as if for a picture. The tablecloth, the matching napkins, my best set of plates and glasses . . . I had even bought two bunches of daffodils, the first of the season. I trimmed two candles with my Japanese blade and stuck them into the candle holder Luc's mother had given us. The effect was fantastic, a true promotional ad for *Foodgourmet*. I was already missing my big teddy bear; quick, quick, I gave myself a vague facelift in the bathroom and went to see him . . .

Lying there on his bed, my loverboy was still a little sleepy, two narrow slits where his eyes were; as soon as he saw the Japanese knife, he opened them as wide as dessert plates. No reason to get upset, though, as the object was not much bigger than a steak knife, but impressive because it was very pointed, a real hole puncher. To show him I didn't mean to hurt him, I sat down by the side of the bed, and scraped my knee with the tip of the ceramic blade, at the hem of my checkered skirt. Beads of blood formed right away; very carefully, I traced a thin red line, a C, meaning Chinese, since I didn't know his first name. The result was very delicate but failed to reassure him. I tapped my heart to show I had feelings for him. He didn't seem to believe me, so I even came up with *I love you*. He must have thought I was out of my mind.

But with one thing and another, my veal was running the risk of sticking to the bottom of the pot. I clapped my hands, *Come on, let's get moving, let's go*. He stood up, staggering; I pushed him under the shower, he didn't respond. He was taking things the right way, the Asian way that is. Zen is Japanese, but they say that the Nippons stole everything from their neighbors of the Middle Kingdom. So Zen has to be Chinese.

I washed him with an almond milk shower gel that smelled very very nice. I was having a terrific time. It's absolutely true: When a man's hands are tied up, his penis becomes more important. He was being very sweet about letting me take care of him and we actually got along rather well. The poor man needed to acquire some experience: What one learns is always beneficial.

I dried him up with a bath towel that had been well heated on the electric towel rack. I dabbed all his little wounds with Q-tips soaked in hydrogen peroxide, smeared some ointment wherever it was needed, rubbed arnica on several bruises. I slipped one of my silk bathrobes onto him and combed his hair. He seemed happy. I was in seventh heaven.

When he saw the nicely set table, he was taken aback; he was probably sick of sleeping. I could read fear in his black eyes hidden under his slanted eyelids. The way experience can make an inexperienced man mature is absolutely spectacular!

I shook my hands frantically, like a mute, so he would understand once and for all that things were over, definitely over: The script was different now. *Sleeping finished, now eating.*

"It's very good food, you'll see! Wonderful French food!"

I went to the fridge to take out the hors-d'oeuvre plates: two slices of duck foie gras from the Gers, along with toast and a slab of fig jam on the side. I removed from his plate one of the slices of toast, spread the smooth paste on it, added a little bit of jam, and took a bite to show him there was nothing to be afraid of. When I brought the slice of bread to his lips, he gulped it down. On and on like that through the whole meal. But I allowed myself pauses so I could get some nourishment too; generosity has its limits after all.

He was going like *Mmm, very good, great.* And honestly, the veal was a complete success; I had slightly spiced it so my darling would feel more at home and it turned out to be a brilliant idea. I pushed forkfuls of meat and vegetables into his mouth. We had found a satisfying rhythm. He was as handsome as when we had first met, his wild strawberry smell lingering on despite the aromas of the meal and the almond-milk scent of the shower gel. My cute little soldier had a strong personality he hadn't clearly revealed yet. But Luc was wrong: I could be patient.

My man had absolutely gorgeous hands and arms. I hadn't seen such perfection up close since Eric, the young swimming champion in the 200-meter freestyle I had abused in the locker room. I had gotten into all kinds of trouble because of that, including being fired from the Swimming Federation and one year of scandalous chemical straightjacket. They talk about human rights for men, but what about the rights of women? No one gives a shit about them.

He accepted coffee without me dipping my lips into it first. Trust had been restored. It just goes to show, it doesn't take much. Then we settled on the couch with small glasses of brandy. He let me do the job. At times, I even seemed to catch a flash of wonder in his weary eyes. *A great cook makes a great lover*: I knew the proverb and I was able to verify how surprisingly true it was.

At 3 a.m., having had my fill, I took him back to his room, certain he would sleep: I had fixed his second glass of brandy with three pills.

As I was going to bed, I thought I recognized the same feeling of ecstasy I'd had with Luc at the beginning of our relationship. Spring had come. I had no doubt about us being able to form a happy couple. Such a thing does exist, whatever they may say; pushing your luck a bit is all it takes.

The next day, I washed and checked my e-mail. No news from Milan. I felt reassured; it's always when everything is going smoothly that the worst happens. I know that well.

I fixed breakfast. When I went into the bedroom, he was asleep. I didn't want to bother him; I just stayed there and watched my little angel without a peep, without pulling the blanket off the bed, an inch away from being the submissive woman, lost in admiration before her man and scared to death at the idea of disturbing his sleep. Finally, I couldn't stand it any longer and my hand shot out. Maybe I wasn't completely stabilized yet.

When he woke up, I was holding his penis firmly in my right hand, with the tip of it in front of my mouth like a mike, and I was singing, *Stranger in the night, I'm so excited* . . .

He gave me a funny look. Okay, I don't sing very well, it's true. I put an end to my recital and gave him his breakfast.

In the bathroom, I filled the tub with water warmed up just right and added a Chanel N°5 bath gel. A pure delight! I sat him up on the edge of the bathtub, what with his feet tied up and all . . . Then *splash!* I was wondering if I would join him right away when the doorbell rang. Bummer!

After the first moment of panic, I decided I wouldn't open the door.

And then: "Sonia, it's Luc, open up, I know you're there!"

Locking and bolting the door had been a good idea. I had to, our home was his home after all.

"What the hell are you doing?" he yelled as he came in.

And who says *I'm* not polite? Not even *Hello, thank you,* nothing. The poor guy wasn't doing so great, actually. He sat down on the couch; there was this scent of wild strawberries and I was wondering when he would notice, but he didn't care; besides, I had already forgotten: Luc has no sense of smell!

"It's all over with Georges!"

What? Over with the macho physical therapist who gave him such beautiful bruises? I had never believed in their story, actually. A massage that turns into marriage, that can't work. So what that I knew it for both of us—it didn't help!

"Any way we look at it, Luc, we can't make it work. We're too different," I said in a soft woman-victim tone of voice that went with my white blouse . . .

"I'm coming back, Sonia, I'm moving back tomorrow . . ."

"Oh! That won't be possible!"

"We have no other choice, Sonia. This is my home."

"It's too late!"

"And why's that?"

"There's someone else in my life!"

He looked at me like *Keep talking, don't even think I'm gonna believe you.* What chutzpah these guys have! They always think that girls are incapable of managing without them. That girls are only good for whining and for begging them to come back home. Boy, did he have the wrong scenario!

"Stop that nonsense, Sonia. You took your pills, right? I think you're weird."

That was pretty incredible! The guy I had was more handsome, younger, fresher. He had traveled thousands of miles to jump into my arms. He was now relaxing in my bathtub, fragrant with Chanel N°5, and the guy who'd just been dumped was putting on macho airs and acting as if he had recently killed the wooly mammoth to save his tribe! The jerk had spoiled my babe's bath! There are limits, after all, limits I cross with gusto, and when I scream, it gets pretty loud.

"Get the hell out of here, you schmuck! I have someone else in my life now, so fuck you, asshole!"

I was starting to turn red. He remembered what that meant so he left, slamming the door behind him.

I remained in the middle of the living room for a good while, just to calm down; even when you are stabilized, sometimes certain people are good at making you fly off the handle. Leaving me for a physical therapist? You had to be really dumb. Being dumped for a man and not for a woman wasn't actually as tough, but . . . I failed to see the connection! What with one thing and another, I was getting all mixed up. Too many things were happening to me in too little time. I had reached the point where I needed a pill. That was smart! Luckily, there was no risk of an overdose as I had only one pill left in my last bottle. The Chinese man had eaten all of them.

As soon as I opened the bathroom door, I was struck by the absence of the wild strawberry scent. Chanel N°5 had punch, true, but still, I was scared. And rightly so: The foam was all alone in the tub, with no Chinese head sticking out. I saw red. Gone? No, he was all slumped in there, white in the red water. My poor baby! I grabbed his head; the stupid idiot was looking up at the top of his head. I pulled him up some more: The handle of the ceramic knife was sticking out of his stomach which was pouring red into the Chanel N°5 . . . Some people sure know how to annoy you! Why go through so much trouble just to die when it's the one thing nobody can escape from? Because really, he did go through a lot of trouble to find that fucking knife and put it through his stomach without swallowing it first. I thought this hara-kiri stuff was Japanese but as it turned out, even that was Chinese!

I was disappointed. To put his honor above my delicious dishes, really! You had to be mentally defective! It didn't make sense. You can't leave such a dangerous thing lying within the reach of children. Even I wouldn't have left the knife just anywhere! I saw myself in retrospect cutting my knee and then . . . then, I totally lost it.

But stay cool! The present was complicated enough, this wasn't the time to get caught in the past; I had to think of the future. My ex would be showing up the next day with a full van. Great! He was going to like the Chinese guy all right. I hesitated. Should I let them do their dirty business together and go on a honeymoon all by myself? I had the money. I could go far away. To Shanghai even. They lacked women there. Okay then, I was on my way! On the other hand, I wasn't sure I was really stabilized, so big trips were not particularly recommended in my case. I felt I was turning red: Worries always make my cheeks glow. I found the prescription in the drawer of the nightstand. Luc was right. I had to start taking my meds again.

It was still nice out. One of the cherry trees thought it was young again and was brandishing its first flower. It's only normal to have your sap rising a little in the spring! You'll get treated for a little while and that'll be that! But I had to admit once and for all that Chinese guys were exactly my type.

Before going to the drugstore, I ran into the kitchen and swallowed the last pill. The guy sure had done a great job.

BIG BROTHER

BY SALIM BACHI

Quartier Latin

Translated by David Ball

M an, it stinks in here."
The commuter station at Saint-Michel did stink. Sour smells slithered along the corridors looking for their prey.

"Let's get outta here."

They were ugly, dressed ugly, but they didn't give a shit, or at least that's what they wanted you to think. Had to pass unnoticed, melt into the gray mass of the buildings in the projects. They didn't change when they went to Paris. They were dressed in war clothes, psychiatric ER style. Watch out, high-voltage box! White Nikes, Sergio Tacchini tracksuits, international class. They were untouchable!

"Your ID!"

Not so untouchable. The cops lined them up against the tile wall of the corridor and began going through their pockets. Then they opened their backpacks. New shoes inside.

"You stole them!"

"No, officer. They're ours."

The younger guy even took out a receipt. One of the cops sniffed the paper as if he'd wiped his ass with it that morning.

"Yeah, sure. Buncha thieves, fuckin' Ayrabs."

The Ayrabs didn't bat an eyelid. Nothing. So little reaction the cops wondered how to stir them up more, let's have some fun. Too bad, really too bad we're not in the middle of the Algerian War anymore when you could pitch the sand niggers into the Seine, not far away, right next door. For these policemen, no doubt October 17, 1961 was a happy day: four hundred towel-heads in the Seine, outta sight! Okay, times change and so do certain methods. But you can still get in their face, make it psychological. But here, nothing doing. You could feel them up, no problem, they were like sheep, the sweat-heads.

"Leave the women alone, Robert. Can't you see they're shy?"

The cops laughed and walked away, waddling on their big feet like belly dancers.

"Actually, *they* are the women," said Big Brother.

The two guys closed their bags and walked to the exit on the Seine side. It was raining out. They walked along Quai Montebello for a bit, across from Notre-Dame cathedral. The elder spoke to the younger in this way:

"You see, Rachid, never, ever play those assholes' game."

"The po-*lice?*"

"You got it. Guys like us turn them on. Gandhi understood all that."

"Gandhi?"

"What school did you go to?"

"Yours."

"Gandhi thought force couldn't accomplish a thing. All it did was legitimize the violence of the occupiers. The cops— they're our English, get it? And we're the Hindus."

Rachid did not understand. In any case he obeyed Big Brother, did like he told him. It had always paid off and it was a lot simpler than getting your head twisted with stories of Indians and English. This guy was an enigma. Sometimes he'd go on for hours about stuff way over your head. To Big Brother's credit, it had always paid off, you gotta admit.

"Do you know, Rachid, that we're in the old student quarter—the Quartier Latin, if you prefer?"

"I don't prefer shit. I don't like nothin'."

"Don't be negative. And you know why it's called the Quartier Latin?"

He had no idea.

"Because in the Middle Ages they talked Latin here and only Latin. All the literate men in Christendom spoke to each other in Latin. Do you know who lived across the river, behind Notre-Dame?"

"..."

"The monk Abelard lived near the Quai aux Fleurs. You heard of Heloïse and Abelard, Rachid?"

"Never."

"Abelard was the son of a Breton aristocrat who gave up his birthright to learn to philosophize. Since the Notre-Dame cloister was getting too small for him, Abelard broke away from his masters and founded a school on the Montagne Sainte-Geneviève. His scholars followed him. He was young, handsome, and very eloquent. At night he would walk down the Montagne to the Seine and return to the house of Canon Fulbert, where he rented a room. The canon had a very beautiful niece, Heloïse. She became Abelard's studious pupil. Naturally, she got pregnant. Abelard married her, but the canon thought he had been betrayed: He hired some thugs to break into Abelard's room and castrate him."

"Castrate him?"

"Cut his balls off, man. Abelard retired to a monastery and Heloïse to a convent. They wrote each other love letters for years. But it was all over, you understand."

And Rachid did understand, for once. He loved Miquette, who would often give him blowjobs in the basement of his building. He went wild when she licked his balls, there, a little lower. Can you imagine having them cut off? He could imagine this guy Abelard suffered a lot after that, alone in the basement of his monastery writing letters to Heloïse. The story also taught him to watch out even more for Miquette's father, the Fulbert in an undershirt who walked his German shepherd through the project every night before going out for a good chat with the crime squad so he could tell them about his Algeria, the one during the war. Her old man didn't talk Latin; he growled at his mutt in French, blew his nose in a dish towel, and gave Rachid dirty looks when he walked by the door to their building. If he had any idea that his daughter and Rachid . . .

"Let's keep going, okay?"

Rachid was beginning to like it there on the banks of the Seine across from Notre-Dame. He lacked the knowledge to put a date on the gothic building. Contrary to Big Brother, Rachid didn't read books. He listened to NTM, Tupac Shakur, 50 Cent, Dr. Dre, and Snoop Dogg, but he never opened a book, no way.

"You know who killed Tupac?"

"Society, Rachid, society."

"They say he was still alive in his producer's car."

"Now he's dead. Mozart is dead too. One day you'll die. No matter how, you will pass away. There are more dead people than living on this earth, Rachid. And Tupac is part of the multitude now."

"But the imam in the projects says that on Judgment Day we will rise from among the dead."

"Who's *we*?"

"Muslims."

"How about the others? The Jews? The Christians?"

"I don't know."

"For Jews, Christians and Muslims are dead for good and they won't rise up at the end of time. According to the Christians, Jews and Muslims are damned because they have the bad luck not to be Christians. And for some Muslims, the Jews and Christians are going to burn in hell to the end of time."

"So they're all wrong?"

"Maybe they don't have the same god. Maybe there'll be a war of gods at the end of time. Ever think of that, Rachid?"

"You're blaspheming. There's only one God. The imam says so."

"The Jews and Christians say so too. So tell me why you're not a Jew or a Christian, Rachid? And why Christians and Jews aren't Muslims?"

"You're driving me crazy, for God's sake!"

"And what about the others?"

"What others?"

"Buddhists, animists, atheists, agnostics."

"They'll go to hell along with the Jews and Christians," Rachid decided.

"That's a lot of people. We'll be in good company in hell."

"Impossible."

"If the god of the Jews is right, we'll burn in flames, because neither of us are Jewish. If it's the god of the Christians, then we'll go to hell with the Jews."

"Allah is the one true God."

"One chance out of three, Rachid, once chance in three. It's mathematical."

"God doesn't play with dice!"

"Einstein thought the same thing, Rachid. May He hear you both! Besides, maybe it isn't the same one."

Big Brother began to laugh as he looked at Notre-Dame over there, so near, and so far away. Sometimes seagulls would fly up the Seine and get lost. They were having fun too, in a way, they were playing as they flew over the work of Maurice de Sully and Louis VII. An endless project; its construction was still going on. It seemed to him that generations were disappearing into the limbo of history, into the nocturne of memories.

"What about people before us, Rachid? What do you do with the Arabs from before Islam? Will they go to hell? Mohammed hadn't taught them Allah existed yet. Mohammed himself didn't exist yet. What do you do with those men, Rachid?"

"They're dead, that's all."

"That's a lot of dead people, don't you think?"

They crossed the quay and entered rue du Fouarre.

"Fouarre means straw."

Big Brother had already gone on to something else. Rachid was still on their discussion about God and his worshippers. It was bothering him some. If Big Brother was right, then nothing made sense. But Big Brother must be wrong, no doubt about it.

"Straw Street. Funny, isn't it, how the streets of Paris always have a hidden meaning, a new story. Here they used to cover the street with straw so the students could sit down on dry spots to take their classes. The whole street was covered by those studious people. It was closed to traffic. And if a cart happened to go through during the classes the monks were teaching, the students would beat up the driver and they'd dump his load on the ground. To avoid fights, the city authorities would close the street off with chains. Classes began in the morning, after mass. Since bums would come and sleep on the straw at night, they had to kick them awake before they changed the straw for the students in the Middle Ages. Hence the expression *the last straw*."

"How d'you know all that?"

"Books. Man's best companions."

Now they were walking along rue Dante.

"Dante is supposed to have lived here after he fled Florence."

"Florence?"

"Shit, man, you really should get out of La Courneuve from time to time!"

Big Brother traveled a lot, crazy as it may seem. He had disability papers that allowed him to take the train free and gave him discounts on most airlines. He had been wounded in Sarajevo while defusing an antipersonnel mine. At eighteen, he had joined UNPROFOR and was sent to Bosnia. After he was discharged, he lit out for Italy, as he told Rachid, who'd never been out of the projects of La Courneuve: The only Italian he knew was *pizza* and *spaghetti*. What's more, he got bawled out by Big Brother whenever he cut his pasta before he gulped it down.

He had traveled, he said, to set his mind aright after the horrors of the war. A kind of convalescence. Rachid couldn't really remember all the places on his journey. But he did know Big Brother had a disability card. And he was very discreet about his war injury. He never talked about it. When Rachid insisted, Big Brother would tell him to read *The Sun Also Rises* by Hemingway. But Rachid never opened a book, everybody knew that. Actually, that was the problem. If Rachid had the slightest bit of interest in anything written, he would have understood his older friend a lot better. But since hanging out with Big Brother had always paid off, Rachid just said forget it, even if his ignorance could fill the Seine.

"In 1309, Dante leaves Italy. He comes here, to Paris, to attend the lectures of Sigier de Brabant. Right here, on the straw of rue du Fouarre, he absorbs those *odious truths, demonstrated with syllogisms.*"

Rachid was feeling the pangs of hunger. A sweet, heady aroma of kebab was tickling his nostrils: The only truth he managed to put into a syllogism was not at all odious to his belly.

"I'm starving."

"One should have an empty belly and a light mind." Big Brother began to recite, in a loud voice, right there in the street: *"Is this the glorious way that Dante Alighieri is called back to his country after the affliction of an exile that has lasted almost fifteen years? Are these the wages of his innocence, obvious to one and all? Is this, then, the fruit of the sweat and fatigue of his studies? Never will the man who is an intimate friend of philosophy suffer the disgrace of being chained like a criminal to be rehabilitated! Never will the man who was the herald of justice, and was offended, accept the idea of going to his offenders as if they were his benefactors, to pay tribute! This is not the way to return to one's homeland, father. If you or someone else can find a way that does not blacken the reputation and honor of Dante, I will take it, without hesitation. If there is no honorable way to see Florence again, I will never return. What then? Can I not see the sun and stars from any corner of the world? Can I not, under every part of the heavens, meditate on the truth, the most precious thing in the world, without becoming a man who has no glory, dishonored in the eyes of the people and city of Florence? Even bread, I am sure, will not be lacking."*

Big Brother fell silent.

Big Brother was born and grew up in Algeria, in Cirta. When he was ten years old, his father, an immigrant he had never known, sent for them, his mother and him, to come live on the outskirts of Paris thanks to the new policy of family entry. Ever since then, he'd always felt exiled: Hence his excessive love for Dante and Joyce, his pantheon of the banished.

Above all, he was drawn to lives that had been ripped away from their childhood, broken by political events, wars, famine. Or simply alienated through an absence of attachment to the environment where they were born and grew up, a bit like Joyce fleeing Dublin, which had become too narrow for his genius. He himself felt that France had become a suit that restricted his movements; this explained his enlistment in the army at eighteen and then his flight to Italy, a copy of *The Divine Comedy* in the pocket of his khakis.

"To return to our conversation, you should know, Rachid, that Dante put men with no religion in Purgatory, that antechamber of Paradise. And do you know where Mohammed is, in *The Divine Comedy?*"

"No."

"In hell! Even Averroës—Ibn Rushd to us—the second Master after Aristotle, is in Purgatory, ahead of our Prophet. You see, Rachid, you have to relativize things. Always relativize."

Big Brother liked to talk. He would hold forth whether or not Rachid was following what he was saying. In fact, he kept himself somewhat aloof in the projects. He didn't hang out with anybody and was utterly discreet about his little trips back and forth to Paris. Naturally he needed Rachid as a foot soldier, but the boy was kind of simpleminded: Only the neighborhood imam had any concern for him. The other kids his age made fun of him and kept him away from their business—making little deals, stealing motor scooters, taking night joyrides that let them extract a little pleasure from their sordid lives between the huge buildings of the project where the only flowers that sprouted from the asphalt were the ones they smoked at night when they hung out and bullshitted for hours.

Now they were walking down rue Dante. They reached boulevard Saint-Germain and took it toward boulevard Saint-Michel. They went into the McDonald's at the intersection, waited a few minutes in front of the registers, and ordered two combo meals from the sexy student in a red apron. They walked upstairs with their sandwiches, fries, and drinks.

"The girl behind the counter, you think about what her pussy must smell like?"

"Rachid, I've already told you not to be vulgar."

"She must smell of french fries and grilled meat. I wouldn't want to stick my nose in it."

"No one's asking you to, you know."

Rachid got out his cell and began tapping on the keys, which lit up and gave out musical notes as he typed.

"What the hell you doing?"

"Sending a text."

"Who the hell to, for chrissake?"

"My lady."

"You out of your head? We're on a job here!"

"I ain't gonna tell her where we are. She's working too."

"Where's she work?"

"At the Quick on the Champs."

"What about her? She smell of fries too, your Dulcinea?"

"Dulcinea? You raggin' on me?"

"No. Or, if you prefer, yes. Show me the message you're sending her."

Miquette huny I digon u big i swair. Will call tonite. Mebbe ur oldman take da dog out. We fuk inna seller. I eat ur apricot. Take shower first. Kisses monamour.

"Rachid, that's poetry! You should write more often. Miquette must be happy."

"My Big Mac's gonna get cold." He pounced greedily on the two-story structure of bread and meat. He gulped it down with gusto, not forgetting to add the mushy, smelly fries. He drowned the whole thing in a quart of icy Coke. He punctuated the end of his meal with a resounding belch that made Big Brother flinch in disgust.

As for Big Brother, he hadn't touched his tray. Ate like a bird, Big Brother. Skin and bones. Dry as a reed. A thinking reed. Who didn't know if he should laugh or cry over Rachid and his lovelife. Over Rachid's life, whose squalor did not escape him. Over the garish, dirty light that permeated the cardboard set of this restaurant, a food factory for all the poor bums in Paris. And over the confused tourists with no place to go, lost *en el corazón de la grande Babylon*. But he wasn't going to cry about their lives. That's the way they were. Okay.

Often he missed his childhood under silvery skies, at the edge of a sea that seemed infinite. And the shimmering of the waves, bursts of sun under the steel blue. But wasn't that just a mirage that hit him in front of these walls covered with Keith Haring reproductions? Little stick figures holding hands on the piss-colored yellow. Imitation leather seats and formica tables had become his world, unique, impossible to steal from. There was nothing to take away. You could die here with no regret, he was sure of this.

He grabbed his bag, stood up, and walked to the restroom. Inside, he locked the half-door and began taking off his tracksuit. Underneath, he was wearing a suit jacket and flannel pants. He opened his bag and took out the new shoes. A world apart from the Nikes he stuffed into his bag with the tracksuit; once he was out of the restaurant he'd throw it away. From the pocket of his Hugo Boss jacket he pulled out a club tie that matched his light blue shirt. When he came out of the bathroom he no longer looked like a young guy from the projects, but some kind of yuppie, almost.

"Your turn now," he said to Rachid.

The same operation witnessed the transformation of Cinderella, but this time the princess had balls, and whiskers on her chin.

"You might've shaved this morning."

"I forgot, Big Bro, I swear to God."

Mickey D's is a very good place for this kind of metamorphosis: You could stand in the middle of the room, unzip your fly, and jerk off without stirring up the slightest ripple in the public. The people who eat there become deaf and blind, concentrating only on their pouch of ketchup or mayonnaise, sort of like the subway, where the greatest indifference is the norm. One of the rules of this kind of place is to never stare at anyone. At most a glance out of the corner of the eye, but no staring. If you scrupulously follow this one rule, you can easily bump off a stranger and get away without anyone remembering your face. That's why Rachid admired Big Brother. He had the gift of identifying the dead spots of modern society.

They went out. This time, they walked along boulevard Saint-Michel. They almost decided to follow boulevard Saint-Germain toward Odéon. But something held them back. Some obscure commandment. Almost as if someone far away was laying out the lines for them to follow, the border not to cross. Big Brother often thought he was merely the protagonist of a story told by an idiot, full of sound and fury. It was probably his reading that blurred his judgment. He often had the feeling that life, his life, was burning in the forests of the night.

They crossed rue des Écoles, kept going up boulevard Saint-Michel, walked by the Collège de France without a glance, not far from the spot where Roland Barthes was run over by a milk truck.

"He let himself die."

"Who?"

"Roland Barthes. He was in mourning."

Rachid had no idea that a man had written books here, taught students—loved some of them—and died because he couldn't bear the loss of his one love: his mother.

Big Brother did not have great esteem for his parents. He blamed them for not preparing him for this life. He had to learn everything by himself, and he had begun late, too late no doubt. He got his education after the army, during his long wanderings through Europe, with his backpack and soldier's pay for all baggage. The pay wasn't much more than an empty promise. But it still enabled him to buy books.

Yes, his parents had been imported from a foreign country; they'd been used by the huge industrial machine and then crushed, like an old version of a computer program.

But their children had never been part of the program. They had proliferated like errors in a line of code. The change in centuries hadn't caused the big computer crash, the huge worldwide bug, but a few individuals who became adults at that time had quite simply tripped out in their corner of the world. Of course, not all of them had gotten on the American Airlines plane one morning in September 2001, but most of them had taken risky paths across the world, since the huge machine had spread over the whole planet, using people like simple material, interchangeable and disposable, just as it had used his parents.

That, he couldn't explain to Rachid. How to explain that the rich no longer needed to import the poor to keep their factories going since they'd now set up the same factories in their own countries—work at home, you might say.

"If you're not part of the solution, you're part of the problem."

"Uhh . . ."

"Malcolm X."

They stopped for a moment in front of the Place de la Sorbonne. Where once again, no doubt to make fun of him, Big Brother gave Rachid a lecture.

"On rue du Fouarre, every house was a school. But how could they house all those people who were piling up on the straw during the day and wandering around looking for a place to stay at night? So they created colleges! They were a dormitory, a shelter, and a cafeteria all in one. Robert de Sorbon, Saint Louis's chaplain . . . May he rot in hell, King Louis. Robert de Sorbon received a house near the Baths from the King. The man took in sixteen poor students who were studying for their doctorates in Theology. That's how the Sorbonne was born, on the very same spot as this late nineteenth-century complex, which is quite ugly, with a seventeenth-century chapel in the middle of it that is quite lovely. Cardinal Richelieu is the one who gave the Sorbonne that magnificent chapel, in which he is buried. A masterpiece of classical architecture."

Big Brother was playing tour guide, pointing to the façade of one of the most famous universities in the world. As for Rachid, he was watching the female students who were coming out of their last classes of the day.

Night had fallen and only the cafés around the Sorbonne lit up the square where these long-haired enigmas were walking by. They intrigued Rachid.

Blondes, brunettes, redheads, tall ones, small ones, some wrapped up in warm clothes, some undressed in spite of the cold or because of the cold, with pink cheeks—they flashed by, their legs like rockets, flashed by like mercury to catch their bus, or to get swallowed up by the Metro, to disappear forever from the face of the earth for at least one night; for the next day, with the first gleam of light, these early-blooming bouquets would swing into motion again, stems in the morning wind.

Rachid was beginning to have a poetic soul. Was he getting all emotional from the contact with Paris, the City of Lights? Were Big Brother's lectures beginning to bear fruit?

As for Big Brother, he didn't give a shit about women, cared for them about as much as his first VD, which he got at fifteen from the wife of the super of his building, avid for youth and exoticism. Since then he'd had no time to waste on all that. He didn't even have the means to do it anymore.

They stationed themselves in front of the first building on rue Gay-Lussac at the corner of boulevard Saint-Michel. Big Brother played the keyboard of the access code box, the big door opened, and they moved into the lobby. A friend in the post office who owed him one had given him the code. Life is hard for those men of letters and a little white powder livens up the deadest days. And then, everybody knows a mailman's salary doesn't cover the needs of a runny nose and a brain above it in withdrawal.

The superintendent wouldn't be in, his cokehead friend had assured him. And it was true.

Big Brother looked up a few names on the mailboxes. He pushed a button on the intercom and waited. Nothing. They shouldn't hang around too long, he knew. He tried another name. Silence. Then a crackle. He heard a sleepy, slow *Yes*, no doubt the voice of an old woman.

"Package for you, madame."

"At this late hour?" said a suspicious voice.

"You *are* Madame Hauvet, aren't you?"

"Yes."

"Special delivery, madame."

"Fourth floor, first door on the left."

The glass door gave out a shrill sound and opened.

They took the ancient cherrywood elevator. A little seat was folded up against one of the walls. There was hardly any room for Rachid and him. They hoped nobody had called the elevator on the second or third floor. It had already happened once. Big Brother had to look at his shoes without saying a word for a few seconds which seemed like centuries.

The car rose, then stopped at their floor. Nobody else had called it.

A second miracle was waiting for them on the landing: The door to the apartment had been opened for them.

What was the point of all those armored doors, codes, intercoms with cameras, if you let your guard down at the last minute, when the danger was at its height?

They walked into the apartment and closed the door behind them without a sound. They heard the old lady asking them to put the package on the table and leave.

Big Brother and Rachid did not have a package to put on the console table with a Carrera marble top. They weren't about to leave the apartment either. Instead, they walked down the long hallway and entered a huge living room, to the great displeasure of the lady; her snow-white, carefully waved hair undoubtedly displayed the finest art of a very chic hairdresser.

"Ah, you probably want a little something?"

The woman got up, lifted her bag, and took out a purse. She opened it in front of them without noticing that they were not dressed like delivery men. She pulled out a five-euro bill and handed it to Rachid. He seemed the most approachable, perhaps because of his youth.

"We don't want a tip," said Big Brother, walking toward her. "We don't want your charity."

The voice that had uttered these words was sinister. The old lady realized this and her mouth opened wide.

"Whatever you do, madame, don't scream."

He showed her his hands and closed them in an oddly gentle way, as if they were already squeezing the woman's neck. Then he motioned to Rachid, who walked over to their prey and began unwinding the string they'd bought in the Everything One Euro store a little further down the boulevard. He tied her hands behind her back, laid her out on the couch, and then tied her ankles together. They did not gag her.

"If you yell, you're dead, you get me?"

The woman nodded, her mouth open and empty. Something couldn't get through, the words remained stuck in her throat.

Big Brother walked out of the living room to explore the rest of the apartment. He went into a big kitchen and walked over to the counter. He opened a drawer and took out a large knife. Then he headed to the end of the hall, opening all the bedroom doors. In one of them, in the back, near the bathroom, he made a discovery that seemed to him, all things considered, rather natural. He came back to the living room and spoke to Rachid in a low voice.

It was Rachid's turn to go out. He crossed the hallway, passed by the kitchen, saw a second living room full of ugly vases and statuettes, then walked into the bedroom darkened by royal-blue cloth covering the walls. His eyes had to get accustomed to the lack of light to finally understand why he had to be there.

At the same time, Big Brother was pacing up and down the huge room with the knife in his hand, examining the paintings on the walls, the little Native American figurines, and even a Berber vase he picked up from its stand.

"That comes from Algeria," said the quavering voice. "You can take it if you like. I'll give it to you. It's my father . . . You know, he loved that country. We had property over there."

Big Brother put the vase down and walked up to the paintings.

"Jean Dubuffet," he said, pointing to a portrait; it was highly simplified, almost mad—broken lines traced by a child of genius.

"You can take that too, you can take everything."

Madame Hauvet was getting more and more restless on her couch. She was coming back to life. She thought she had identified a ransom. Everything would be all right again soon. He would take the painting and go away with his horrible sidekick. Perhaps she would offer him a few trinkets and it would all be over with.

"It's fine right where it is," Big Brother answered. "I won't touch it. These works have a soul, madame. They belong to no one. They should be in a museum. And museums should be free."

She didn't understand: These drawings belonged to her

and she could wipe herself with them if she wanted to. Her ransom had been devalued by those stupid words. These guys were total morons!

"You see, madame, I was sent to Yugoslavia during the war."

"Oh! It must have been frightful," she said, feigning great compassion. "You must have suffered a great deal."

"Me? Oh no, don't worry. But the Bosnian farmers, yes. They suffered a great deal, as you say."

He stopped talking for a moment.

"Have you read Dante, madame?"

"When I was young. How boring!"

"Too bad," he said, very curtly.

She was sorry she'd given her opinion about Dante. She had almost forgotten she was at their mercy. At *his* mercy. He terrified her. He was not like the others. Not like the ones you see on TV. The ones who had burned cars for two months. Those people were far from her world, far from her. This one was getting too close to be harmless, like the sun to the earth. He was in her home! In her home, my God! She'd been so dumb she felt like crying.

He interrupted her thoughts and began speaking again.

"Yes, madame, hell exists. I saw it with my own eyes. I saw it in those devastated farms where everything had been looted, destroyed, trampled on. I'm not talking about human beings, I'm talking about objects, madame, just objects. Believe me, they have a soul. Like you and me."

He was preventing her from thinking. He was trying to distract her—worse, he was lecturing her. He horrified her now.

"So leave the paintings and take my jewels, take all of them. They're in the safe, behind the Dubuffet you like so much. The key is stuck to the bottom of the frame."

She was on the verge of hysteria.

"That is not very prudent, madame. Anybody could find it there."

Rachid came back into the living room. He wasn't alone anymore. When she saw him, Madame Hauvet began blubbering softly.

"Silence!"

He was accompanied by a pale girl. For Big Brother, she seemed to have come out of a Modigliani. For Rachid, she was just kind of skinny and tall. Above all, she was scared to death.

Her whole body was trembling, her eyes still foggy with sleep. She couldn't be more than sixteen.

"That's my darling granddaughter!"

The old woman was sobbing now.

"Shut the fuck up!"

She stopped sobbing and Big Brother turned the portrait over, removed the key, and opened the safe. Inside, an ebony box: He lifted the cover. Necklaces, bracelets, several pairs of earrings. He examined the contents under the light of a lamp and closed the little box of black wood again.

"I thought I could trust you," he said. "You're really disappointing me."

"I don't understand . . . no, I don't understand."

But she did understand. The jewelry was fake. That's why she wasn't protecting it. The Dubuffet was a copy as well. Big Brother knew that too. But he liked to give any human being a second chance, even a third one. In Bosnia he had learned that men and women in some places never even got the slightest chance.

He walked up to the old lady, turned her over on her belly, grabbed her hand, and cut off her little finger with the large knife. He threw it onto the white carpet. A spot of blood began flowering like a rose. He had stuck her head into the couch cushion to stifle her screams.

Rachid hardly had a chance to hold her up in his arms—the girl who looked like a Modigliani model fainted. He laid her gently out on the carpet.

When the old woman stopped moving, Big Brother turned her over so she wouldn't get smothered to death. When she came to, he said, "Now let's stop playing games. Where are the jewels?"

The old woman was trying to speak through bloody lips. She had bitten them out of pain. Pink bubbles welled up in her mouth and exploded on her chin. Big Brother had to put his face up close to hear her tell him where the jewels were.

He got up and this time walked over to a little writing desk. He ignored the only visible drawer, kneeled down, and stuck his head under the desk. He groped around and found it. He slid a little wooden panel and the precious objects tumbled onto the carpet. He picked them up and shoved them into the pocket of his Hugo Boss jacket. What cop would search a man dressed like him? Especially if he was coming back home in a taxi.

"I have some bad news," he said to the old lady. "My friend and I cannot allow ourselves to be recognized. By anybody."

"Oh my God! Oh, my God! I beg you. Please, I'm begging you. Let me live, please! I won't say a word. I swear to you. I'm imploring you. I don't deserve to die."

"No one deserves to die, madame. And yet, one day or another . . . And just think: You have lived well up to now. You have never wanted for anything."

"I implore you, for the love of God, take *her!* Take her. Take my granddaughter. Isn't she beautiful? You'll like her a lot, I'm sure of it. Please, please don't kill me. I don't deserve it. I'm giving her to you, take her!"

This kind of reaction no longer surprised him. It was, after all, a very human reaction. An old she-bear would have reacted differently, but not a grandmother.

"She deserves to live too," he said very gently. "She's so young. Consider what a long way she has to go in life. All the good things she can do for humanity. And believe me, I know something about humanity."

The old woman began to spit blood.

"She'll be of no use to anybody. She's a slut. A lousy bitch. She's, she's . . . she's a whore, that's what she is."

Big Brother had heard enough and took care of the old woman.

The girl was still lying on the carpet, languid as an odalisque. She was beautiful. And she was sleeping like a princess in a fairy tale. Big Brother was happy she hadn't seen all that. He was happy for her. Perhaps she would even sleep through her own night, a night without end, a night without glory.

BERTHET'S LEAVING

BY JÉRÔME LEROY

Gare du Nord

Translated by Carol Cosman

1.

Berthet and Counselor Morland are having lunch at Chez Michel on rue de Belzunce. Berthet and Counselor Morland have ordered fricassée of langoustines with cèpes as their first course, and grouse with foie gras as follow-up operations.

It's autumn.

Berthet and Counselor Morland are men of the world *before*. Berthet and Morland favor only restaurants with seasonal products, and Berthet and Morland still believe in History, loyalty, and things of that nature.

Berthet and Counselor Morland know that they are out of step, but that's just how it is. Berthet and Morland were born before the first oil crisis, and Morland way way before. Berthet and Morland are among those Europeans over forty who've been spared the microchip submission implant.

It would never occur to Berthet or Morland to find a temperature of twenty-seven degrees Celsius normal on the third of November.

It would never occur to Berthet or Morland that the market economy and its related carnage are not one big lie.

It would never occur to Berthet or Morland to eat sandwiches standing up or to listen to MP3 players plugged directly into their brains.

Berthet and Morland are informed of the coming end of
the world.

Sometimes Counselor Morland jokes. This is rare for
this high-ranking operative; also Protestant. Very rare. But
it happens.

"Berthet," Morland says, "I have a mistress who's not even
thirty, and you know, sometimes I feel like I'm gonna find myself in a USB port instead of her pussy."

Berthet says nothing. Berthet is nervous. Berthet does not
know Morland's mistress and Berthet is not even sure Morland has a mistress.

What Berthet knows about Morland:

he has a cover as a European bureaucrat;
he has a tall, fuckable wife who teaches philosophy at
    the French high school in Brussels;
he has no children;
he has twenty-five years' service in The Unit, at a very
    high level;
he has a predilection that does him credit for the liter-
    ature of the unlucky, forgotten '50s writers Henri
    Calet and Raymond Guérin;
he has a slightly less honorable predilection for the
    complete repertoire of the singer Sacha Distel;
he's Berthet's boss;
he's a good guy, almost a friend.

"What's wrong?" Berthet finally says. "It's not like you to
talk pussy."

"The Unit's ditching you," says Morland. "They're after your hide. And fast."

Before the fricassée of langoustines with cèpes, Berthet and Morland had ordered a bottle of champagne as an aperitif. Drappier brut, zero dosage.

Berthet and Morland are eating some excellent charcuterie and drinking the champagne, which actually tastes like wine—something always surprising in a totally ersatz era.

"When?" asks Berthet.

"Say what you will," says Morland. "When they start making pinot noir with this kind of expertise, there's almost hope for the survival of the human race."

"When?" repeats Berthet, who agrees on the zero dosage and the pinot noir as a sublimation of the vinous quality of the champagne and who even enjoys it, but who's nevertheless somewhat upset by Morland's information.

"When what?" says Morland, who pours them each another glass of champagne. "When are they going to kill you or when was the decision made?"

"Both," says Berthet.

Berthet might say, *Both, mon général,* as the joke goes in the French army. Except that it wouldn't be a joke. Morland is a one-star general, though not many people know it, and he probably hasn't worn a uniform in thirty years. Morland's cover is counselor to a European Commission member in Brussels.

Berthet and Morland look at each other.

At Chez Michel, you always feel you could be in the provinces. Rue de Belzunce is calm—a small, clean, narrow tear in the continuum formed by the Gare du Nord, boulevard Magenta, and rue Lafayette. The setting is pure Simenon. Berthet has never liked Simenon. Morland always has.

"I'm going back to Brussels on the Thalys train—come with me. We'll plead your case . . ."

"That way, you'll just have an easier time bumping me off."

"You're making me sad. I'm risking my life to warn you."

They finish the champagne, the charcuterie. The fat of a Guéméné sausage relaxes Berthet, reassures him for a moment about the possibility of his body's enduring power, almost as much as his 9mm Glock in the shoulder holster and his Tanfoglio .22 in its ankle case.

Berthet doesn't answer. Berthet asks for the wine list. A blond waitress comes over. Berthet gets a hard-on. This is a sure sign. Death is on the prowl. Berthet concentrates on the choice of a white to go with the fricassée of langoustines with cèpes. Berthet decides on a Vouvray. Dry. La Dilettante, from Cathy and Pierre Breton.

The blonde says it's a good choice, and Berthet wants to tell her that he'd be glad to eat her pussy.

"You'd be glad to eat her pussy, right?" says Counselor Morland.

Strange and specific kinds of telepathy exist between men who have been together a long time in close contact with state secrets and violent death.

Berthet thinks he's going to die. Berthet knows he's going to die, or is about to. The sudden hardness of his dick is a somatic sign that never fails to warn him. An even surer sign than Morland's announcement.

Berthet gets hard for anyone, for anything, when death is near.

This began when Berthet was twelve years old, well before Saint-Cyr Coëtquidan military school, well before The Unit. His grandfather was being buried in a village in Picardy.

They'd had to take a train, from Gare du Nord to be precise. Berthet was as sad as if he were the one who had died.

Getting out of the taxi with his parents, Berthet had looked up through the rain at the statues with big boobs on top of the building. The statues represented international destinations. The ones lower down, in front of the vast windows, represented more local destinations. Their boobs were not so big, of course. Berthet had preferred the international ones. The big-boobs cities.

Cities where Berthet would go later on behalf of The Unit—London, Berlin, Vienna, Amsterdam—cities where he would manipulate, destabilize, lie, torture, assassinate, and cities where after all this, he would fuck desperately, seeking out women who resembled those statues, women huge, massive, firm.

To get to his grandfather's funeral, they'd taken an old mainline train with sleeping compartments. Berthet, distraught by the first death in his life, had spent his time walking annoyingly back and forth past his sobbing mother to go jerk off in the train car's toilet, mentally replaying to the rhythm of the tracks the images of the railway caryatids, their hard breasts, their arms against the gray sky.

When they buried his grandfather in the rain, which played its role perfectly in that cemetery on the outskirts of Abbeville, Berthet wept hot tears because he liked his grandfather, but also because his martyred prick was bleeding a little and he was afraid it would show on his black corduroys.

At the time, the Gare du Nord didn't look like an airport you'd take to fly to the fourth dimension, a platform for freaks bound to the parallel worlds of dope, an accelerated state of homelessness, and social death. Their medieval-looking faces, their ulcers, their missing teeth, their foul smell of mass graves, their barely articulated speech, all of this was like living blame for thirty years of failure on the part of the welfare state.

At the time, the trains at the Gare du Nord were not designed for high speed, for the exclusive use of global elites. Blue, gray, Bordeaux trains, phallic enough to make a Lacanian laugh out loud. And from these trains, men and women pour every hour now, looking busy with their laptops, their cell phones, their bodies full of benzodiazepines, antidepressants, alcohol, come, shit, and the latest figures marking the return on their investments in start-ups in Amsterdam or Copenhagen. Their bodies full of all these things, but not nicotine. You've got to draw the line somewhere: Cigarettes stink and smoking can kill you.

At the time, to intervene between those two mutant species, the Gare du Nord did not have mixed patrols of soldiers and uniformed cops, which always makes you think a coup is not far off. Besides, at The Unit, they know that a coup is never far off, that perhaps one is happening at this very moment, though no one knows it. A postmodern coup.

At the time, there were no battalions of special riot police either, transformed into ninja warriors meant to make the new market gap materialize once and for all—a digital divide to the end of time, unbridgeable, an end of the war of all against all. Neck-protecting helmets, opaque visors, Kevlar vests, padding at the joints, walkie-talkies constantly crackling.

And Berthet thinks that he has never liked the 10th arrondissement, and the Gare du Nord even less, the Gare du Nord as:

antechamber of the coup
prelude to civil war

back room of electronic fascism
warehouse of the death trade
laboratory of the apocalypse

Once again, Morland is telepathic: "When I arrived from Brussels a little while ago, I said to myself, walking along the platform, that everyone is now living in a permanent state of emergency and everyone thinks this is normal. No one can even remember what this place was like only twenty years ago. Better they don't, or they would seriously start to panic."

Morland interrupts himself. Morland burps from the charcuterie, but discreetly because Morland is a high-level intelligence bureaucrat, a classy one, not a bum.

"Fucking hell, Berthet, they're really after your hide at The Unit . . ."

The blond waitress brings the bottle of Dilettante.

Berthet is still hard, Berthet tastes. The Vouvray is perfect, heartbreakingly perfect, even when you know that The Unit is ditching you and drinking wines like this one cannot go on much longer.

"You know why?" Berthet asks.

"Hélène. Hélène Bastogne," says Counselor Morland.

They bring the fricassées of langoustines with cèpes. Berthet and Counselor Morland sniff.

It's like a forest in autumn by the sea.

And then the windows of Chez Michel explode.

2.

Berthet is lying on the ground. The fricassée is all over his suit. Berthet sees:

Morland, his skull topped off like a soft-boiled egg,

holding his glass of Dilettante halfway to his
  mouth;

the well-endowed blond waitress, who has no more
  face but is still standing with a bottle of Châteldon mineral water in her hand;

the other couple who were having lunch at Chez Michel, quite dead, their shredded heads on their
  plates of grouse with foie gras, still tempting despite two manicured feminine fingers, cleanly cut
  off, lying on the meat;

a cat right next to his face, a cat meowing as if to express its displeasure, but a cat that Berthet can't
  hear.

Berthet is thinking two things:

first, cats are not democrats, which must be a vague,
  Baudelairean reminiscence;

second, I'm deaf because of the explosion. Probably a
  defensive grenade. They're going to come back to
  finish the job. Shit. Shit. Shit.

Berthet gets up. Berthet stinks of langoustines and cèpes.
Berthet is annoyed. Berthet has a romantic notion of the last-
ditch stand. And it does not fit the image of a man in a ripped
Armani suit that smells of langoustine.

Hélène Bastogne, what do you know?

A car somewhere blares its antitheft alarm.

Counselor Morland's topped-off head is dripping into the
Dilettante from Cathy and Pierre Breton.

Barbarians. Bunch of barbarians. To do that to a practically unadulterated wine.

A motorbike makes a half-turn at the end of rue de Belzunce. Two guys in helmets. Petty subcontractors. The Unit subcontracts now, like any other big firm in the private sector. It's pitiful. The driver of the bike leans against the buttress of Saint-Vincent-de-Paul church before skidding to a halt.

The passenger pulls the pin out of a second grenade.

Fucking subcontractors, I'm telling you.

Professionals would have stepped right into Chez Michel, come up to Berthet and Counselor Morland's table, shot them simultaneously through the back of the head with low-caliber weapons, like the Tanfoglio .22 against Berthet's ankle.

Farting noises. By the time everybody has reacted and understood that the strike wasn't really a stroke, they're far away.

Come on! Stupid temps. Even The Unit has accountants now. Even The Unit is into budget cuts. Part-time work in the intelligence services. Assholes. Berthet knows that he's living in a system in which, even on the day the world ends, there will be guys complaining about deficits.

Berthet takes out his Glock. Berthet puts a clip in the barrel. The nondemocratic cat is still silently yowling at him. Berthet would have liked to be sure the bullet is properly in place. You can always tell by the sound, but Berthet is still deaf.

Berthet opens fire. Berthet does not hear the irritated gunship-like noise the Glock lets out.

Berthet hits the grenade-throwing passenger first. Who is theatrically thrown off, who falls, who explodes all by himself on the pavement of rue de Belzunce.

Then Berthet changes his line of fire.

Then Berthet shifts into a new target acquisition phase.

Then Berthet thinks: *Motherfucker!*

Then Berthet punches holes into the driver's helmet. Four times.

The bike wobbles, the body rolls over, the bike keeps going on its side and stops at Berthet's feet.

Now the enucleated waitress is sitting on the banquette, the Châteldon water is spreading, the Châteldon water is fizzing on the moleskin seat.

Counselor Morland is still and forever waiting for the nervous impulse that would allow his arm to bring the glass of Dilettante to his lips, which move spasmodically.

Berthet understands that his hearing has returned when Berthet hears:

the yowling of the reproachful cat;
Counselor Morland humming Sacha Distel's song "La
    Belle Vie" through a reddish mush;
the bike's motor running in neutral;
the police sirens.

Hélène Bastogne. Shit.

And to think that Berthet missed the grouse with foie gras.

Berthet puts the Glock back in its holster, gulps down the last of the Dilettante directly from the bottle.

And Berthet takes off.

Hélène Bastogne.

3.

Unlike Berthet, Hélène Bastogne loves the 10th arrondissement. Hélène Bastogne lives there. An apartment on Place Franz Liszt, beneath Saint-Vincent-de-Paul and the charming little Cavaillé-Coll park. Not very far from where Counselor Morland is almost done spilling the top of his skull into the

Dilettante, where Berthet rushes out of the carnage scene and heads toward the Gare du Nord.

Hélène Bastogne is an investigative journalist, and like all investigative journalists Hélène Bastogne is being manipulated. Hélène Bastogne does not know this, but even if Hélène Bastogne did suspect it, Hélène Bastogne doesn't give a damn because Hélène Bastogne is going to come.

The solution would be a novel, thinks Hélène Bastogne. There is a blue sky out there. A novel in which Hélène Bastogne would tell everything. The blue November sky and the wind in the trees of Cavaillé-Coll park.

Hélène Bastogne concentrates on the cock inside her. A novel would be the solution for a number of problems. But Hélène Bastogne does not know the names of the trees. Hélène Bastogne regrets this. Actually, a novel would solve nothing. Hélène Bastogne feels the cock inside her getting soft.

Hélène Bastogne is going to come.

Let's hope he doesn't come before she does. The cock belongs to Lover #2. Lover #1 is a graying publisher from rue de Fleurus. Lover #2 is his editor-in-chief. Lover #2 has come to check on Hélène Bastogne's work. Confessions of a secret service guy. Lover #2 has promised to take her to a new bar on Canal Saint-Martin. Hélène Bastogne doesn't know the name of the bar. Hélène Bastogne doesn't know anything right now, except her oncoming pleasure.

A novel. A novel that would speak of pleasure, of the wind in the trees whose names she does not know. Of the bars along Canal Saint-Martin, of the 10th arrondissement, of Lover #2's prick, Lover #1's prick too.

Hélène Bastogne is going to come.

Lover #2's prick is regaining some strength. Or perhaps it's because Hélène Bastogne, who is riding it, has slightly changed her angle. And that's better for him. Don't go soft, please, don't go soft.

Explosive confessions, as they say. The guy came to the paper two weeks ago. The guy was wearing a beautiful Armani suit. Forty-five at most. Soft eyes, deep voice, close-cropped hair. The guy began to talk.

Wind in the trees, wind in the trees of Cavaillé-Coll park, still. The top of the one Hélène Bastogne sees through the large window is moving to the same rhythm as Lover #2's cock.

Hélène Bastogne is going to come.

The guy might have been a good lover too. The guy said really interesting things in this preelection period. From the Ivory Coast to the riots in the projects just outside Paris, the true, bloody poetry of secret intelligence.

Names too.

Then he left. Then he came back the next day. And he said really interesting things again, the game with the dormant Islamist cells, the journalists abducted in Iraq, and he gave names again, and numbers.

Hélène Bastogne is going to come.

Things come and go, which is normal in a consumerist society. The wind in the trees of Cavaillé-Coll park, Lover #2's cock inside her, the confessions of the secret agent in the Armani suit, everything comes and goes in Hélène Bastogne's world. A novel to say that. But Hélène Bastogne wouldn't know how. Hélène Bastogne could almost kick herself for not knowing.

Hélène Bastogne needs redemption. Quickly. Hélène Bastogne needs to come. Quickly. Like everyone else, she no longer believes in God. Perhaps a novel. But Hélène Bastogne wouldn't know how. To begin with:

she doesn't know the names of trees;
she doesn't know how to pray;
she doesn't know if the spy hasn't conned her a little;
she doesn't know if she can write.

Hélène Bastogne is going to come.

Yet Hélène Bastogne is no fool. Lover #2 is an editor-in-chief first and foremost. When he listened to the MP3 recording of the operative, he found it so wild that he danced around Hélène Bastogne's office at the paper—"It's a bombshell, baby!"—a pitiful parody of rappers by a fifty-, soon sixty-something baby boomer with an indecent income.

And afterward, he had wanted to fuck Hélène Bastogne. Logical. For the moment Hélène Bastogne, thirty-two in a month, likes the cynical animality of it. Lover #2 is no longer that abstract power managing the editorial board like some tyrannical Nero, who makes trips to New York and back in one day, who meets tired and greedy faces in the drawing rooms of luxurious hotels, who takes telephone calls with a cell nickel-plated like a handgun.

No, Lover #2 suddenly had a body. Hormones, adrenaline, cologne. Slightly trembling hands, moist temples: the flashes of amphetamines, the flashes of triumph, the flashes of his exultant gonads. A spy who's ratting, a spy spilling names, dates, evidence, a spy who's going to explode the paper's circulation.

Hélène Bastogne is going to come.

A stronger gust of wind. The nameless trees in Cavaillé-Coll park are moving. Lover #2 is coming. By distilling all this little by little, they can double the sales over two weeks.

Hélène Bastogne topples onto Lover #2's torso. Then slips down beside him on a Bordeaux spread. Crumpled La Perla underwear. A Mac screen is pulsing. Hélène Bastogne buries her face in a sweaty neck, near a madly beating carotid artery.

"So, baby, can I take you to this new bar? It's on Quai de Jemmapes."

"If you like."

Lover #2 is a typical baby boomer. Lover #2 likes to exhibit girls who are half his age with a third of his income in lame places like Canal Saint-Martin, which has completely turned into a museum by now. Always in the hope of bumping into the ghost of Arletty. Asshole. For her trouble she'll play the whore a little and get him to buy her some stuff at Antoine et Lili, a trendy clothing boutique a little farther down, on Quai de Valmy. The fact is, Hélène Bastogne is not in a very good mood.

Because Hélène Bastogne did not come. As usual.

4.

"We missed Berthet, sir."

"You're really dumb, Moreau. Did you subcontract again?"

"Yes, sir."

"With your tightwad savings, you're going to land us up shit creek. Was that you, the killing in the 10th? I just heard it on France Info."

"Yes, sir."

"Who are the dead?"

"My two subcontractors, three civilians, and Morland."

"You killed the counselor? You're so stupid, Moreau."

"If the counselor was with Berthet, it means the counselor was talking, right?"

"You're an idiot, an asshole, *and* a moron. And on top of that, you wrecked one of the nicest restaurants in Paris. Where are you calling from?"

"From the Brady—"

"The alley or Mocky's movie theater?"

"A movie theater, actually, yes, sir. The room is full of black guys jerking off, sir. Whose movie theater did you say this is?"

"Mocky's, Moreau, Mocky's. You're completely ignorant on top of it all. Stay there, Moreau, and wait for orders. I'm going to fix your dumb blunders."

They hang up.

Moreau is not happy. Moreau is forced to sit in the dark movie theater.

Moreau is forced to watch a film in black-and-white with the young Bourvil who steals from church collection boxes.

Moreau is forced to stay there with black guys who are jerking off.

Berthet will pay for this.

5.

Berthet goes into the Gare du Nord. The caryatids are making fun of him in the blue November sky. Especially the Dunkirk one, it seems to him. A train to Dunkirk, why not? And then a freighter.

And then what?

Berthet is totally losing it. Berthet knows he's got to get a grip on himself, and fast. This isn't Conrad. This isn't Graham Greene.

Berthet has The Unit after his ass. Berthet has a torn suit that smells of cordite and langoustine. Berthet still has one clip for his Glock, two for his Tanfoglio. Berthet knows that going home isn't an option. The Unit is waiting for him, of course.

Berthet doesn't live far from here, though, Passage Truil-lot in the 11th, but rue du Faubourg du Temple, the border between the two arrondissements, suddenly seems to him impossible to cross, like the Berlin Wall must have been for Morland before. Poor Morland.

But listen, all this is kind of Morland's fault.

It was Morland who told Berthet to talk to that journalist, Hélène Bastogne. Saying this was going to be a big help to The Unit. To pass himself off as a guy from the Service. To destabilize the Service by ratting on the Service. Because during this preelection period, The Unit is still loyal to the Old Man, the President, while the Service is rather in favor of the Opposition Candidate, the Pretender. And the Old Man wants to take down the Pretender.

At least that's how Morland explained it.

Internal politics, what a pain in the ass, thinks Berthet, as he steps into a terrifically impersonal neon and stainless steel café.

Inside there are people with that strained look of all departing travelers, and other people who have that strained look of people who aren't departing travelers but who have nothing better to do than watch the ones who are.

Yes, internal politics is a pain in the ass, thinks Berthet, who doesn't mind dying in Algiers, Abidjan, or Rome, but not two kilometers from home in an arrondissement where there are nothing but train stations, hospitals, and whores.

In other words, an arrondissement for hypothetical departures to rainy places, incurable diseases, and paid orgasms with spots of melanin on callipygian asses.

Yes, internal politics is a drag.

And Jesus, talk about those train stations! Berthet thinks the Gare de l'Est is even more depressing than the Gare du Nord. The Gare du Nord plays it futurist and Orwellian, but the Gare de l'Est still reeks of the draftees who went off twice in twenty years to get slaughtered on the Eastern fronts.

Furthermore, the paradox is that Berthet has hideouts even The Unit doesn't know about in a dozen European and African cities, but here in Paris, in the 10th arrondissement—nothing, nada, zilch.

Berthet finally understands, though a bit late, a precept from *The Art of War* by Sun Tzu. A book that everyone at The Unit claims to be reading, it's their bible and the pretext for seminars after Commando Training in Guyana.

Berthet used to think that reading Sun Tzu was a bit of a show-off, a little "We-at-The-Unit-are-philosopher-warriors," a pose, really.

But now Berthet has to admit that the old Chink was right: "*What is essential is to ensure peace in the cities of your nation.*" In other words, peace would be a studio known only to himself, equipped with:

clean suits
weapons with no serial numbers
a set of false identity papers
medicine in the bathroom cabinet
some cash
cell phones with local numbers

These studios do exist. The closest is in Delft, between Brussels and Amsterdam. Delft—that sure does Berthet a lot of good.

The road might be a possibility. Straight toward Porte de la Chapelle, the highway to Lille. Yeah, right.

Berthet orders a coffee at the counter. Berthet thinks this over. Berthet understands. The Unit wants him dead to eliminate the source of leaks to the Service. The Unit, once the dirty work has been done, wants to keep its hands clean.

Berthet feels very depressed. If The Unit has decided to do away with him like that, it's because The Unit must think he's outdated, old, a loser.

Berthet could call Hélène Bastogne, tell her about having been conned. That wouldn't do much good, just piss off The Unit. Whatever he does now anyway, he's definitely out of the game.

Berthet wants to take a piss. Berthet goes up to the first floor of the café. To get into the john, you have to put fifty euro centimes into a kind of piggy bank on the door handle.

Clearly, a homeless bum is waiting for Berthet to go in and for Berthet to leave the door open when he comes out. The stinginess of this café, the bum's stinginess, the stinginess of internal politics, all this irritates Berthet.

In the world as it was before, you didn't pay to piss. To accept this is more proof that a submission chip has indeed been implanted in all people born after the oil crisis.

Berthet looks for exact change. Next to him, Berthet feels the bum's need to piss as pressing as his own. This irritates Berthet even more.

Then Berthet blows his fuse.

Berthet takes out his Glock and breaks the bum's nose with the butt. Then Berthet finally manages to find the right coin, Berthet goes into the john, Berthet drags the body of the bum along with him, quite easily given the drug-addicted thinness of this economically deprived individual, and once the door is closed, Berthet crushes the bum's face with a stomp of the heel of his Church's shoe, thinking about:

those Unit shits
those Service shits
that shit Sun Tzu

that grouse with foie gras he had to skip
that internal politics crap

The bum is pretty quickly disfigured and dead. In place
of his face there are shards of bone, bits of rotten teeth, torn
flesh, and even an eye popped out of its socket looking disap-
provingly at Berthet.

Berthet takes his leak, Berthet farts, and Berthet wonders
what got into him.

Berthet washes his hands, Berthet splashes water on his face,
Berthet wipes off his Church's and the bottoms of his trousers.

Berthet remembers, then, that he forgot to take his Haldol when he was having lunch at Chez Michel. And this is
the upshot.

Berthet swallows two pink gel tablets and is about to step
out, when one of his two cell phones vibrates.

6.

"Hello, my friend!"

Lover #2 immediately recognizes the Voice at the other
end of the cell phone. Lover #2 loves this Voice. A top bureaucrat's phrasing, a cabinet minister's unction with media
appeal to boot because the Voice publishes two essays a year
on globalization, always the same ones, and because the Voice
is invited everywhere to receive all the journalists' compli-
ments and bows. The Voice is one of the ten or twelve most
powerful Voices in France.

"Hello, sir."

Lover #2 tries to stay cool, relaxed. To deal equal to equal
with the Voice. Lover #2 is the editor-in-chief of a major daily,
after all.

"I have a favor to ask you, my dear friend . . ."

Lover #2 puffs out his chest. Lover #2 forgets that he is stark naked on Hélène Bastogne's bed, and that his fingers smell of Hélène Bastogne. As for Hélène Bastogne, she's taking a shower so long it might be insulting if Lover #2 didn't have other things on his mind.

"Go on, sir."

"You have a journalist on your paper called Hélène Bastogne, I believe?"

"Indeed, sir."

Lover #2 restrains himself from saying, *That's funny, what a coincidence, I just fucked her, rather well if I must say so myself, and now we're going for a drink near Canal Saint-Martin. How about joining us? We'll make it a threesome. These thirty-year-olds do enjoy a good fuck, you know. Probably because of their poor spending power in relation to the older generation.*

But Lover #2 doesn't know the Voice intimately enough. That's too bad. One day.

"Mademoiselle Bastogne has gathered some rather sensitive information, I believe, from an agent belonging to our services, hasn't she?"

Uh oh. Uh oh. Careful. Careful, thinks Lover #2.

"True. And we're about to bring it out soon. But if this is a problem to you, sir, I can postpone it."

"Out of the question, my dear friend, it's not our style to control the press. On the contrary, I'm going to tell you something in confidence: We ourselves encouraged this agent to talk. It has to do with internal stability, it's very complicated, one day I'll tell you about it. We are in favor of transparency, my dear friend. Only here's the thing: This agent still has things to tell Mademoiselle Bastogne, some very interesting things."

"He can just come by the office again tomorrow."

"Now here's the problem. A rival service has spotted him in your offices. We are in a preelection period. He's risking his career and even his life if he visits you again. Your journalist does live in the 10th, right? Tell her to go home. Our man is in the area. He will meet her at her place. He will feel more secure there. Do this quickly, my dear friend. Let's say within the hour. It's urgent. We'll send our man to a quiet place right after."

"For security purposes, I would also like to be present at the interview," says Lover #2. "You never know."

"Your ethics and your courage are to your credit, my dear friend, I was going to suggest the same thing. But our agent is very nervous. The idea should seem to come from Mademoiselle Bastogne, that would make him feel secure. I'm counting on you, my dear friend, and I won't forget to thank you after the elections."

The Voice hangs up. Lover #2 rises, walks over to the bedroom window. Lover #2 looks down at Cavaillé-Coll park. Kids are playing before night comes, which won't be long now. Lover #2 scratches his balls, Lover #2 looks toward the façade of Saint-Vincent-de-Paul's. Oh, not a great example of a faux Greek temple.

Lover #2 scratches his ass. Lover #2 has the feeling they've got him just where they want him. But come on, that's paranoid, too much coke. Change dealers, must think about changing dealers.

Hey, Lover #2 says to himself, the place where my dealer wants me to meet him is not very far away, as a matter of fact. Near Saint-Louis Hospital. I'll go as soon as everything is settled with this Berthet. I'll have a blast with the Bastogne girl. I'll order bo bun from the Asian restaurant on avenue Richerand. It's the best bo bun in Paris. Coke, bo bum, and sex. If you're going to spend an evening in this lousy area, you might as well make it a good one.

Behind him, the shower has stopped. The bitch has finally finished washing her ass.

Without turning around, Lover #2 senses the damp presence of Hélène Bastogne. Lover #2's cock swells a little. This isn't the right time, even if at a good fifty-plus years it's always heartening to see that the machine can react in a split second.

"I got a tip over the phone while you were scrubbing yourself; I was told Berthet still has a bunch of stuff to spill. And fast. After that, he's gone. He's in the neighborhood, apparently. That's lucky, don't you think? We could ask him to meet us here. Do you have some way of reaching him?"

Hélène Bastogne looks at the soft buttocks of Lover #2. Hélène Bastogne wants to send this lousy fuck packing. But this lousy fuck is sometimes a good journalist. Not often, but sometimes. So Hélène Bastogne says: "I have his cell number, I'll call him."

7.

"Moreau?"

"Yes, sir."

"You're still at the Brady?"

"Where, sir?"

"At Mocky's, moron."

"At whose place?"

"Fuck, in your movie theater."

"Yes, sir, and there are still black guys jerking off, sir."

"You're dismissed now, Moreau. You're to go to an apartment on Place Franz Liszt, number seven. It's near a bar called l'Amiral. The entry code is 1964CA12. Top floor. The apartment belongs to Hélène Bastogne."

"And?"

"You clean up. If Berthet isn't there, clean up anyway and wait. Until Berthet arrives."

"Okay, sir."

"Say, Moreau, what's the film at Mocky's?"

"What?"

"The film playing on the screen."

"Something with the young Bourvil who filches from church collection boxes. I don't understand anything. The actors are all terrible. Plus, with all these black guys jerking off—"

"Moreau, you don't understand anything about film. And this nonsense about black guys jerking off—are you racist or what, Moreau? Or did you forget to take your Haldol? Forgetting to take Haldol makes you do stupid things, you know."

"I took my Haldol, sir, and there really are black guys jerking off."

"Okay, fine, though I don't see why anyone would jerk off watching *Un drôle de paroissien,* unless they're really serious film buffs. So, your mission?"

"Top floor, Place Franz Liszt, code 1964CA12. I clean up."

"Good, Moreau. All right, get moving."

8.

In his pay toilet at the Gare du Nord, Berthet puts his cell phone back into his pocket. Hélène Bastogne. Who wants to see him. Maybe it's a trap, maybe not. Actually, Berthet doesn't care. Berthet has a headache. Berthet looks at the bum's disfigured corpse. Maybe they're right at The Unit, maybe he's gone totally rotten. The fact that he lost it just by skipping one dose of Haldol proves it. Shit.

Might as well go see Hélène Bastogne. Berthet leaves the

john. Two people are waiting. Berthet takes out a red, white, and blue official ID card.

"Health services, closed for the moment."

And Berthet smiles. And Berthet signals with a broad, competent, and pleasant gesture that everybody must go back down, that he'll be coming down too, right after them.

Berthet leaves the café. Berthet leaves the station.

The 10th arrondissement is falling into the warm November night. Global warming. Heading back home to the suburbs, the commuters are starting to flock in. Since Berthet has been bipolar—no, actually, since he's become completely psychotic—Berthet remembers all the figures he sees. It's terrifying.

Just today, for instance, glimpsed on random posters and newspapers, Berthet will always remember:

Portugal's debt, which is sixty-three percent of their GNP;

dial 08 92 68 24 20 to talk uninhibited with very hot babes;

349 euros per month, no money down, for a Passat Trend TDI;

sixty percent of the young Senegalese woman's skin was burned after the bus attack in the projects outside Paris.

So Berthet, who is moving against the human flow, almost automatically converts everything into numbers, and it's no longer people he sees entering the Gare du Nord but:

180 million travelers annually
27 tracks

2 metro lines
3 regional railroad lines
9 bus lines
247 surveillance cameras
1 special police precinct

All this because a few years ago The Unit named Berthet head of a study group to mastermind terrorist attacks on the Parisian transportation system.

People bump into Berthet. Berthet wants to vomit now. Berthet's headache is getting worse and worse.

Berthet avoids rue de Belzunce, taking a different route along boulevard de Denain, rue de Valenciennes, rue Lafayette. Berthet is hot. But it's November. Shit. The end of the world is coming.

You might wonder what's the point of still playing cat-and-mouse in this arrondissement sinking into twilight now, what's the point of this squabble between the Service, The Unit, the Old Man, the Pretender.

To take over a country doomed to defeat, on a planet in its terminal phase?

Berthet remembers another lunch with Morland at Chez Michel, maybe a year ago. Then, too, figures, secret numbers. Berthet doesn't want all these numbers to come back to him. Berthet takes another Haldol.

A pink pill against the apocalypse. Poor fucker.

Berthet reaches Place Franz Liszt. Berthet thinks of knocking back a glass at l'Amiral before going up to see Hélène Bastogne. Berthet hesitates, gives up the idea even though the Haldol is making his mouth terribly dry.

The code. The stairs. He draws the Glock and then bends down to take the Tanfoglio from its holster on his left ankle.

An intuition. The intuition of an operative. The intuition of a psychotic.

Top floor. Berthet gives a small push to the half-open door. Hot light from a lamp. He says, "Hélène Bastogne?" No answer.

Berthet gives the door a hard kick.

Berthet does a roll, head first.

Berthet hears the flatulent noise of a silencer. Berthet feels bullets going into his abdomen, his thorax, and also ripping the lobe off his left ear.

Berthet sees a Combas reproduction on the wall—that's thirty-year-old taste for you!—and fires blind. To his right with the Glock, to his left with the Tanfoglio. It sounds like badly adjusted speakers, a broken stereo. Berthet empties his clips.

Berthet gets up. Berthet is spitting blood. Berthet is coughing in the smoke.

Berthet stumbles into a living room furnished in second-hand chic and sees Hélène Bastogne on a ratty club chair with her throat cut, and an aging Romeo he's noticed at the newspaper as he vaguely recalls. He's had his throat cut as well, and he's been emasculated for good measure. His balls are in a vintage Ricard ashtray, on a low table, Vallauris style.

That's why Berthet is hardly surprised to see Moreau stretched out on a threadbare kilim, with two round openings in his forehead, the Tanfoglio's signature bullet holes. Moreau was also taking Haldol, but Moreau was probably skipping pills. Otherwise, Moreau wouldn't have screwed up the job at the restaurant like that. Moreau wouldn't have castrated the Romeo guy. Moreau would not have left the door half open.

Berthet coughs. Clots of blood. Not to mention his ear that's hurting like hell.

Well, at least Berthet got Moreau. Berthet sits down in

another club chair. It's night now in the 10th arrondissement. Berthet sees the tops of the trees in Cavaillé-Coll park, the top of Saint-Vincent-de-Paul's façade.

Berthet is afraid. Berthet is in pain. He hopes it won't be too long now.

He seems to hear the wind in the trees. But that would be surprising, with all the traffic and all those sirens down below.

Two minutes later, Berthet dies.

9.

Three days later, purely out of curiosity, the Voice walked around the Gare du Nord, rue de Belzunce, Place Franz Liszt. The Voice came back up through Cavaillé-Coll park, went into the church of Saint-Vincent-de-Paul, and the Voice prayed, quite sincerely, for the souls:

of Counselor Morland
of the blond waitress from Chez Michel
of the couple who were lunching at Chez Michel
of the two incompetent bikers
of the bum in the john at the Gare du Nord café
of Berthet
of Moreau
of the emasculated editor-in-chief
of Hélène Bastogne

Then the Voice walked out.

Autumn was still warm in the 10th arrondissement.

And the Voice said to himself that, all things considered, the operation had been rather successful.

PART II

LIBERATION LOST

LIKE A TRAGEDY

BY LAURENT MARTIN

Place de la Nation

Translated by David Ball

> *I hold the world but as the world, Gratiano;*
> *A stage where every man must play a part,*
> *And mine a sad one.*
> —William Shakespeare, *The Merchant of Venice*

1.

Still the same smell same view same disgust. Nothing's changed.

My bedroom window looks out on the night. The night where the lights of the city all around are shining. The night where hidden men are patiently waiting for the next day. When I was a kid, I used to think dead lights left the earth and went up to the sky in the form of stars. Dinner's over. They've left. My sister Sophie and her husband. In actual fact they're getting married tomorrow. That's why I'm here.

A few groggy steps around my room. Nothing's changed. The worn-out furniture. The wallpaper. The dreary smell. Took a whole day to get here. The fatigue and boredom of being here, I'm going to collapse.

When I got here, the table was already set. They had already come. His name is Patrick and my sister's in love. That's all I know. Mom made soup for us. Soup's a family tradition. It's lasted thirty years. "Eat while it's hot." Mom doesn't look any older. Or hardly any. Still something sad in her eyes, and pink cheeks and jet-black hair. Not like me, verging on brown and now white. Man, do I look older. Dinner. Pretend to be interested in Patrick. With a bitch of a headache. Patrick is tall and kind of good-looking. My sister's pretty too. The years seem to have made her look even better. Say anything at all to fill up the time and now Sophie's urging me to tell them some of my adventures. My adventures, when I was in the submarine corps. "That's such a different life!" "So tell us about it." So I tell about it. The dives, the trips, the ports of call. The danger-ous situations that make you shudder when you have no idea how a submarine works. I worked in the engine room. A very important job and Patrick thought I was interesting. Everybody was happy I was back, happy with my stories, and I played the prodigal son come home, as if nothing had happened, whereas I would have liked to have been very far away from here. Pat-rick asked me why I'd left Paris. "To see how it is somewhere else." He could feel I was lying. There are stories I'd rather not tell. Discreetly, Sophie thanked me for coming. "Without you, something would have been missing from my wedding."

We all separated. Till tomorrow. I was alone again in my lousy room where I spent so many shitty years looking at the stars leaving the earth, wondering if someday I'd have the courage to leave. I had to have a good reason to run away from this city and find myself in a submarine, sealed in half the time. No wonder I already have white hair and tired eyes.

2.

The first morning. Up early, first one. A Navy habit. Six o'clock, every day, never lose crappy habits. Mom's still sleeping. I feed the cat. He must be fifteen or sixteen. I'm the one who found this cat. Lost and wet right outside the building. The only good deed I've ever done. I believe. I make myself a cup of coffee. Mom's coffee's still just as bad. From the kitchen window you can also see the city the railroad tracks the high-rises that stand out and try to wake up. It's still almost night. I grab an old issue of the paper lying on the table. Pages are missing. I skim through some news items as I drink my coffee.

In the silence of the early hours I look for the iron. It hasn't moved. In the hall closet. Nothing has moved. I wonder if I really left, if it's not the morning after a rocky night of drinking that made me think I'd disappeared for ten years. My only suit has to be ironed. Keep up appearances. Patrick's parents have money. They rented a big room in a restaurant in the Bois de Vincennes that has a little garden. We don't have the money for that. So we keep up appearances. A family tradition. Like the soup. But I don't hold it against her: Mom did what she could when my father died. A perfectly pressed suit. A wedding in September when the days are getting shorter, what an idea. I put it in my room on the bed and I close the door so the cat won't come in and sleep on it.

Mom's up now. She's surprised. She forgot I was here. Yet it's the first time I've been here in ten years.

"Did you sleep well?" "Yes! You left the room just like it used to be." "What did you expect me to do with it?" "I don't know." She grabs a cup and helps herself and takes a sip. "Your coffee is very strong." "That's the only way I like it." She adds a little water. "I ironed my suit for the wedding." "I could have done it for you." "I'm used to it. We did everything ourselves in the subs." "So it's not like it used to be." She smiles sadly and adds: "Are you okay?" What can I answer? I lie: "Sure! Work, life . . .

everything's okay." She finishes her cup. I tell her I'm going out for a walk. "Do you need something?" "No! I feel like taking a walk." "You'll see, there've been some changes." "I'll bet."

I walk downstairs. Fifth floor. Fifty-seven steps. I still remember the jerky tempo of the descent. Back in the day, the light used to go on the fritz a lot and you had to keep count of the steps in your head so as not to fall. Outside. A kind of square where two buildings face each other. Ours and Olivier's. Olivier was a friend of my father's. Anyway he doesn't live there anymore. The air is cool. A strange feeling that this new old world is much smaller than the one I left. A few shouts in the distance, and the background noise that never goes away. A mix of all the activities of the city. Never have I heard silence around here. I go up rue de Fécamp, cross boulevard Daumesnil, and I take rue de Picpus to reach the little park where I used to hang out a lot. The place where I smoked my first cigarettes with Marco and the other guys. The mix of new and old apartment buildings gives a rhythm to what I see. Nothing has really changed, but everything is different. Ten years is an eternity. After the little park I walk up to Place de la Nation. I leave the neighborhood. Our neighborhood our universe where we thought we dominated the city and the world. What a laugh. We were just fragile little insects running around in a space that was too vast and noisy for us.

And the back streets around there, like little islands, where life was organized around a café. That's where we would meet, in those cafés. We rarely went any further away. Rarely to the other neighborhoods—for us that was elsewhere, too far away. I gulp down a cup of coffee in one of those cafés. I don't know if the sign has changed. It's a little blurry in my memory. A few old guys are talking over a beer. They were already there in the same spot ten years ago, a hundred years ago.

Store after store, like everywhere else. The same signs, the same colors. Standardization settling in and taking over. Just shadows. Buildings, cars, men, women, these people. Just shadows I ignore.

I walk back toward Daumesnil, until I find another sad café to sit down in. A young woman barely twenty comes to take my order. Just a coffee. This return to the past is awful. It forces me to think about myself, and all I've done so far is hide, in order to forget myself. I'm the same. Nothing has changed. The main thing is the only thing you hold onto. Thick heavy vapors coming from the souls of things. Light, superficial, intoxicating things . . . I've forgotten all that. I come up to the surface again, suffering from a painful illness. Stinging nostalgia.

Mom was getting worried. "You could have said where you were going." "What for? I'm here." "The wedding." "D'you think I've come six hundred miles to miss my sister's wedding?" She made me a dish of meat in sauce. I hardly ate any. "It's not good?" "I'm not really hungry." "But it's sauté of veal, you used to like that."

Yes! I used to like that. She thinks I'm pale for someone who lives on the Riviera. "You know, at my job we're not outside a lot." And she makes some comments about my white hair and my father who didn't have any at my age.

We get ready for the wedding. Mom doesn't want to be late. She has even ordered a taxi. "We're not going to your sister's wedding by bus!" "She could've left us her car." "She still needed it." Mom bought herself a dress for the occasion. She asks what I think of it. I say it's fine without looking.

3.

About a hundred guests. Eight to a table. I'm entitled to the table of honor. I occupy the seat of the father of the bride. The worst table at a wedding. I listen politely to what Patrick's parents say. Real assholes who own a business. "Our children are so charming!" Sure! He's their only son, so they wanted to do things right. And you can tell. A band. Food, and more food. Drink, and more drink. At this moment I hate my sister but I send her loving smiles. Between two yeses and two meaningless comments, I look the guests over. All of them from Patrick's class. A business school. You can't change yourself. I don't know any of them. And a few of my sister's friends I met years ago; their faces are totally dark in my memory. Time. The feeling that I'm falling headfirst into what I wanted to leave for good. I gulp down wine, good wine, to get drunk. Patrick plays the nice brother-in-law. I gulp down wine. I hardly listen at all. I gulp.

And suddenly I see her.

Sitting at a table, vaguely smiling at the people around her. She wasn't there at the start of the celebration. She just came in. The same somber face, the same sad smile, and her short hair shorter. I ask my sister: "Is that Valerie over there, in blue?" "Yes." "You still in touch with her?" "A little. Why?" "Just curious." A strange emotion in my sister's face. Fear, almost. I don't know why. My heart stirs, jumps, the way it jumped ten years ago. I watch Valerie for the rest of the meal. I'm pretty sure she has seen me too.

Before dessert, we're entitled to a pause for the champagne. I take a bottle and two glasses. I get up. Valerie is there, alone, absent. I walk up to her. A feeling of staggering, plunging into a bottomless pit, one of the dark places alcohol generously throws you into before it asks you to pay the toll. Charon works on earth now. Three breaths. I'm at her table.

> [*He walks over to her with a bottle in his hand. She's sitting at a table.*]
>
> HIM: Hello.
>
> [*She jumps.*]
>
> HER: Hello . . . I haven't had the courage to go up to the table of honor yet . . . You came back?
>
> HIM: For the occasion. That's all.
>
> HER: I didn't think I'd see you again. Sophie hardly ever talks about you.
>
> HIM: I've been kind of quiet these past few years. I have some champagne. Want some?
>
> HER: Yes, please.
>
> [*He serves her. They drink to cover their embarrassment.*]
>
> HER: What are you doing now?
>
> HIM: Not much. A few years in submarines. Now I'm working at a garage in Toulon. How about you?
>
> HER: I stayed here. Not much either. It's a nice wedding.
>
> HIM: I don't know what "a nice wedding" means.
>
> HER: Your sister and mother seem happy.
>
> HIM: That's true. Are you alone? No escort?
>
> HER: No! No one.
>
> [*Silence.*]
>
> [*They cross glasses.*]
>
> HIM: Cheers.
>
> HER: Cheers.
>
> [*The potion acts.*]

We spend the rest of the night together. Talking a little about our memories. She talks to me about submarines. What's with all these people with their submarines? Valerie. Years ago, we went out together. She was a friend of my sister's. She was beautiful. She still is. A rather sophisticated charm that contrasted with my raw, almost animal state. We finish the bottle of champagne, we take another one. The world fades out around us. We're alone, surrounded by the deafening crowd that sings, howls. A nice wedding.

I agree to dance with my sister. She's worried. I'm merry. I wish her moments of happiness. "Just moments?" "Could be worse, right?"

In the restaurant garden. With Valerie. Outside, drunk, staggering, facing infinity and fresh air. She takes my hand.

4.

I remembered her body perfectly. And yet we only stayed together for a few weeks. It was just before I left this city. But her body is deeply engraved inside me. With acid, almost.

I watch her slow breathing. Then she wakes up. It is 6 a.m. We've only slept a few minutes. The emotional silence of our first morning. Bodies still palpitating. Hands graze each other, push each other away, are pulled toward each other. Doubts. Questions. Who will dare to speak first?

[*They are lying pressed against each other. Silence.*]
HER: I have to go.
HIM: Already?
HER: Yes. It's late. It's early. I'll call you today or tomorrow. I really have to leave.
[*She gets up, gets dressed, and scurries offstage. He remains alone.*]

* * *

She goes away. I don't move. I hear the door slam. Close your eyes. Forget. Dream. But nothing happens. Except for this need, here.

She didn't call, not that day, not the days after.

Hanging around the house, and outside. Looking for her name in the phone book. Nobody with the name of Valerie Mercier. See and see again the place she lived before. Near boulevard Michel Bizot. A guy tells me he doesn't know her. She doesn't live here anymore. My sister is on her honeymoon on an island in the Caribbean, I'm not going to bug her about this.

Slow to come to life again after the death that accompanies Valerie's painful silences.

5.

Marco. He learns I'm back. "You could've told me." "I was going to." Marco. The guy, the friend, the near brother I used to see all the time before I left. Not the kind of guy you really want to be seen with, though. If I hadn't left, I might have really turned out badly with him.

We'll meet at Place Daumesnil. A square where we used to hang out when we were younger. A square like in my memory. Sad and gray.

Cars are driving around a fountain where stone lions are spitting out water. He's late. I walk around a little. Emptied out, tired from the nights spent turning over in my bed, waiting, feverishly, for the phone, for Valerie's voice, her breath. That fucking need. He arrives in a pretty little English car. Marco hasn't really changed. A tall blond guy with a smile in his eyes. We kiss each other on both cheeks. "Glad to see you." "Me too." We look for a café to have a drink.

"So! How are you, what's up?" "I managed to integrate into society, like they say. I run a security agency. I supply tough guys for big parties, concerts, things like that." "You didn't have any problem getting started?" "No, I knew some people who helped me." "That's good." "How about you?" "I tinker around. I spent a long time in the submarine corps, in Toulon." "Your mother told me, at the time." "Now, with my savings, I bought a little apartment and I found a job in a garage." "A calm life." "Kind of. Kind of too calm." "Why don't you come back here? I'll fix you up with something." "You know that's not possible." "Anything's possible. Especially now." We talk about years past. Lost years. "I'm going out tonight. Want to come along?" "Sure."

A fine clear night. It's for us, to celebrate our reunion. That's it.

Everything, or almost everything, has changed around Bastille. We start at a spot with a tropical atmosphere and a touch of class. Then a new bar with an Indian theme. We end up in a big three-story club. Marco knows everybody. He introduces me as his childhood friend who's come home. I'm treated with respect. From time to time I see him talking discreetly with people. Marco must be a little more than just the head of a security agency. I don't ask him about it because it's none of my business. We got real drunk. Especially me. I want to forget I exist. To forget Valerie exists. But it's not easy to forget things like that.

We find ourselves at the place of a friend of his. He's having a party in a big, completely renovated loft near rue Crozatier. I sprawl out for an hour on a leather couch with a bottle of rum in my hand. I'm flying, until I go vomit somewhere. I can sense the friend's been kicking up a fuss. Marco tells him to calm down and we walk out.

* * *

Car at the shore of the lake in the Bois de Vincennes, outside the city. Day's dawning. Drunkenness going slowly away, giving way to beatitude. The sound of water. The sound of steps. The sound of urban silence. Marco in front of me. Suddenly he stops. "Look!" A field mouse, at the edge of the water. Marco grabs an old piece of wood lying there. He walks forward, stops, then starts to hit the poor beast. The surprised mouse bursts into pieces. Marco keeps going. "What are you doing?" No answer. He keeps hitting. Again and again. Then I understand we don't belong to the same world anymore. Our minds have grown apart. Finally he stops. He's breathing heavily. "Want to go home to bed?" "Yes!"

On the way back, the question. The question I didn't dare ask. "You didn't get into trouble?" "About what?" "Ten years ago." "No! Nothing. I forgot all about that business." "I didn't forget it." "You were wrong. And you shouldn't've left. Nothing happened." "We had no idea. And leaving was good for me. I don't know what would have become of me if I had stayed here."

6.

Marco calls me up. "What're you doing tonight?" "Nothing, nothing much." "I'm taking you along. I'll come by and pick you up around 10." "That late?" "Yeah." He hangs up.

I spend the end of the day with Mom. She needs help wallpapering her bedroom. She was hesitant. I advised her to do it. "Your father liked this wallpaper." "My father died over fifteen years ago." "Yes, that's true."

Around 10 p.m. I hear a car honking. I lean out. Marco is sticking his head out of a dark BMW. He waves to me. I go downstairs. "You make enough to afford this thing?" "No. It's a loan. Get in!" I get inside the machine. He puts a CD on

at top volume and the bass makes everything vibrate. I yell:
"Where're we going?" "You'll see."

We leave the neighborhood, and Paris, for the suburbs.
He lowers the sound. We get to Rungis, in the industrial zone.
There isn't much traffic at this time of night. We drive between
big sheds, warehouses. Black-and-white, like in old films. We
turn. Marco hangs a right. We roll up to an open shed. We enter. Inside, an English truck and two small vans. Guys bustling
around. I'm getting worried. "What's happening?" "Nothing.
A business operation."

"What the fuck is this?"

"Come on!" We get out of the car. We walk over to the guys.
Marco gives out a few hi's. There are four guys; they look at me
strangely. "No problem, he's a friend." The guys are taking big
boxes out of the English truck and putting them in the vans.
"What's in them?" "Stuff like cigarettes and hi-fis." "You're
bullshitting me. Didn't I tell you I didn't want anything to do
with crap like this?" "Don't worry, it won't take long." "Are you
the manager here?" "No, I'm watching it for a boss." "Who?"
"Remember the Café du Commerce?" "On rue de Wattignies?"
"Yes. The boss had a son, Frederic Dumont." "Could be." "He's
the one I'm working for. I supply the manpower." "You're not
sick of this shit?" "What else do you expect me to do? Work on
trains like your father, or in a factory like mine, and croak like
an asshole just for a pitiful salary?" "You don't have to do that."
"I don't know how to do anything else."

A cell phone rings. One of the guys answers. All of a sud-
den he gives an order. Everybody starts moving. Marco grabs
me by the arm. "Come on! Gotta leave." We run back to the
BMW. "You want to drive?" "Why?" "Because you're the best."
He flips me the keys. I start the car. "Got to get outta here.
There's a Customs patrol going around." I accelerate. He's my

copilot. "Right. Left. Now *hit it!*" I keep the lights off. We can make out something in the distance. "Park in the shadows." I turn off the engine. Silence. A halo of light slowly approaches. A car goes by. Customs. I watch it in the rearview mirror. As soon as it turns I start up again and I speed toward the exit. Marco keeps looking back. "You worried?" "Not about us. About the merchandise. My cut." "You never should've dragged me into this job." "Sorry. I thought you'd enjoy it. How was I supposed to know?" "Stop breaking my balls."

7.

A strange sun over the city. Something warm and restful. I walk for a long time before I get to Lycée Paul-Valéry. That's where I told Marco to meet me. The high school we went to. Especially me, because Marco didn't go to school very often. But I tried my best. Especially in French and History. So how did I end up a mechanic?

Marco's already there. Sitting on the hood of his BMW. We look for a nearby café. We sit outside. We order, then exchange banalities.

That's when she appears. For the second time. Valerie is striding ahead, as if she's late. I call her. I get up. I run after her. She finally turns around.

[*She walks rapidly across the stage. He calls her. She turns around.*]

HER: What are you doing here?

HIM: Nothing. I'm having a cup of coffee. You have a little time?

HER: No, sorry. Someone's expecting me.

HIM: You never called me.

HER: I know, I was really busy.

HIM: I waited. I didn't know how to reach you.

HER: Forgive me.
HIM: I have nothing to forgive you for. I'm only passing through.
HER: I promise you. As soon as I can . . .

Then I hear a voice. "Mommy!"

[*A voice calling offstage.*]

Valerie turns around. A little girl is running toward her. Maybe eight years old. Valerie glances at me. I see a painful form of despair in her face. Behind the little girl, a guy, a tall guy. He looks familiar.

HER: I've got to go.
HIM: I understand.
HER: I'll call you.
HIM: Don't bother. I understand completely.
HER: I don't think so.
[*She turns around and exits.*]

She leaves. Wobbly legs, exploding heart, I think I'm going to collapse on the ground. Two breaths. I go back to the bar. Marco questions me. "You know Valerie Dumont?" "What?" "The girl you followed." "She's a friend of my sister's. We saw each other at the wedding. I didn't know her name was Dumont." "That's her husband's name. I told you about him already, at the warehouse. I do some jobs for him. If you want, I'll introduce you."

"Don't bother. Really, don't bother."

8.

Flattened, hurt, smashed. Aching belly. Back from the station. My train ticket. Tomorrow I'm going back to Toulon. The phone rings. A few words of conversation. Steps. Mom through the door. "Phone for you." "Marco?" "No, it's a woman."

I rush over to the phone. It's her.

[*Each at opposite sides of the stage. They talk to each other on the phone.*]

HER: Antoine?

HIM: Yes!

HER: I'm sorry.

HIM: You didn't tell me you were married.

HER: I know.

HIM: Or that you had a daughter.

HER: I know. Forgive me. When we met . . . it was so sudden . . . I didn't know what to do.

HIM: And now?

HER: I still don't know. But we can see each other, if you want to.

HIM: That's not a good idea.

HER: What are you talking about?

HIM: You're married, you're a mother, all that.

HER: That's not a problem.

HIM: I'm going to go away.

HER: It's your decision.

HIM: Right. When?

HER: Now.

HIM: It's nighttime.

HER: I'll wait for you at my place. Nobody's home.

[*They hang up and exit from different sides of the stage.*]

I call out to Mom. "I'm going out for a little while to see a friend." "So late?" "It's the only way she can do it." "Okay, son." "I'm taking Sophie's car."

9.

Through the darkened city. Just one thought leads me on. Her. Speed to her. Speed. A nice apartment on boulevard Diderot. I ring. She opens the door.

[*Doorbell. She hesitates, walks forward, straightens her hair with one hand, and opens the door.*]
HER: Come in.
HIM: Thanks . . . Nice place . . . Money's no problem, is it?
HER: It's not me.
HIM: It's your husband.
HER: Yes. Do you want something to drink?
HIM: Something strong.
HER: Cognac?
HIM: Perfect.
[*She fixes him a glass.*]

I close my eyes. What am I doing here? I should have left today. Shouldn't have come. She's pouring me a drink.

[*She brings him a glass.*]
HER: Here you are.
[*He swallows.*]
[*Silence.*]

I drink almost the whole glass. Then silence. Like two strangers in an elevator.

[*She takes him by the hand and they exit.*]

So she's taking me by the hand. She leads me slowly upstairs, into a bedroom. Not the master bedroom. A guest room. She only leaves a little lamp on. She strokes my face. Her hand is trembling. And we make love. Entwined in each other, breathless, exhausted, neither of them dare to say anything yet.

[*In a big bed, they are lying pressed up against each other, out of breath. We can guess they're naked under the sheets. Silence.*]

HER: Why did you leave?

HIM: Why? Because I couldn't stand this city anymore.

HER: You don't like Paris? The neighborhood?

HIM: It's complicated. I love this city and I hate it at the same time. It's the city of my childhood. That's a terrible thing! Years . . . painful years . . .

Silence.
She puts her hand on my cheek.

HER: You know, I was in love with you.

HIM: I was in love with you too.

HER: We've missed each other.

HIM: You said it!

HER: And you left.

HIM: Yes . . . And now what?

HER: Stop it.

HIM: Stop what?

HER: For a long time, I dreamed of your body.

HIM: You're not answering me. Now what?

HER: I can't answer. You wouldn't like the only possible answer. I wouldn't like it either.

HIM: I know that answer.

HER: I'm not so sure.

HIM: How about your family?

HER: What about my family?

HIM: I don't know.

[*She puts her hand over his mouth.*]

HER: Shhh! Don't talk about the future. It doesn't exist.

[*They embrace.*]

10.

I decide to stay in Paris longer. My mother is delighted. I meet Valerie the next day. We go for a walk. Moments wrenched away from the rest of the world. Moments for just the two of us, with that permanent threat, that ending getting nearer.

[*They cross the stage holding hands.*]

HER: I can't come tomorrow. But later . . .

HIM: Later?

HER: In one or two days. I don't know yet. It's complicated.

HIM: I'm not asking you for anything.

HER: I know. It's not easy for me.

HIM: Not for me, either.

[*They exit.*]

Evening. Marco comes by to pick me up. "Where're we going?" "A nightclub near Bastille." "I really don't like all that." "I gotta tell you something." "What?" "You'll see."

It's not really a nightclub. Just a big bar with music playing in the back room. We order cocktails. "What did you want to tell me?" "Just wait a little. Actually, I want to introduce you to someone." "I don't like your mysteries. Last time, I was really mad at you." "Last time, everything went okay." We drink and we order again. Then a group comes in. Three of them. Marco waves and they walk toward our table. I recognize one of the guys from the warehouse and I recognize Dumont. What the hell is he doing here? The three guys stop. Marco introduces everybody. Dumont stares at me. "Haven't we met somewhere?" "Could be. I'm from the neighborhood but I've been away for a while."

Marco praises my skill as a driver. Dumont becomes interested in me. "And what are you doing now, my man?" I don't like it when somebody calls me "my man" just like that. "I work in a garage." "I might need you." "I don't see how." "A good driver." "I don't do that anymore." "Marco, you should persuade him." "I'll take care of it." "No way." Dumont gives me a piercing glance. He doesn't like to be contradicted. "I have a feeling we'll meet again." "I don't think so. I'm leaving in a couple of days." He doesn't answer. He goes away with his two bodyguards. Marco doesn't say anything.

"Why did you bring me over here? Why'd you introduce me to that guy?"

"So you can stay here. He can find work for you."

"I'm not looking for work. You really don't get it. I don't want to stay in Paris. I can't stay here. I'm going to leave as soon as I can."

11.

Eyes diving into the night. Valerie comes over to me. I can feel her breath and then her arms around me.

[*She comes over to him and puts her arms around his shoulders.*]

HER: What are you thinking about?

HIM: What I missed in life.

HER: Did you miss me?

HIM: Maybe. Hard to say. I didn't know if you still existed for

me, but when I saw you again at the wedding it all came
back to me. You had never really left me. You were hidden somewhere, ready to spring up again.

HER: You still haven't told me the real reason you left.

HIM: I never told anyone because the reason is too ugly.

HER: Tell me.

HIM: Truth burns.

HER: It's as bad as that?

HIM: I think so . . . Ten years ago, I used to hang out with
Marco a lot.

HER: I know.

HIM: We did a lot of shit together. Real hoods, almost. On my
end, I was still kind of hanging on to what I thought was
a normal life. But him, I felt he was going over the edge.
And then there was this problem with a guy. Marco asked
me to go to a meeting with him. He had some business
to settle. One night, a little after 12. Actually, the guy
owed Marco a bunch of money. He was supposed to give
some of it back to him. It was near the wine warehouses
around Bercy. Before they knocked them down. In a deserted spot . . . The guy was there, waiting for us, sitting
on his moped. We'd come in a car. I was driving, as usual
. . . Marco got out and began talking with the guy. Then
they started yelling at each other. The guy shoved Marco
to the ground and jumped on his bike and started it . . .
Marco got up. He came back to the car and told me to follow the guy. That's what I did. He had no chance of getting away from us. And suddenly the guy braked, turned
around, got off the bike, and pulled a gun out of his jacket.
Even in the night, with the moonlight and all, we could
see he was aiming at us. We ducked. I hit the gas pedal . . .
He didn't have time to fire and I crashed into him . . . I

felt the shock. We backed up. The guy's body was lying on the ground. Dead . . . I decided to get out right then and there. Marco wanted to stay. We promised never to squeal on the other guy if one of us got busted.

[*Silence.*]

HER: For a long time I thought I was the one you were running away from.

HIM: No, I was running away from that business. I had blood on my hands, I didn't want to pay for it. But, in fact, I did pay. Ten years—a kind of exile.

HER: It was an accident. It wasn't your fault at all.

HIM: There's no such thing as an accident.

[*Silence.*]

HER: Do you want something to drink?

HIM: No.

[*Silence.*]

HER: I'm scared.

HIM: Why?

HER: You shouldn't have come back. We shouldn't have seen each other again. We're going to make people unhappy.

HIM: People? Who?

HER: Us, maybe. And then there are our families . . .

HIM: As far as our families go, all we have to do is leave.

HER: What about us?

[*Silence.*]

HER: I'm cold.

HIM: Let's go back.

[*They exit.*]

12.

Three in the morning. The phone. I get out of bed. Mom too. She's worried. I pick up the phone. She must think it's Sophie.

Marco's voice. I reassure Mom. "That you, Antoine?" "D'you know what time it is?" "You gotta help me." "Where are you?" "In the country. Seine-et-Marne. A village called Ferrière." "What're you doing there?" "I crashed the BMW." "Anyone hurt?" "No." "What do you want me to do?" "Come get me." "Now?" "Yes! I'm at the main square, in front of the church, in the middle of the village. I already walked two miles. I've had it." "I'm on my way."

I get dressed fast. I grab the keys and papers for Sophie's car. Two minutes later I'm heading east on the highway. Moving forward through the night. Marco, what an asshole. I drive for half an hour. Then I get on a road toward Marne-la-Vallée. Little roads and villages go by. Don't get lost. Never been around here before. Finally, a sign says *Ferrière*. Turn left. What the hell am I doing here again? Go back to Toulon. As fast as possible. Go back to Toulon. Finally I'm there. The village is asleep. I slow down, drive up to the phone booth. Nobody. Where the hell is he? I turn off the engine. I'm about to get out. Marco gets into the car. "Thanks! I owe you one!" "You don't owe me a thing." I start the car again. "What about your car?" "We'll see about that later." "Someday something's gonna happen to you." "Someday. But not today. You're here. You saved my skin."

I drop Marco off in front of his house. He left rue de Fécamp for a more upscale apartment on rue Montgallet. He thanks me again. "That's your last word, about Dumont? You don't want to work for him?" "No! Absolutely not." "Maybe you're right." And he adds: "How does it feel, sleeping with his wife?" "What?" "You know what I said." "What are you talking about? You on the vice squad?" "One day, people are going to find out about it." "So what?" "Dumont's not soft-hearted. He's going to fuck you up, and his wife too." "He'll

never know." "That's what you think. I know, and I didn't
have to try. G'night!" He slams the door. I really have to leave
this city. ASAP. Before things turn nasty.

13.

Noon. Valerie's waiting for me. She wants to talk. Not at her
place. In some out-of-the-way café. I take my sister's car. The
fatigue from the night before still weighing on me. I go in. I
look around for Valerie.

[*He walks in. She's sitting at a table. He comes over.*]

HIM: What's up?

HER: I had to see you. Last night I spoke to my husband.

HIM: What?

HER: I told him I was having an affair with someone.

HIM: You didn't!

HER: What else could I do? He thought I was acting strange.
He would have tried to find out and he would have succeeded. He came back pretty late. I waited until it was 1
in the morning. He looked as if something was bothering
him. I drank two glasses of cognac to get up the courage. And I told him everything. I didn't tell him who you
were. He insisted, he threatened me, he yelled. Luckily,
our little girl woke up. He calmed down.

HIM: And then?

HER: I told him I was going away with you.

HIM: With me?

HER: Remember when I was telling you about the only possible answer for our future? The answer wasn't what you
thought. I'm not staying. I'm leaving. I'm leaving because
it's the only thing to do, even though I know it's not something good for me, or for you. I want to spend the next

days, the next weeks far away from here, with you.
[*He walks over and puts his arms around her.*]

I take her in my arms. I'm almost crushing her. I know she's right, we're lost, but it's too late for us to give each other up.

HIM: What about your daughter?
HER: My mother knows about it. She's going to take her for a while.
HIM: How're we going to do this?
HER: I packed some things. Just two bags.
HIM: We run away like thieves?
HER: We're stealing love, and we'll be punished for it.
HIM: Come on!
[*He grabs her by the hand and they exit.*]

I drive her to the station. Gare de Lyon. I tell her I need an hour, max. The time to go back to the house, get my things, explain everything to my mother, and return to her. She tells me she'll wait for me at the Train Bleu. I take the car and drive back to the house. I know I'm seeing the neighborhood for the last time.

14.

Inside the building. Up the stairs four by four. The door. The living room. I explain things to Mom. "They just called me. I've got to go back to the garage. An emergency. The boss is in the hospital." "You're leaving me?" "Not for long, this time." "You'll be back soon?" "I promise." Does she believe me? I walk quickly into my bedroom. I cram my stuff into my bag. A last look around this bedroom. Goodbye. I kiss Mom. "I'm going down there with Sophie's car. I'll leave it in the parking lot of the station and I'll mail the keys." She sniffs. Goodbye.

I run down the stairs. Into the hallway. Marco's there. "What the hell are you doing?" "I was waiting for you." "Why? You got more problems?" "I think you're doing something really dumb with Dumont." "Me?" "Yeah. He's not happy." "He sent you over here." "You have to give back what you took from him." "I didn't take anything." "His wife." "What're you talking about? He doesn't own her." "She's still his wife." "Marco! Stop this shit. We're not in the Middle Ages anymore. She can do whatever she wants." "That's not what he thinks." "I don't give a shit what he thinks. I came to get my stuff and I'm on my way." "I'm telling you, you're doing something really dumb." "Marco! And I thought you were my friend." "I *am* your friend. That's why I'm here. You can't leave with her. He'll stop you. Believe me." "How?" Marco lowers his eyes. A voice behind me.

"Your friend is right."

I recognize the man who just spoke. It's Dumont. I turn around. He goes on: "Marco explained the situation to you." "There's nothing to explain." "My wife." "She can do what she wants." "She has always done whatever she wants. Except leave me." "I think that has changed." I turn back around toward Marco, who's blocking my way. "Move, I've got to go." He doesn't budge. "Marco, let me through!" He closes his eyes and seems to be murmuring an apology. Then I feel a kind of shock. Something violent on my skull. And then nothingness.

I wake up. It's dark. I'm cold. A smell is irritating my nostrils. A sticky smell. My head's exploding. My eyes hurt. Hand on my skull. My hair is glued down by blood. Where am I? I try to get up. I retch. I vomit. I spit. I cough. I stagger forward a couple of steps. I collapse. The pain makes me scream. I'll make it. I get up again. The walls are freezing. Concrete stairs.

The cellar. Crawling. I vomit again. Bile and blood. At last the hallway. At last I'm outside. Air. Goddamn air's going straight to my head. For the first time in my life I like the Paris air. The keys to Sophie's car in my pocket. Valerie must still be at the station.

[*He is alone onstage. He falls and gets up again.*]
HIM: [*shouting*] Wait for me, I'm coming!

Night is falling. The car. The keys. Start. Can't see a thing. Blood and tears blur my vision. Rub my face with the sleeve of my sweater. Everything is blurry. Drive.

Hard to sit up straight. Drive. Light. Red? Green? Doesn't matter. Retching again. Nothing else to vomit but bitter bile. And that blood flowing from my skull. The wound has opened again. I really feel bad. Arriving in the middle of nowhere. Can't recognize anything. Ah yes! The avenue of the station. Can't hold the wheel anymore. Trembling.

HIM: [*shouting*] Wait for me, I'm here!

The car's on the sidewalk. I try to get out. Take a step. Fall on my knees.

HIM: [*shouting*] I'm here . . .

A breath. A strange sensation. Cold taking hold of me. A tear flows, then nothing. That's how I die. On a dirty sidewalk, while Valerie is waiting for me.

[*He collapses on the ground. We hear a cry offstage.*]
[*Curtain.*]

CHRISTMAS
BY CHRISTOPHE MERCIER
Pigalle

Translated by Nicole Ball

> *Faith has been broken*
> *Tears must be cried*
> *Let's do some living*
> *After we die*
> —Keith Richards/Mick Jagger

There are better places than a restaurant in the 9th arrondissement to be spending Christmas Eve, that's for sure. Even though I've been a regular there and a pal of the owner—the successive owners—for the last twenty years, for as long as I've lived in the neighborhood.

Actually, Chez Léon is not exactly near my home, but going there gives me a reason to walk a bit. Well, it's not that far, really . . . I live on rue de la Grange Batelière—a well-read client, there are some, told me that George Sand had lived there as a child, I think—and Chez Léon is at the corner of rue Richer and rue de Trévise, almost across from the Folies Bergère, where busloads of American and Japanese tourists in search of "Gay Paree" pour out every summer. It makes for a 200-yard walk and allows me to get cigarillos at the café-tabac on the corner of Richer-Montmartre. That café is run by a couple, both tattooed and particularly unpleasant, but fun to watch. And watching people is what I do for a living.

Because I'm a private detective. A "private eye," as they say in American novels. But there's nothing glamorous about my life: I don't have a fedora and I don't wear a trench coat (well, yes, I do wear one, because it often rains in Paris.) Nobody thinks of Humphrey Bogart when they see me; I don't go see his films anymore since the Action Lafayette movie house closed (to be replaced by a cut-rate supermarket) because they're not shown anywhere else in the neighborhood, and I don't watch them on TV either because I find them irritating. I find them irritating *now*, I mean. But thirty years ago, I used to like the dark romanticism of those movies and sometimes I tell myself that without *The Big Sleep*, I wouldn't have picked this line of work. Back from the Algerian war, I probably would have been a pastry cook like my dad, and I would have been disgusted with napoleons by now. Good thing I finally saw *The Big Sleep*. Although . . .

It really is a rotten job, especially after thirty years, and it does wear you out. Now, whatever's left of my hair is white, I have trouble walking (arthritis, from too much time keeping watch in the rain, hidden behind the column across from the Ritz, waiting for an unfaithful wife), and I look more like Maurice Chevalier in *Love in the Afternoon* than Bogart; Maurice Chevalier plays another movie private eye but this one is closer to reality. To mine at least. Now there's a movie I would gladly see again. But the first time I saw it—a terrible copy with Italian subtitles showing at a small film festival at the Action Lafayette—it somewhat depressed me. (Originally, it was because of the two movie theatres—the Action Lafayette on rue Buffault and Studio 43 on rue du Faubourg Montmartre, now replaced by a hair salon—that I chose this neighborhood in 1985, a time when you could still find a rare film by combing all of Paris.) It's a comedy but it's only funny to non–private detectives—or private detectives who don't raise their daughters alone—which still gives it a pretty large audience.

Now that my daughter no longer lives with me and she's with her mother in Nantes, I wouldn't mind seeing it again, with a touch of nostalgia even. For without Lola—my daughter's name is Lola, not Ariane like Chevalier's in the movie—I'm bored. She's been gone six months, studying Public Relations at a school paid for by her mother (and her rich step-father) in Nantes, a city her name predestined her to, probably. A dirty trick from my ex-wife to lure her there, obviously. She was supposed to come back for Christmas but the rich step-father invited her to Chamonix and she'll only get here on the second week of her break, after New Year's.

All this to say that, as far as Christmas Eve goes, I had no choice. If I was to spend it by myself, I might as well go to Chez Léon instead of staying all alone with my TV, my canned foie gras, and my lukewarm champagne. I was told they wouldn't have any mother-in-laws going yackety-yak or revelers celebrating there.

So, on that Christmas Eve, the first one without Lola, it was raining. And what's worse than Christmas alone in a restaurant to escape from an old two-room apartment in a dark building in Paris' 9th arrondissement, except Christmas alone in a restaurant to escape from an old two-room apartment in a dark building of Paris' 9th arrondissement in the rain.

It had been raining for the last two days. I had spent them hanging around the Royal Monceau to catch a super-rich but unfaithful emir whose wife had hired my services, and I had been gazing at the gloomy twinkle of the garlands in the trees of avenue Hoche, under the indifferent eyes of the passersby;

sheltered under their umbrellas, they were looking down to avoid the puddles on the sidewalk, busy with their last-minute Christmas shopping. The Arc de Triomphe, way at the end, never seemed so dismal, and my arthritis had flared up.

On that day of December 24, I had returned home late in the morning, after a stake-out of several hours, and I had made myself a hot Irish toddy (boiling whiskey and cloves). After that, I had buried myself under the eiderdown quilt passed down to me by my great-grandmother.

I had slept a good chunk of the day and after I woke up, I listened to some Bach Christmas cantatas to get into the spirit of the day, comfortably settled in my Voltaire armchair, bundled up in three blankets with a Jack Daniel's. Keith Richards listens to classical music too, I suppose. He did break a leg when he fell from the stepladder in his library . . . We must be about the same age. I fantasized for a while about old Keith listening to Bach, then I put on some Stones for good measure. I started with "Time Waits for No One" because of Mick Taylor's solo (he's the greatest guitarist they ever had) and because the bourbon, the rain, Christmas by myself, arthritis, and my elusive Arab sheikh and all had put me in a morose mood. After a third Jack Daniel's, a very hot bath, and the complete recording of *Exile on Main Street*, I felt a little tipsy, no longer in the Christmas spirit, but reinvigorated and even combative. A combative melancholy, so to speak, an energetic melancholy like in "Let It Loose."

I slipped into gray pleated pants, white shirt, bow tie, and the narrow-waisted, shiny dark red jacket with thin black threads that makes me look like a pimp, according to Lola; then, armed with my huge red umbrella and a dry raincoat, I was on my way to Chez Léon.

It was 9 p.m., the festive Parisians were celebrating at

home, and rue de la Grange Batelière was empty.

I felt like having a drink somewhere, to take part in the upbeat mood of a crowded bar on a holiday evening, or to take in the gloomy atmosphere of an empty bar on a holiday evening. I've always liked to hang out over a beer, at night, in train station bars, preferably in the suburbs right outside Paris.

But the wine bars across Drouot were closed, and the dark, dismal glass walls of the auction hall loomed against the sky blurred by the vague drizzle that had followed the afternoon rain. I had rarely seen the neighborhood so dead. More than dead even, deserted, as if the inhabitants had fled to escape a Martian attack, as if they all had been stricken by the plague.

I kept on walking along rue Drouot up to the Grands Boulevards. After a day spent softening in the warmth of my bed and a half-bottle of bourbon, it felt good to walk a bit and my arthritis was no longer bothering me. On boulevard des Italiens, a group of lost, jolly Americans swooped down on me—I was the only living soul in view—and asked me where the Grand Café was. It always gives me pleasure to speak English, as I don't get to use it often in my profession, so I gladly gave them the information. Grateful or completely drunk already, they made as if to drag me along; I had a really hard time declining the invitation without offending them. I finally convinced them that I was expected somewhere else. A white lie which was hard to tell. Not because I mind lying, but it made me realize how poor my English is, even though I like to use it.

In this state of mortification, I turned left toward the Faubourg Montmartre and Chez Léon. I thought I could take a shortcut through the alleys. They have the feel of Paris in the old days, they give you the illusion of breathing in the smell of its old lampposts. They remind me of Céline and his Passage Choiseul and I was looking forward to seeing the storefront windows illuminated on a Christmas night. Never turn down your nose at simple pleasures. I love the store that sells replicas of old toys on the left of Passage Jouffroy: It brings back my soppy side and the good little boy I used to be. There's also the cane store on the other side, near the Musée Grévin (one of Lola's greatest pleasures). I'd love to get a cane someday but they're too expensive. Or more simply, I'm embarrassed to open the door and wake up the old gentleman with tortoise shell glasses who always seems to be dozing off behind his counter.

As I could have guessed, the Passage Jouffroy was closed, its gates down. Gloom was creeping in and on an impulse, I nearly went back home to finish myself off with Jack D. while listening to the Stones and Johan Sebastian Bach. The thought of the next morning's hangover stopped me. I know too well how getting smashed on bourbon makes me feel. I had my share of that in another life, before Lola was born. But now, no thanks. Morning hangovers stay with me for the rest of the day and it's enough to sober me up. So I kept on walking toward Chez Léon.

The novelty store was also closed, of course. I used to buy surprise bombs for Christmas and New Year's Eve there, and fake mustaches that Lola found hilarious. On those evenings, I would be reminded that I was a single father, and once she was in bed, I would get plastered on whiskey and cry in my glass. The Chirac and Spider-Man masks flashed morose smiles at me.

The café of the tattooed couple, on the other hand, was still open. Because of the festive occasion, she was displaying, instead of her usual biker T-shirt, a low-cut one that enhanced her fake pearls and her Jane Mansfield breasts, as unappetizing as a soft block of butter. Not that it made her any more pleasant. She was grumbling at a short Asian man who insisted on paying for a cigarette lighter with a two hundred–euro bill; I thought I heard her call him a "Chink," as in *Tintin in Tibet*, and that made me laugh. Coward as I am, I answered her mumbles with a fake, knowing smile. I'm one of her old regulars but I'm always afraid she might put me down.

Her husband, thin mustache, all dressed up too—black leather pants and orange tie—refused to serve a beer to a lonely old lady adrift in the neighborhood. He was bullying the waiter. "Come on, Marcel, move it! You know we're invited to Mimine's sister's for Christmas dinner. That asshole told us they'll start the oysters without us if we're not there by 10." He calls all the waiters Marcel—I've seen many pass through here, all sickly looking and underpaid—like in the old aristocratic families where all the maids were rebaptized as Marie. I hate those old aristocratic families.

Rue Richer, devoid of street lights, was dark—its pizza places were closed, its kosher butchers (*Chez Berbèche, served better*) had their shutters drawn, its travel agencies (also kosher) offered dream vacations sprawling all over faded posters at bargain prices to the rather scarce customers.

I heard the screams of the crazy woman across from number 46 (I learned from an erudite client of mine—another one—that Alexandre Dumas had briefly lived at that address). She's famous in the neighborhood; some people complain and want to have her committed. She apparently lives in a hovel at the top of the stairs of the building where the Goldenberg grocery store used to be. (It closed down a few months ago and its front is now blinded with cinder blocks.) You can see her stroll about, dirty as a pig, always wearing the same thick woolly petticoats that she doesn't pull down to take a piss (she doesn't squat either, does everything standing up, like an animal), the same heavy, filthy sweater, with her old wino face. The supers of the nearby apartment buildings give her a little money to do chores for them, scrub staircases or take out the garbage in the middle of the night. Sometimes one of them, Maria, an old friend of mine who takes care of the 46 building, pulls her inside her home and forces her to shower. I know the woman through her. She must have been very beautiful once. When she leaves Maria's place, when her gray hair has just been washed and isn't greasy or all tangled, you notice how beautiful it still is and what a sweet, rugged face she has. Her name is Elena, she came from Italy (Ferrara) before the war to flee Mussolini, and later, her whole family, with the exception of one son, died in Auschwitz. Maria knows all this because she was already here twenty years ago and because Elena, who lived in a studio apartment belonging to Goldenberg, was still talking at that time. Then her son died, she became a bag lady, and she stopped communicating. Well, she didn't exactly stop: She still expresses herself: She lets out terrifying howls at night, from the window at the top of the stairs in her building; that's where she took her rags after she stopped paying her rent.

She bays at the moon, like a dog, like an animal, as if she has no language, as if she can no longer articulate and the howling comes from a huge red hole deep inside her mouth. Like the desperate woman she is, to whom nothing matters anymore. Those who want to get rid of her or commit her are the young yuppies who subscribe to special cable channels like Canal+. They've invaded the neighborhood in the last few years, like rats in pin-striped suits. I hate young yuppies who subscribe to Canal+. The people who've been living here for a long time—old Jews with payess and yarmulkes you see on Saturday mornings hurrying to the synagogue with lowered eyes, in white shirts, black suits, and hats—pity her. She's one of them, only in more despair than they are perhaps. According to Maria, she may have a grandson who's "very successful," no one knows in what capacity; he would like to move her into an apartment of her own, somewhere else, but she doesn't want to; she wallows in her loneliness and misery.

When she screams, you can hear her in the silence of the night for blocks around. In the summer, if I have my window open, her animal cries split the air above the rooftops like a witch's broom and come to me.

She doesn't howl every night, only when she's scared or when she remembers that day during the German occupation when she came back home to find out that a roundup had taken place and that all her family had been taken away.

Her screams don't bother me anymore, but on that Christmas Eve, under the thick drizzle that had started up again, in that deserted street whose sidewalks would tomorrow be lined with garbage cans overflowing with oyster shells, they made me shiver. I started to walk faster.

Chez Léon is a big, long room with a bar on the right side. I sometimes go there at the end of the evening to have a drink with the owner, a cocky young guy from Morroco I like; he suggested a couple of years back that we go into business together: The idea was to set up a car deal between North Africa and France. His name is El-Hadji; he's a fun-loving Muslim with a sexy walk and a soft way of looking at you. Conversations are rather limited with him—sex and money—but it doesn't matter because you can feel friendship behind the words and occasionally even something like tenderness.

Our friendship nearly suffered a major blow three years

ago when he got it into his head that Lola, whom he had known since she was very little, was becoming "a real knock-out," as he put it. I had no desire to see Lola be a member of El-Hadji's harem even if he's my friend and a nice guy. But I stuck to the principles of education I've always given Lola and I didn't prevent her from going out with him when he invited her to dinner. A good decision really. After the third time, she said he was the biggest asshole, that he was so fucking thick, and how in the world could a guy like that be my friend. She didn't set foot in Chez Léon for several months after that and I was able to go back to my routine there, without ever bringing up the business with my pal El-Hadji.

I happened to help him out, professionally, once or twice, and since then, it's friendship for life between us, he says. I'm not that committed; I only hope he stays here; I don't want him to drop everything and move to the suburbs—he talks about doing that sometimes. I just want to keep coming here like tonight, like I've done for the past ten years since he showed up as a young waiter. I want to keep bathing in the milk of human kindness, as Shakespeare wrote, more or less.

El-Hadji got married six months ago (after I did a little investigation on his bride to be, at his request, to see if she was faithful) and he stopped talking about women for a while. (It's sort of coming back now.) He's a complete egocentric: A week after his wedding, he had his sexy head of curly hair clipped because it was more comfortable for wearing his bike helmet; and now that he'd found a serious woman, he didn't care about being good-looking anymore.

His wife is pregnant now and for the last two or three months he's been complaining about her big belly and letting his hair grow back. Something's cooking but I have no business trailing him.

Chez Léon: There's a pale-blue ceramic fountain standing in the middle of the room, always dry, and on each side of it, along the wall, tables for four are enclosed in little booths that make you feel at home.

On that Christmas Eve, El-Hadji had made himself a kind of bullfighter costume and over his white shirt, he was wearing a black satin vest discreetly embroidered with pink silk, bullfighting style. When I got there, the place was empty. He came over with two glasses of champagne and sat down in front of me. He was in a confiding mood so he explained that he had opened tonight not because he was hoping to make money, but because he didn't want to go to Christmas dinner at his in-laws' and could go see his babe later. My guess had been correct. His green eyes were shining.

He only had one dinner reservation, two people, around 9:30. He knew he wouldn't have any unexpected customers, not on a night like this, on such a deserted street, so he would close early.

El-Hadji knew very well that I had come here, by myself, to escape the gloomy festivities, the ready-made, jolly good time you were supposed to have tonight. He didn't take my order but brought me, as usual, five or six little plates of assorted spicy vegetables. I knew that my traditional tajine chicken-olives would follow, along with a couscous dish. That's the advantage of being a regular, you don't have to talk too much. I would wash down my tajine with a Boulaouane rosé, followed by a little glass of fig brandy, courtesy of the house. On Christmas Eve, it's reassuring to find a place where you can forget you're all alone on a holiday.

El-Hadji was back at his post behind the bar. He had a beaming, distracted, fixed smile on his face because he was thinking about how his evening would end, and I was daydreaming in front of my hors-d'oeuvres when they arrived.

It was like an apparition. She was very tall (six-two, as my professional eye automatically informed me), very long; her sublime, never-ending legs were sheathed in soft leather thigh boots studded with fake pearls at the hem.

When she took off her long fur coat, I nearly choked at the view of her back; an oval was left bare by a thin, very short dress of red wool that also let her thighs show. When she got rid of her hat, her curly, jet-black hair fell down to the middle of her back. She had magnificent green eyes and lucky teeth—a space between them, that is. I love women with a space between their upper front teeth, like the actress Maria Schneider. This girl was a cross between Brigitte Bardot '69, an erotic year, and Maria Schneider—my fantasy women when I was thirty.

The man was up to her—no pun intended: He must have been six-six, like that character in *Lucky Luke* comics named Phil Defer. I'm not one of these men who claim he's incapable of telling if another guy is handsome or not, for fear people might think he's gay. I can tell when a man is handsome, which has nothing to do with the charm that attracts women—I'm a bad judge of that—but that man surely was handsome. It's all the more praiseworthy for me to admit he was handsome because he had an Italian kind of beauty, handsome but vain and dumb-looking, which I've always hated for no particular reason. He was immense, well-built, curly smile and frizzy hair, the typical playboy you picture in your mind, shades on his nose, muscles flexed on his Vespa as he drives along the beach to pick up all the chicks.

In short, that couple made a major impression. Even El-Hadji, who is pretty tall himself, only came to his customer's shoulder. When he brought my tajine, his annoyance was evident through his forced smile: "Who does that broad think she is? She handed me her coat like I was her servant." She probably didn't even see him.

What do you do, alone in front of a tajine on a Christmas Eve, when such a spectacular-looking couple sits down at the next table? You look at them. And if you are a good private eye, you look at them with your ears pricked up without them being aware of it.

It kept me busy for a while. She was truly extremely beautiful and when I heard her speak, I thought I was hearing Lauren Bacall in *The Big Sleep*. I'm not an unconditional fan of Lauren Bacall, I even find her a bit stupid to tell you the truth, but I love her husky voice.

The handsome guy—very chic: gold watch and chain bracelet, pocket handkerchief matching his tie, chic like I myself could never be—was looking lovingly, with ecstatic eyes, at his sweetheart. Behind his façade of young businessman, it was easy to see a kid in love. He was no more than twenty-five, too young to be a businessman really, or else he was a particularly gifted one; he looked like a sweet boy.

The couple was rather nice, actually. Busy watching them as I was, I had forgotten my tajine, which was getting cold, as well as my Christmas blues, and the fact that I had taken refuge at my friend El-Hadji's so I wouldn't be alone.

The young man's name was Nico. Hers was Teresa, Teresa, Teresa, a name he kept repeating to get closer to her, to possess her, to convince himself she was his. She looked at him tenderly, as if he were a puppy-like little brother who happened to be her lover too.

After El-Hadji had served each a mayonnaise lobster, he brought me my fig brandy and sat down. I kidded him a little: "Since when have you been serving lobster? You bought it frozen?"

He shrugged. "I bought those lobsters just for them. Fresh. I know how to cook them perfectly. The guy insisted on having lobster when he made the reservation. I told him this was a Tunisian restaurant; he said yes, he knew that, he used to come here a long time ago, but he absolutely needed to have a lobster dinner here tonight. What could I do? The customer is always right and I wanted to open the restaurant tonight anyway. Besides, it was the only reservation I had . . . Shit! I forgot to bring them their Chablis."

Apparently, they hadn't noticed and El-Hadji, holding the bottle with his eyes lost in space, had to wait a solid minute so as not to interrupt a passionate kiss. The girl was so beautiful that there was nothing indecent about the kiss.

El-Hadji came back to my table to tell me at length about his plastic Christmas tree. He hadn't set it up because he didn't want his place to feel too much like Christmas; it felt dumb. He was wondering if he would set it up tomorrow morning to make the place feel like Christmas after all, but the tree was in the attic, all dusty and one branch missing. Just to attract a few customers (because, you see, tonight is actually okay, but if it's empty like this till January, business will suffer).

I was sort of listening while enjoying my second glass of fig brandy when suddenly I saw Nico turning ghastly pale as he peered toward the entrance.

A man had walked in. He was shabby-looking: short, almost dwarflike. His grayish complexion, under a two-day beard, was as rumpled as his suit, which was too big, floating around him with a faded pink that reminded me of that particular color my first grade teacher vividly depicted as "drunk vomit."

He could have been fifty as easily as seventy. His greasy, thin gray hair was showing from under his felt hat, which he hadn't removed. You felt like giving him spare change to go get a sandwich.

Everything happened very fast. Handsome Nico turned pale, I glanced at El-Hadji, expecting him to get rid of the intruder, but the aforementioned El-Hadji was petrified: He turned red and lowered his head, concentrating intensely on the few grains of couscous in the congealed sauce on my plate. Nico got up from his seat, abandoning his sublime Teresa, and walked over to the visitor.

Nico, the handsome, flamboyant Nico who had entered Chez Léon just a little while ago, was no more. He was taking little steps with his head down. Next to him, the visitor seemed to be a real midget, but a midget with authority.

The older man made a sign with his finger; Nico bent down so their heads were at the same level. I think the guy whispered something to him but I couldn't be sure. What I'm certain about, though, is that he smacked Nico on his left cheek with his right hand, a pat really, like in the game where you hold each other's chin while singing that little song and whoever laughs first gets slapped on the cheek. Except this was no game.

Nico didn't return to his table. Suddenly hunched, crushed, aged, he left the restaurant. The old man didn't move. He watched Nico leave, then walked to my table where El-Hadji had remained, as white and rigid as a wax statue.

"Give the lady whatever she asks for. Here's the money."

He put a small wad of two hundred–euro bills on the table and walked away. El-Hadji, his eyes still down, didn't check, but clearly there was enough cash there to cover all of his evening expenses, and even if he served caviar by the ladle to his customer, he could close the place and reopen after the holidays without losing anything.

"The mafia," he stammered.

The old man had left.

The whole thing hadn't lasted more than two minutes and Teresa still hadn't reacted, as if she hadn't realized that her beau had abandoned her there.

Funny things happen in Paris, that's for sure, whispered the little provincial guy from Savoie (my father's pastry shop was in Albertville) sleeping inside of me. But his big brother, the one who grew up and became a private eye, had to find out more.

I jumped from my seat and left with my dark red jacket with black threads.

The old man seemed to have vanished in the deserted street, but I spotted a spineless, raggedy shape who was throwing up on the garbage cans. It was Nico. He hadn't walked more than fifty yards in two minutes. He was dragging his feet, on his way to doomsday.

On rue Richer, there was no sign of the crazy woman and everything was silent. You could see garlands on Christmas trees twinkling through windows. The rain had turned into a light snow that evaporated when reaching the ground, just as the old man had. The shabby old guy was like a genie, like a snowflake, I said to myself jokingly. He evaporates, disappears, doesn't exist anymore.

But Nico's ghost still existed and was sticking to the asphalt. He looked like he was dragging an invisible ball and chain. And then I saw him negotiate a quarter-turn to his left (with difficulty, as his body wouldn't obey him anymore), and go into the Goldenberg building, the one with store windows blinded by cinder blocks, the building where the old Italian woman, the desperate, crazy Jewish woman lived.

I followed him. The building, ready to be torn down, was

deserted and sinister. The marble lobby smelled of mold and at the bottom of the large stairwell, a yellowish stone goddess covered with black and blue graffiti proudly displayed a nudity no one was interested in anymore. The rise and fall of elegant Hausmannian architecture. But I wasn't there to write about the history of the 9th arrondissement.

Following him was so easy I was almost ashamed. He paused on each step of the large, pompous stairwell. (In other times, young romantic men must have climbed it already on their way to becoming paunchy bankers with pear-shaped heads à la King Louis-Philippe.) I said to myself, and I thought it was funny, that I shouldn't have been a private detective or a pastry cook like my dad, but a scholar, a historian.

In the dark, barely lit by the snow falling behind the broken transom windows, Nico kept going up, with me trailing him. We were two characters in a silent, black-and-white film, screened in slow motion. It was bitterly cold. A rat scrambled between my legs; I held onto the banister and felt the paint peeling. Falling would be all I needed. *Hello! Merry Christmas!*

The stone staircase ended at the fifth floor but Nico took a smaller wooden one spiraling up to the next floor which, in another era, must have been where the maids' rooms were located. I stopped at the bottom of that ladder of sorts which ascended to the heavens. Everything was dark up there.

So that's where the crazy woman lived, then, and she was the one Nico had come to visit. A picture, a little blurry still, started to take shape in my mind.

And suddenly I was sure of it. The famous grandson who "was doing real well" was Nico, and that's why he wanted to have dinner in this neighborhood. Childhood memories, probably, from the time his father was still alive and his grandmother still sane. And I also understood how he was getting his money, his suit, his golden jewels, and why El-Hadji had seemed to liquefy when the old guy had stepped into Chez Léon. I had crossed paths with the 9th arrondissement mafia before. I knew Nico was doomed. He had come to say goodbye to his grandmother.

Careful not to make the wooden steps creak, I continued up. There was a sourish smell, a smell of urine, of a stable where the straw is never changed.

Nico was at the top. He groped his way in the dark to find a big flashlight that pointed at a bunch of rags under the slanted roof. The old woman was sleeping like a tired baby, all red and wrinkled. Her face appeared strangely at peace. Again I could see the former beauty my friend Maria had talked about. She didn't wake up.

Nico set the flashlight down and bent over inside the halo of light. He took his wallet out of the inner pocket of his jacket and came up with a wad of bills that he deposited next to the pallet. He did the same with his wallet. Then he took off his watch and his gold arm chain, and after undoing his tie, the big chain and pendant he was wearing around his neck followed. He placed everything next to the bills and the wallet. At the end of this strange ritual of stripping, he crudely cut a handful of his curly black hair with a kitchen knife he had found by fumbling around in his grandmother's stuff, near the cheap wine bottles. He deposited the curls next to his other offerings. When his face came back into the halo of the flashlight, I could see he was crying silently.

He remained there motionless for a good ten minutes, looking at her with great tenderness. Then he kneeled, kissed her hand, and went down the stairs again.

I hardly had time to hide in the darkness of the sixth floor landing; and then I followed him. I knew there was nothing anyone could have done for him but I was moved by a kind of sick curiosity, professional as well as romantic.

When he got to the street, he took off his tie, stuffed it inside the pocket of his jacket, and dumped the jacket in a garbage can. It would soon be covered with oyster shells and lemon peels. Wearing only his shirt with the collar open under the snow that was now falling hard and sticking to the ground, he was walking faster than before, as if eager to put an end to the whole thing.

He turned left and took the Cité de Trévise. I love that park with its fountain and trees, its old, solid, and very bourgeois buildings. The balconies around the square were decorated with white garlands that twinkled under the snow.

Nico stared at them for a few minutes, shivering; he was standing in front of the old store that sells theater wigs at one corner of the square (it seemed right out of a Balzac novel), he was smoking a cigarette he'd had trouble lighting because of the snowflakes. He looked like he was filled with a vague longing for a life that could never have been his. Then he started walking again, along rue Bleue, then the dismal and deserted rue Lafayette, that cold thoroughfare that cuts the 9th arrondissement in two, between the first slopes of Montmartre and the flat, Hausmannian part where I live.

I followed him up to rue des Martyrs and I was almost happy for him that his last walk—for I was sure this was his last—was taking him to a more lively, joyful part of the neighborhood that I've always liked. On a night like this, you could feel the magic of Christmas. The windows of the antique stores on the little square Saint-Georges were still lit, and because I was walking very slowly, I spotted a magnificent barrel organ that reminded me of the one in Jean Renoir's *The Rules of the Game*. Which made me wonder if people who live in the bourgeois 16th arrondissement are so happy or at peace with themselves after all.

The cafés on rue des Martyrs were still brightly lit, and down the street, on the right, the beautiful produce store—managed by a Moroccan guy who couldn't care less about Christmas—was open. After reaching boulevard Rochechouart, Nico turned left toward Pigalle. The sex shops splattered the night with their bright lights, but the whores, freezing under their much-too-short synthetic fur coats, didn't even try to seduce that strange passerby wearing only his shirt in the snow, disheveled, lonesome, and disgraced, already a shadow.

On Place Blanche, Nico got into a big black limousine that seemed to be waiting for him there. It went around the traffic circle and down toward the Opéra. The snow on the ground was so thick by now that the limousine had a hard time moving forward and I could easily follow it. My feet were freezing inside my cowboy boots and I said to myself that at least Nico was out of the cold. Rue Blanche, La Trinité Church, less forbidding than usual under the snow, and the huge Christmas tree twinkling in the little park. The doors of the church were wide open, a well of light, like the mouth of hell. A loudspeaker played "Silent Night" over and over for the few faithful who were cautiously walking to midnight mass. But I don't like hymns or mangers anymore. I've lived too long.

The limousine was moving forward, solemnly, silently, like a black whale lit by the bluish whiteness of the snow. Behind the Opéra, without slowing down—granted, it wasn't going very fast—one of its doors opened up and a body fell out. Finally, the car accelerated in the mud and disappeared in the direction of boulevard Haussmann.

The intersection was completely empty; the Santa Claus of the Galeries Lafayette, tucked away inside the warmth of its department store window, was moving his arms mechanically for nobody, with his ugly, hairless papier-mâché reindeer standing in the cotton snow.

I walked up to Nico. He had stopped breathing and his confession, scribbled in a shaky handwriting—*I have betrayed*—was pinned to his chest with a knife. He looked like a frightened little boy. I closed his eyes and left.

The Godfather, one of my favorite movies, only came to my mind when I was in front of the Opéra. I thought of all the killings and the death of Al Pacino's daughter at the end, on the steps of the Palermo opera. The scene amused me and I think I even smiled. How theatrical these Italians are! But really, it would have had more panache if they had disposed of the body in front of the Opéra, at the foot of the majestic staircase rather than behind it. The way they had done it here, it looked kind of lame. The 9th arrondissement mafiosi were small-time gangsters.

Cars were scarce on Place de l'Opéra but you could already see a few dressed-up silhouettes: early revelers in suits and long dresses returning home after the twelve strikes of midnight; frail silhouettes against the snow carefully making their way—they could have been right out of a Dauchot painting.

I came to know Dauchot well, at the end of his life. I had paid him a visit twenty years earlier in his studio towering above Pigalle and we had become friends. I would drop by his place sometimes in the morning and have a drink there, when I was depressed after a night stake-out. He was the only friend of mine who could give me a dry pastis, like Robert Mitchum, apparently, when he was on a shoot in Corsica, at 8 a.m. He would show me the painting he was working on, though at the end, the poor guy wasn't painting much. We didn't talk a whole lot but we were fond of each other. I love friendship. I sure miss that poor old drunk.

Rue du Faubourg Montmartre was almost magical, surreal, in the quiet of the snow. But my heart wasn't into dreaming.

Fifty yards beyond the intersection, flying over the snow, the screams of the crazy woman pierced the silence. I had never heard her howl so loudly, to the point of exhaustion. You could feel she was breathless. A few seconds of silence and it would start up again, a long, strident sob, inhuman, so human, unbearable. The nearer I came, the more I felt for her. I was sorry that she hadn't died in her sleep, that she had seen the things her grandson left. Nico, out there, under the dead gaze of Santa Claus, had probably turned into a vague snow heap by now.

A police van came skidding along the buried street. It stopped in front of the crazy woman's building. People in the neighborhood must have called to complain, finally. Nobody's very patient on Christmas Eve . . .

On my way up to my place, I heard Tino Roastbeef's stupid "Petit Papa Noël" song trumpeting out from under a door. I wasn't in the mood. I nearly rang the doorbell of my downstairs neighbor, an eviction officer with ugly daughters, and acted tough, like a private dick, threatening to smash his face if he didn't turn the sound down. But then, why bother? I was too tired, even to talk.

When I got home, I sank into my Voltaire chair and bourbonized. I finished off everything I had left. And I listened to "Wild Horses" over and over again, not the Stones' version but my buddy Elliott Murphy's *Last of the Rock Stars*, last of the bluesmen, the ultimate *loner*, like Dylan, like Neil Young. He lives not far from here, on rue Beauregard, on the other side of this arrondissement. Sometimes when I feel blue, I go visit him; he takes his guitar and plays some Willie Dixon for me. Beautiful, my friends, just beautiful.

But tonight, it was Christmas and it was too late. And El-liott, after all, is a married man and a father.

So I kept on playing "Wild Horses," all alone.

On Christmas morning, I had a terrible hangover.

THE REVENGE OF THE WAITERS
BY JEAN-BERNARD POUY
Le Marais

Translated by Marjolijn de Jager

The whole neighborhood called him Zatopek.

Every morning he'd trot five times around the Place des Vosges at a slow pace, keeping under the archways even though it's a lot more exciting, humanly speaking, to be running beneath the linden trees of the park when it's nice out.

Something every other stupid jogger in the area actually does.

But he was nothing like any of those fitness fanatics who sweat in their name-brand, pastel-colored, see-through jogging suits, their iPods in their ears, rings of perspiration under their armpits, and the stupid look of someone forced to read Derrida.

He didn't really look like your basic 4th arrondissement bourgeois bohemian who works himself up into a sweat before he gets on the sweaty backs of the employees in his start-up company. His shaggy head, his strange and frightening grimaces, his intimidating glances, his tramplike clothes, they all stood out in this temple of outdated good taste. He spoke to no one. Not even to himself. He never bumped into anyone, even when passing right by the tables of Ma Bourgogne from where a group of apprehensive Italian-American tourists watched him go charging by, breathing hard and staggering on his skinny legs like a frenzied duck, as if he intended to send their tea and pastries crashing down.

His ritual was unchanging: On his third loop he would stop in front of me and I'd hand him a glass of water, which he'd gulp down like a camel. In my old-fashioned black-and-white waiter's livery, I felt like a magpie or, on weekends, like a stork giving a drink to a muddy and exhausted fox.

When he'd completed his five rounds of the Vosges Stadium he would disappear, literally melting into the ancient stones of the rue de Birague, passing beneath the archway of the Pavillon du Roi, and no one would see him again for the rest of the day. But at 9 on the dot the next morning, summer and winter, Zatopek would reappear from the rue de Béarn, on the other side, emerging from the Pavillon de la Reine as if he were charging down onto the cinder track in Prague.

Several of us, true professional barkeepers, had figured out that he'd been working out like that for three years. Five times, or about two kilometers, around the square each day over three years adds up to a total—another round, boss!—of 2,190 kilometers in all. Hats off. Here's to you.

Zatopek.

And then one clear Tuesday in late September he didn't show up. Nor the following day. The neighborhood was in turmoil. Worse than if a thimble signed *Buren* had been found in place of the huge, hideous Louis XIII statue planted smack in the middle of the park. We waited. Maybe Zatopek was sick. Or maybe he had corns on his feet. Or his tibias had perforated his knees—who knows what might have happened with that stupid obsession with jogging.

Going from bar to bar, from store to store, we began a speedy little investigation, questioning neighbors like the cops do when they're out to piss everybody off. No one around had heard anything about an accident. No old folks run over by a bus, not by the number 29 or the 96. No firemen or EMS personnel had been called anywhere. Nothing special had occurred.

It was as if Zatopek had suddenly left for the Olympic Games to defend the honor of the 4th arrondissement before the whole world. Our patient concern lasted a good week. No news at all about our anonymous champion. I waited every day with my glass of water in hand.

A strange panic came over all those who truly loved the Place des Vosges. It was something of a catastrophe. The appeal of the place had suddenly lost one of its vital components. An appeal we had created, protected, and sheltered inside us. In spite of the droves of tourists, guides, and the dismal parade of rich people from the 16th arrondissement who come bursting onto the square every weekend, from rue des Francs-Bourgeois—where else—with gullible faces and teeth sharp enough to cut through the asphalt in search of a duplex to buy. In spite of the avalanche of new galleries under the arcades, filled with ghastly art geared to the lobotomized, showing nothing but pathetic naïve art, lascivious nudes in soft bronze, and hyperrealist paintings of Bordeaux bottles. In spite of all the children tearing at each other in the park's sandboxes; in spite of the homeless who camp out right beside Miyake's.

We missed Zatopek.

As if in a small village in the Creuse, the mailman was no longer coming by.

My job as waiter at Ma Bourgogne provides me with free afternoons. After the lunchtime rush, my replacement arrives. Then I leave to join my colleagues in the neighborhood bars.

The International League of Barkeepers. Very pleasant to be served. For once. But hey, we don't bug the waiter all the time. And we leave a tip.

We had gradually formed a group held together by superglue. For professional reasons, of course; as a group it was easier for us to stay up to date on vacant positions, replacements, and little extras to earn on the side. But we were also attached to our little community for reasons of survival: There were about ten of us who were sick of hearing about soccer games and having to silently put up with the vaguely racist conversations of customers barely awake in the morning or half-sloshed in the evening.

I presented the problem to them and I must have talked like Victor Hugo in exile, for they got on board very quickly. We decided to reach out to everyone we knew to try and find out a little more about Zatopek. Where did he come from? Where did he live? Where did he go? All the questions that had never really occurred to us over the last three years. Our mascot was so reliable. Every day, at more or less the same time. Like the mail. Like a radio broadcast.

If we, seasonal sidewalk waiters, had spotted Zatopek, other people must have seen him too. Janitors, street sweepers, storekeepers, we were going to approach everyone. Strangely enough, we really missed this weirdo who came shaking his little legs on our turf every day. Some uneasiness about using the past tense when speaking of him. It just goes to show how concerned we were about what might have happened to him.

There was a sense of drama in our activity, not sure why, it was pure intuition. But something didn't feel right. The whole neighborhood was being hacked away, the old residents dropping off one after another, replaced by young heirs with slicked-back hair; the former notion stores and wrought-iron workshops were turning into clothing stalls which then turned into restaurants where you paid twenty euros for a radish salad.

To take stock of the situation we picked 3 o'clock on Saturday at Jean-Bart on the corner of Saint-Antoine and rue Caron, a cool, bustling café-tabac filled with unintelligible young people and Keno addicts.

In less than a week the job was done.

Three janitors later, we knew where Zatopek lived. Number 12 rue Saint-Gilles. A cavernous, paved courtyard full of ancient workshops, old and crumbling apartments, makeshift shelters, the poor man's idea of a loft.

I used to walk around there sometimes during my break in the hope of finding an attic room to rent. I was sick of having to cross all Paris every morning.

With Jean-Louis, who slogs away at the café-tabac on the corner of Saint-Claude and Turenne, I went to check out the place, our hearts in our mouths, afraid of finding out that the old jogger had died. Surprise. Impossible to enter beneath the old-fashioned arched entry: A huge wooden fence barred the doorway. Demolition permit. To be followed by the construction of a group of apartments, some of which would be "affordable housing." Project manager, the IMPACTIMMO Society with the City of Paris as its client, at least for the public housing part. Behind the boards, a construction site, gigantic.

So that's what it was. Real estate. Plain, dirty real estate. That moral scourge. With its cynicism set in cement. As for Zatopek, they had found him another pad. Somewhere. Far away no doubt. Maybe in a nursing home. Maybe in a shelter, who knows?

Bastards! The heartless sonsofbitches!

An old guy. He'd spotted us scrutinizing the official notices with disappointment. Cap, cane, the type who spends all day hanging around trying to find someone to talk to.

"I used to live here, they threw me out, I won't tell you how, those bastards, nobody budged, I was one of the first, they didn't care . . ."

"Can we buy you a drink?"

"I won't say no, boys."

The old fellow was as endlessly talkative as his gullet was bottomless. We learned a ton about the Place des Vioques—the Old Squares Square—as he called the Place des Vosges. He knew everybody. And more importantly, Zatopek. Whose real name was Monsieur Girard, as it said on his mailbox. But he had never made friends with the old madman, a retired railroad worker—that had to be why he was galloping all day long, probably took himself for a locomotive. The only one who managed to talk with him was old Marthe, the one who took the garbage out and sometimes cooked for two. She had vanished as well. No mystery there. Pushed toward the exit little by little, everyone had left. Those bastards from IM-PACTIMMO had succeeded in evicting all the residents of number 12 in less than a year. How were they doing it? By negotiating, supposedly. With a little dough—very little given the neighborhood—but the poor who lived there didn't know any better. Or else, with the oldest and the nearly bedridden, a placement in a home for the elderly, impossible to get un-der normal circumstances. For this guy it was different, he'd jumped at the money even knowing it was a rip-off, but he had a weak heart. He had given it all to his daughter, who let him have her maid's room on rue de Turenne. With his puny retirement pension, he could hang on until the grave.

The strange thing was that we suddenly had the feeling we knew it all and yet had learned nothing. The only lead we had was old Marthe. The garbage woman. She might know a little more about Zatopek. But she had left without saying where she was going. She might well have returned to the provinces. Stashed away in some slum, a country dump twenty kilometers from the nearest grocery store. Our marathon man, too, for that matter. Running through the fields wouldn't be too terrible a sentence.

We let our old timer keep stewing about those rotten real estate sharks a while longer, then left him in front of his fifth Picon beer.

We were stuck.

To get any further, to try and find more traces of the former tenants of number 12, we would have needed an armada of muckrakers. It was hard to feel reassured by the possibility that Zatopek had been safely put away somewhere. In view of the state he was in, that somewhere could be a stinking shelter, a place like a prison where they'd slowly anesthetize you, where they'd just let you croak. Because it costs society too much to take care of its relics. Even the daily *Parisien* says it, and that's saying something.

The days went by and the Place des Vosges was looking hard in the direction of Versailles. And to think that I'd known that square as a little kid, a real rough place then. With the opening of the Picasso Museum everything had changed. Consequently, the Spanish paint-splasher had pushed the whole area toward the classical era, chic, conservative, with a platinum checkbook. Even if the joint where I work, my Bourgogne, had always been classy. It used to be a gem in a rugged setting. Now it was a gem among other gems. With Jack Lang practically living above it.

It was Joseph, who worked nights at the Elephant du Nil by the Saint-Paul metro station, who reopened the hunt. There was this old woman, a funny one who hung out at his bar every morning; she came from the rue de Fourcy senior housing. She'd attack her first glass of white wine and lemonade at 10 in the morning and get steadily soaked until noon. She's soaking up her coffin, the owner would say. A real chatterbox. A nasty one too, angry with the entire world.

We went there the following Saturday as a delegation, a group of union representatives. And we sure weren't disappointed. It was good old Marthe, the garbage lady of number 12, the one who knew Monsieur Girard—Marcel to his friends, Zatopek to us. A poor devil. Retired from the railroads, gone half-crazy after he'd pulled parts of a woman who'd been run over by a freight train car. Crazy, for sure, but only halfway, completely with it at other times. Together with her, Zatopek had been the only one to truly fight the real estate jackals. He owned his small two-room apartment in the back of the courtyard and screamed that he'd only go feet first, they wouldn't mess with him. The old guy was borderline straightjacket. And in excellent health; he even went running, can you believe it?

"Where does Monsieur Girard live now?"

"What do you want with Marcel?"

"Nothing. We don't see him on Place des Vosges anymore so we're worried. He was a friend, an acquaintance."

"Oh really? Did he talk to you?"

"Not really. He'd smile. We liked him."

She observed us, her glass of white wine in hand. With her blue smock, her red cheeks, and her eyes an opaque white because of cataracts. Cute as hell, like an old enamel coffeepot. Which could burn your hands if you didn't watch out.

"Why are you worried?"

"We don't know. That's why we'd like to know where he is. So we can stop worrying."

She scrutinized us for a long time. Time enough to empty her glass and order another.

"One morning he wasn't there anymore. He'd left during the night."

"He moved?"

"I don't know. Anyway, he left everything. Two days later, two guys from Emmaus came to load up his stuff. Nothing much. Rickety furniture, some old things, borderline homeless stuff. He must have taken everything worth something with him. Clothes probably."

"Did he have family elsewhere, like, I don't know, in the provinces?"

"I don't think so. Besides, he was a Parisian, a real Parisian, a Parisian down to his toes."

And so on. She kept talking for quite a while, she couldn't let go of us. She felt important at last, and that pleased her. Late in life, almost at death's door, she'd found an audience. But for us it was just padding. We let her talk, we had the basics. Zatopek had suddenly disappeared.

A bit too suddenly.

That Saturday, as we prepared to leave rue Saint-Antoine— already overrun with leisured people stopping every twenty meters to study the restaurant menus and real estate ads—we decided to change our approach. We sat down around some blazing hot pizzas and very quickly, without anyone taking the lead, decided to kick into high gear. No one dared to openly express the negative thoughts that had just entered our heads. The rotten smell of a shady operation. The stench of a dirty trick.

Somberly, we divided the work. It looked like a meeting of anarchists plotting the stormy end of the Republic. Each of us knew we had to get rid of that bad taste in our mouth.

Maurice from the Dôme had a cousin who worked at City Hall. He'd asked her. No trace. Marcel Girard had never asked for any assistance at the municipal offices and always paid his residence tax. He had recently provided a change of address: in Montargis, rue des Hirondelles. He was therefore no longer of concern to the Paris administration. We checked Montargis; rue des Hirondelles didn't exist.

Same story, more or less, at the Railroads Pension Fund. It was Samir, from the Fontenoy at the corner of Saint-Gilles and Beaumarchais, who had the job of investigating this. Marcel Girard had not cashed his last two money orders. The post office had declared them *Unknown at this address*. The French national railway company had no new address listed. They were waiting. Had to. Without a death certificate, the law required them to wait one year before closing the account. As soon as anything new came up, they'd let Samir know. Thanks, that's very nice of you.

We saw Marthe again. After thirty liters of white wine, she agreed to take us to the person in charge of her residence who, very kindly, began an inquiry among similar institutions. Nothing. There was no one in Paris or the surrounding area by the name of Marcel Girard living in a nursing home, senior housing, or the like. No one with an extended stay in a hospital either.

All this took us about two weeks. Two weeks during which we kept going forward despite the tiny spark of hope getting hit with more bad news, bad but not definitive. Perhaps he was now homeless, living in one of those camper tents that keep popping up on the banks of the Seine and the Saint-Martin canal.

Two weeks for our hearts to sink deeper and deeper, avoiding the thought of the old runner having passed away.

But a village is always a village, even inside a big city, even buried inside the City of Lights, that unavoidable city which people from all over the world come to admire, their eyes sparkling and smiles frozen on their faces by the blinking Eiffel Tower. In a village everyone knows everything about everything and the shutters are never closed. Bernard, the waiter at the Mousquetaires on the corner of rue Beautreillis, serves beer to all the fans of The Doors who come ogling the banal façade of the building where Jim Morrison kicked the bucket. He's been hitting on the lady mail carrier who told him that the headquarters of the DAL—a leftist group that focuses on housing issues and has been battling the real estate sharks for years—is right near rue des Francs Bourgeois.

I got the job. They appointed me to sniff around in that direction. The lefties might know something about the number 12 rue Saint-Gilles scheme.

The activist was practically a grandma. Not the leader but a key person. Very interested in our story, even over the phone. I set up a meeting with her at Ma Bourgogne. As she settled down in the back of the room, slipping in behind the white tablecloths, she grew wide-eyed; no doubt the first time she'd ever dared enter this place reserved for the platinum card holders.

Full of fun, bubbly. A *Pasionaria*. Who was probably getting revenge for something, maybe her previous life. The DAL knew—those were her words—the monstrous, disgusting scandal of number 12 inside out. They had opposed it, tried everything, even a surprise occupation, quickly repelled by the cops, but nothing had done any good, the press had barely mentioned the scandal, a clear reflection of the new, cynical harshness of the ruling class. The white-collar gangsters of real estate capitalism were acting somewhat legally, but it was a legality that was infinitely variable, for they were protected by the government. This explained why the former residents, even though they knew they were being ripped off, had all, or almost all, accepted the skimpy bit of money. So they could leave as quickly as possible.

And one of the main reasons, according to this pugnacious old lady, was that the negotiating team was led by a retired police chief named Henri Portant, a sly and devious fellow, using a mix of kindness, threats, understanding, and harshness as he must have used throughout his career. For a fellow who'd spent thirty years getting the toughest of the tough to talk, dealing with scared old people with no support was a godsend.

She herself had met him once, only once, the day when the DAL had been alerted that he would turn up with his assessors to try and persuade the tenants in the back courtyard of number 12. She remembered him as a guy who breathed calm strength, very calm, incredibly calm, like someone with no scruples whatsoever, absolutely no reservations, doing a job that undoubtedly paid him twice as much as what he was offering his victims.

The rebellious grandma asked us to let her know if we were able to dig up anything. The story of number 12 was sticking in their throats. The DAL had legal resources. Any proof of embezzlement could be taken very far, no reason to give up. It's not because the enemy wins every battle that the war is lost.

Our meeting at the Jean-Bart on the following Saturday was morose. We laid it all out. Bernard was the first to speak.

"It's very simple. Zatopek doesn't want to leave. He has no

family. They see him as a crazy man and no one else at number 12 gives a shit."

"Except Marthe."

"But what can that old hag do? No, Zatopek doesn't count. And that old wreck is certainly not the one who's going to throw a monkey wrench into the system or even slow it down."

"Time is money."

"And who's on the other side? Tough guys, handsomely paid to throw everyone out."

"With a former cop in command."

"We should find out more about this guy."

"We already have. The quiet, kind Inspector Maigret fond-of-his-veal-stew type is gone."

"Right. Cowboys now, that's what they are . . ."

"So? Come on! What're you thinking?"

"The old guy, he must have left in a truck, buried under rubble. Or he fell inside the foundation and they poured concrete on him. Who would know?"

Bernard had said it. He'd said what everyone was thinking. Once it had been said it seemed true. It was no longer a foolish thought. It became a plausible reality. Awfully plausible. An anonymous grave.

And now what? What were we supposed to do with this bitch of a quasi-certainty?

"We need to check it out."

"Check what out?"

"Portant. The cop. We need to—"

"Torture him? So he'll spill the beans? How do you expect to do that?"

"No. Meet with him. To find out more."

"He's a cop. We're not cut out for that. Look at us: a

bunch of bored waiters, nice guys crying over a poor old mad-man, not even a customer. The Cartier-Bresson type . . ."

"Still, we managed to dig up some shit."

"Okay. But what are we up against, poor forty-year-old slobs with little potbellies that we are? The pigs. City Hall. Plenty of powerful guys whose arms are so long they could slap us from thirty kilometers away."

We looked at each other. We knew Maurice was right. From start to finish. But we also knew that being right wasn't good enough. That's the way it was.

"It won't cost us anything to find out a little more," I said slowly.

We wasted no time. It was so obvious. The Internet. The phone book. There were several Portants. But only one Henri. He lived at 22 rue de l'Insurrection in Vernon-sur-Eure. I called him, claiming to be an employee of the CNAV Pension Fund. I talked about a file issued by the police department that was confusing me because the addressee was already retired.

He fell for it. He began to yell. There's the administration for you! He wasn't surprised, it's a mess over there! He was yelling so much that when he asked for the file number so he could give them all hell, I hung up.

So now we knew where he lived.

So what?

So nothing.

Except that two days later Samir got a call from the lady at the Railroad Pension Fund. Marcel Girard had just reap-peared. He had asked that his small pension be sent to his new address, 22 rue de l'Insurrection in Vernon-sur-Eure.

Saturday.

We were all there.

With the same findings, worthy of a detective story but one that's hard to finish.

"On top of wasting him he's now grabbing his money."

"He buried Zatopek in the garden of his stupid house, for all we know."

"Sounds like the Landru case. Or Petiot. That kind of shit isn't new."

And then we looked carefully at each other. Testing each other. Silently. For a long time. The time it took for two more glasses of kir. In an hour I'd have to be back at work at the Place des Vosges. To serve all those rich fucks who look at you as if you're ectoplasm. An ectoplasm who never works fast enough. They call you by snapping their fingers. They bellow from beneath the archway: "Garçon!"

So I made up my mind.

"Tomorrow I'll go to Vernon. To take a look at the scum-bag's face."

"I'm going too," Samir said.

"Count me in," Maurice added. "I like action. In memory of Zatopek. We'll see what happens."

We left very early. In Maurice's car. That guy is a gadget freak, his entire salary goes into anything new. He even had a GPS on his dashboard. He drove well and he drove fast, nearly risking points on his driver's licence. We ate up the 130 kilometers like you gobble down a ham sandwich and reached Vernon by 9.

Thanks to the GPS we easily located rue de l'Insurrection. In a residential development built in the '80s. Imitation modern houses with lawns decorated with ceramic dwarfs, sculpted hedges, and at least one araucaria tree every fifty meters. It reeked of money, but not too much. It had the smell of retired civil servants' money. With cars primly parked in front of the outmoded mansions of their owners. The cushy life. Far from Darfur. Nothing to do with all those wretched, helpless, old folks who vegetate in the big cities, sometimes eating out of the same cans as their mangy dogs.

In a silence that spoke volumes, we waited for a solid hour, sitting in the car without knowing why, vaguely hoping to see the cop. Nothing. Other people were coming out of their houses with swarms of kids, rushing to their cars. A picnic. A walk in the woods. Perhaps mass. Sunday lunch at a restaurant and then a movie. Well-deserved peace.

And then he came out. Small and fat.

Without thinking, we disembarked from the car, approached him like the brothers Earp at a pathetic OK Corral. Three against one. We just wanted to talk to him. I started three meters away from him.

"Monsieur Henri Portant?"

He stopped. Same reflexes as before. Inspecting us. Weighing what could be happening here. Who we might be. He was thinking, that was obvious. Perhaps we were ex-cons he had caught before who were coming to take revenge. Or highway robbers about to rip him off.

"I beg your pardon?"

"Are you Henri Portant?"

"What is this about?"

We hesitated. We didn't know where to begin.

The former cop moved his hand toward the inside of his jacket. Samir reacted very fast, jumped him, smashing him with the head butt of the century.

Portant fell backward screaming. I pounced on him to pull him up and drag him off. Into his house. All of this taking place right in the middle of the street, a major mistake.

He was bleeding, his crushed nose was leaking like a fountain. His startled blue eyes were barely visible behind that red river.

I grabbed him by the lapels of his jacket and pulled him up to his feet with difficulty. He was moaning and blowing bubbles.

"Bunch of assholes," he muttered.

I smacked him. He groaned. He was in pain.

"Oh my God, I can't believe it!" Maurice cried out behind me.

I turned around.

Some twenty meters off, Zatopek was moving toward us, grunting, trotting along down the sidewalk.

LA VIE EN ROSE

BY DOMINIQUE MAINARD

Belleville

Translated by David Ball

1.

On rue de Belleville, Japanese tourists who had come to see the steps on which Edith Piaf entered the world lingered under the April drizzle, protected by odd little hats of pink, translucent plastic with the logo of a travel agency on them. All the way to boulevard de Belleville, two hundred yards further down, the bright red signs in Chinese characters gleamed through the mist. Legendre turned left into the labyrinth of little cobblestone streets leading to the park, swung the wheel hard to avoid the kids playing soccer in the puddles. Arnaud was trying to drink out of the thermos of coffee his friend made when his radio had started crackling half an hour ago. They had gone to bed very late and he had a hard time waking up, but his heart jumped when he saw police cars stopped a few dozen yards up the street with their lights flashing.

Legendre parked the car at the end of the street and winked at Arnaud.

"I have to be careful," he said. "They've seen me hanging around the neighborhood too much, one of them threatened to give me a ticket for obstruction of justice. You coming?"

When Arnaud hesitated, Legendre held out the car keys with a theatrical gesture.

"Okay, you'd rather stay warm," he said. "That's your problem. You'll find CDs in the glove compartment. But I'm telling you, man, if you want inspiration for your book, this is the place to find it."

Arnaud shrugged with a forced smile. He was almost sorry he'd told Legendre about it a few days ago, out of boredom, out of loneliness; but the truth is, even if he hadn't seen the guy since college, there was no one else he could talk to about it. At the beginning of the winter, Arnaud had gone on unemployment insurance to start writing the novel he'd been thinking about for a long time; 181 days, he'd counted them, and he hadn't even succeeded in finishing four chapters. All winter he'd paced through his apartment watching the leaves fall from the chestnut tree under his windows and onto the sidewalk, soon to become invisible. He'd felt himself sinking into the inertia and calm of his little town in the suburbs—what a cliché, he thought, a former Literature major, the ambitions, the powerlessness.

After a meal washed down with a lot of wine—he'd accepted the cigarette Legendre had offered him, and since he didn't smoke very often he was dizzy and laughed as easily as if it had been a joint—he had dropped a few words, negligently, about this novel he'd given himself till spring to finish, adding that it was coming along, it was coming along nicely. Legendre had tried to get it out of him and finally he admitted it was a *noir* novel, but he didn't want to say very much more. Even if he'd wanted to, he couldn't. He had only said his hero would be a private detective, his victim a woman, she'd live in Paris and work in the world of the night, a stripper or a prostitute. And who'll be the murderer? Legendre had asked, and Arnaud had raised his eyebrows with an air of mystery. If I tell you, there won't be any suspense, he'd answered; but the truth was, he didn't know himself. He didn't have a feel for crime, he hated to admit, and the five months he'd spent going through short news items in the newspapers hadn't changed a thing. When he tried to understand what could drive a man to close his hands around a woman's neck, he couldn't imagine it and he told himself this was a terrible start for a novelist. Would his murderer be a pimp, a customer, a serial killer? It was absurd to already have the victim and the setting and be unable to find the murderer, as if a writer could be worse than a bad cop.

He knew Legendre worked for the newspapers and that's what had led him to get back in touch with the guy: the confused hope that since his old friend had written stories about ordinary daily dramas, he had pierced this secret and could reveal it to him.

When he spoke to Legendre about his novel, his friend had slapped him on the shoulder, pointed to the radio on a shelf, and said: "Dig that: It's a police transmitter. When something happens in the neighborhood, sometimes I manage to get there before they do and I sell my photos for five or six hundred euros. Come sleep over next weekend and if something happens, I'll take you along. With a little luck you'll get to see him, your ideal killer. Don't kid yourself, though, there's not much going down right now."

But the transmitter had started crackling early in the morning, and hearing the code the police use, Legendre jumped to his feet and shook Arnaud, who was sleeping on the floor of the two-room apartment situated over an Asian produce store with its fetid stench of durian. Come on, he'd said, this is the real thing, and twenty minutes later they were turning onto rue Jouye-Rouve.

Several of the entrances to the Parc de Belleville hadn't been closed off, so they got in without difficulty. They were not alone; onlookers were crowding the paths, teenagers especially, standing on tiptoe to peer over the metal fences and the yellow police tape stretched from one tree to another. Despite the gray sky you could see all of Paris, just slightly veiled in mist, even the Eiffel Tower to the west. The catalpa trees were in bloom, tulips were standing straight up in carefully spaded triangles of soil, and the park's little waterfall was murmuring; but in the middle of the roped-off space there was a slight swelling under a gray tarp. The fine drizzle had almost stopped; only the smell of moss and undergrowth remained hanging in the wet air. The spectators crowded behind the yellow tape in a warm, motionless mass, and Arnaud almost felt good: It was the first time he had ever been so near a crime scene and he was discovering the silence interspersed with whispers, the strange complicity of the crowd, that morbid fascination, the almost superstitious fear—but also the hope that a corner of the gray tarp would be lifted to reveal a hand or a leg.

Legendre had gone off. Arnaud heard him murmuring a few yards away, moving from one bystander to another. After two or three minutes his friend came back, grabbed him by the arm, and led him away from the crowd.

"I got some information," he said in a low voice. "It's a kid, a mixed-race girl seventeen or eighteen years old, Layla M. She grew up here but she'd been living with a guy for a year. She danced in a nightclub in Pigalle and they say she also slept with the customers. She was strangled to death. See, you've got your story now! All you have to do is find out who did it and you've got your book." He glanced at the gray tarpaulin and went on: "Got something to write with? Go question the neighbors, the people who live in the old building over there—the one with the Hotel Boutha sign on it—they might've seen something. I'm gonna stay here and try to grill these guys—discreetly. Hurry up, you got to be the first to question them. If you go in after the cops they won't want to say a thing."

Reluctantly, Arnaud walked away from the crowd. He was cold in his light jacket and he would have liked to stay in the circle, the cocoon of onlookers. "But I can't," he protested, "I've never done that. What the hell gives me the right to question them?"

And Legendre threw open his arms, exasperated. "I thought you wanted to get involved. If you'd rather sit in front of your computer tearing your hair out, that's your problem."

Arnaud felt ashamed to have hidden his secret so poorly. "But what am I going to tell them?" he insisted, and Legendre answered with a wink before he turned away:

"Tell 'em you're a private detective. They should like that and it'll give you something to think about."

Arnaud waited until Legendre went away; then he groped around in the vest pocket of his jacket, took out the notebook and pen he always carried on him, and walked to the gates of the park. Hotel Boutha was a bit higher up, and Legendre had a point: It was the only building whose windows let you see out onto this part of the park. On the façade, a notice was nailed under the old hotel sign—*Condemned Building*—but the apartments were obviously inhabited. In the lobby, overflowing garbage cans almost prevented him from going in, and the mailboxes had been broken into so often that their doors were dangling from the hinges; the names on the boxes were all faded out, illegible. Arnaud wrote down these details in his notebook and even copied the red graffiti on a wall. He felt a vague sense of shame, taking advantage of the situation to get his hands on these fragments of reality, like a petty thief. Then he made his way between the garbage cans and walked up the stairs.

He rang the doorbells on the second and third floors but nobody answered; a baby was crying behind one door, but no one opened it. A little girl in pajamas opened the door next to it. Her hair was made up in dozens of braids; she looked at him in silence, but before he had a chance to say a word, her mother appeared, with hair braided the same way, and as quietly as her daughter, pulled the child back and closed the door. He started up the stairs again. The stairway smelled of urine and vegetable soup but he didn't have the heart to write it down any more than he'd had the heart to note the serious silence of the child and her mother. For a moment he thought of going back down and telling Legendre the building was empty, but then he heard a door open on the fourth floor and when he got up to the landing, he saw an old man watching him intently from the threshold of his apartment.

The man must have been waiting for him—or the police, more likely—because a plate of cookies was sitting on the kitchen table next to the entrance, as well as cups with coffee stains in them.

"Good morning, sir," Arnaud said, holding out his hand, "I'm a private investigator looking into the crime that just occurred down there." And the old man shook his hand with surprising gentleness.

He was wearing a big plaid jacket even though it was quite hot in the apartment, and a woolen cap he immediately took off with an embarrassed look: "I don't even know when I'm wearing it anymore. Come in, come in."

Arnaud remained in the doorway with his notebook in

his hand, tapping the cover with his pen. "I don't have much time, sir," he said. "I have to question the whole building."

But then the old man smiled knowingly, as if he was well aware that no one had opened their door for him on the lower floors, and simply repeated: "Please, come on in."

Arnaud hesitated. Later, he wouldn't be able to recall how he'd guessed the old man knew something; maybe because just as he was about to refuse again, the old man's smile had hardened and he'd looked Arnaud straight in the eye. So he nodded and said, "Just five minutes," and with two steps he was right there, in the kitchen. An old dog was sleeping under the radiator, stretched out on a plaid blanket the same colors as the old man's jacket, and he didn't even open his eyes when Arnaud pulled a chair over for himself.

As the old man puttered around in the kitchen, checking that the coffee was hot, putting the sugar bowl and a glass of milk on the table, he said: "She's a kid, right?"

"Yes," replied Arnaud, looking out the window at the trees in the park. Between their branches, blobs of color—the onlookers—were pressing against the yellow tape. "Layla M., seventeen or eighteen years old, they told me. She died from strangulation." He was trying for the neutral voice of the private detective he claimed to be. "That means she was strangled, see."

The old man had his back turned. His hands were in the sink; he was mechanically running spoons and knives under the faucet. He didn't say a word.

"Seems she grew up near here," Arnaud continued. "She hadn't been living in the neighborhood for a few months, but I thought some people would be bound to remember her. You yourself—did you know her, by any chance?"

The old man still had his hands in the sink. He seemed

to be washing the silverware under the faucet for an interminable length of time, and Arnaud, thinking the sound of the water might have prevented him from hearing, repeated more loudly: "You know her, by any chance?"

The old man kept his head down, but stretched out his hand and shut off the water. Finally, still without turning around, he said: "Yes, sir, I knew her. I knew her very well. I loved her like a daughter."

Arnaud remained silent for a moment. He cursed Legendre for having put him in this situation; he had no more idea how to console a man than he knew how to grill him or judge his guilt, and he remained silent until the old man finally turned around and leaned against the sink, drying his eyes with the back of his hand. Then he spoke again, clumsily: "She probably didn't suffer, you know, she must have passed out when she couldn't breathe anymore. And the police are there, they're going to find the bastard who did it. Don't worry, they're animals but they always get caught in the end."

The old man raised his head and stared at Arnaud without answering. He picked up the coffeepot, brought it to the table, and filled the two cups. He sat down in front of Arnaud, right next to the dog; he scratched the animal behind the ear for a long time. Then, as if he'd just made a decision, he sat up, put his two hands down on the table, and said: "I'm going to tell you a story."

2.

You see, sir, in two or three months this building's going to be torn down. I think about it every time I see it. Every time I turn the corner I'm glad to see its old walls still standing, and then the potted geraniums of the old lady on the third floor, they're old as the building. She takes cuttings from them and puts them in glasses of water, they're all over her kitchen. During the summer, with the flowers and the wash drying outside the neighbors' windows, you'd think it's a street in Italy. That's what I tell myself, you see, even though I've never been to Italy. Every time I see the building from the street I'm happy, and relieved. As if the demolition crew might come in with their bulldozers and jackhammers before the date they've set, and there'll be nothing left of my house but a pile of rubble. They're going to build what they call a "residence," you know, one of those high-class buildings they sell to young people for a fortune because you can see the trees in the park, as if you couldn't go live in the country when you feel like seeing trees. Twenty years ago it was a hotel—you can still see the sign painted on the front—then they knocked down some inside walls and turned the rooms into apartments to rent to people who didn't mind sharing a bathroom with four other apartments and a toilet out on the landing. Yes, people like me and Layla's mother.

But I'm always afraid they'll knock down the building without any warning, and every time I go out I take a bag with my most important things in it: my papers, the money I've saved up, my watch—I don't like to wear it on my wrist—my social security card, some letters from my mother, and . . . these photos. That's Layla. Take a look. She got these snapshots done in the Photomaton at the supermarket; she gave them to me on her fifteenth birthday. You can see how beautiful she is. Nobody ever knew who her father was; her mother got married and had three other kids but Layla was the oldest, from the years when her mom was going out and having a good time. The kid was conceived who knows where and she was born who knows where, in the street, she was in a hurry to see the world, the neighbors didn't have the time to call an ambulance.

For a long time she was ashamed of it, being born in the street. The other kids in the neighborhood knew—kids always know everything—and you can bet they made fun of her. Then one day I took her by the hand—her mother asked me to watch her a lot when she was a little girl and the kid was used to coming over my place—and I took her to rue de Belleville to show her the marble plaque on number 72, where Piaf was born, you know, five minutes away from here. And then I took her to the library to show her what a great lady Piaf was, I showed her books and I made her listen to recordings too, she looked like a little mouse with those earphones—she was . . . oh, not more than five or six. I never had a record player and neither did her mother.

That story of Piaf who was born in the street like her . . . it was a good thing for her—and a bad thing too. Because she decided right away she'd be a singer, and she did have a nice little voice. She started singing all the time. Since they couldn't handle her anymore at her place, with the three other kids squealing, she'd come to mine. She used to give me sheets of paper with the words of the songs and I had to check if she was making any mistakes, and me, I hardly know how to read, sir. When it was nice out we'd go down to the park, right next door, I'd spread out a sheet or a blanket under a tree and I'd give her what I'd made to eat, sandwiches usually, cheese or chicken sandwiches, and sometimes she'd run off to get Cokes at the nearby Franprix. Those days, when I listened to her sing, with the smell of the flowers all around, stretched out on the blanket with a piece of grass between my teeth— sometimes she sang so softly I'd fall asleep—yes, sir, no doubt about it, those were the best days of my life.

They should have given her singing lessons, of course, and taught her to play an instrument too, but they didn't have any money for that either. For a while she thought she'd pay for them herself and she sang in the street, especially in summer at the sidewalk cafés around Ménilmontant, and there too, I'd go with her to make sure nothing happened to her; I used to take along a folding chair and I'd roll myself cigarettes until I decided it was time to go home. Yes, you see, I never had a kid, so naturally it was like she was mine, almost, what with her mother always busy with the three little ones. But she was never able to collect enough money to pay for lessons or a musical instrument.

When she grew up things got difficult. At fourteen she started changing her name all the time, saying she was looking for a stage name. She used to go to the library a lot, first with me and then alone, that's where she learned all those names of singers and opera heroines, Cornelia, Aïda, Dorabella. Plus, you had to watch out: You couldn't make a mistake, confuse her most recent name with the old one, or she'd get mad; it was like mentioning somebody she'd had a fight with. One day, just kidding around, I told her she was like an onion adding skins instead of taking them off, but after that she wouldn't talk to me for a week. Maybe what the girl really missed was bearing the name of a man who was a real father to her.

She hung onto the idea of becoming a singer. Her parents wouldn't hear of it, of course, they wanted her to get a real job, with a good salary. But she stuck to her guns. Then it began to go to her head, and it's my fault too, because I always encouraged her. Those years, when she was fourteen or fifteen—they were the worst. Layla wasn't going to school anymore—we learned this by pure chance because she'd steal the notes from school and imitate her mother's signature. Her stepfather gave her a beating and she went back, but not for long, she never stopped cutting classes, she'd leave in the morning with her school bag but she'd hang out in the street all day.

Things were so bad at home that she got used to sleeping here from time to time, then more and more; her parents felt secure knowing where she was. I wanted to give her my room but she said no, she made her bed on the living room sofa, over there, she'd sleep with Milou at her feet. She said she didn't want to bother me but mainly I think she wanted to be able to go in and out without my hearing her; I've gotten hard of hearing in my old age and it wasn't so easy to watch her, she wasn't a little girl anymore. And then, I didn't have the guts to bawl her out, I was afraid she'd leave, that's the way it is when you're not really the parent, you don't dare to be too strict. And then she started disappearing for days on end. We didn't know where she went. I had a feeling she was traveling with a bad crowd—when she came back her breath smelled of cigarettes and even liquor, but you see, sir, she still loved to sing. So I used to tell myself that would save her, I always thought that in the end it would save her from the worst, that's how naïve I was!

A year ago, she started telling me about people she'd met who worked in television. She told me there were shows that helped young people like her become singers or actors and she was going to try her luck, and for the first time she asked me for a little money to buy herself a dress and shoes. For the audition, she said—she's the one who taught me the word: *audition*. She told me it was going to be in a suburb of Paris and she'd sleep over at a girlfriend's place, a girl who dreamed of going on stage too. She told me all that sitting right where you are, with Milou's head on her lap, pulling his ears the way she liked to do when she was a little girl. At the time we already knew the building was going to be torn down and she told me that when she was famous she'd buy a big house with a garden and there'd be a room for me and a basket for the dog. Yes,

that's what she said. Then she asked if she could sleep on the
couch and of course I said yes. When I went to bed, she kissed
me. She told me she'd keep in touch, because she'd probably
have to stay a few months there in the TV studios, after the audition. She was laughing. I hadn't heard her laugh like that for a
long time. The next morning when I woke up, she was gone.

Right away I knew she'd left for a long time. She'd been to
her place very early and took some money from her mother's
purse. Everybody was still sleeping. They thought one of the
kids had left the door open and someone had snuck in. I didn't
say a thing, but I was sure it was her, even if she never stole
before. I was hurt, less because of what she did than because
it meant she wouldn't be coming back for a long time. And
also because I told myself that if I'd only given her more she
wouldn't have had to steal.

I began to spend my evenings at Samir's, the grocer on
the corner of rue Piat. He had a TV set in the back room and
when he had customers he let me watch whatever channel I
wanted. I watched all the shows Layla told me about, those
shows for young people. I never thought there were so many
kids who wanted to be famous, and that made me afraid for
her. It's true she had a nice voice and she was very good-
looking, but there were lots of other kids with nice voices
too, just as good-looking. I just hoped it wouldn't ruin her life,
hoped she wouldn't be afraid to come back. I got five post-
cards from her over the next year, look, you can see them over
there on the wall. She wrote the same thing on every one of
them, or just about: *I'm fine, Grandpa. Love you.*

One evening I really thought I saw her on a show. I'm
almost sure of it. By that time I'd lost hope, I kept going to
Samir's mainly because I wasn't used to staying home alone
anymore, especially without much chance of Layla dropping

by. The girl I saw only stayed on stage for a few minutes, they didn't even give her time to finish her song. She said her name was Olympia but that doesn't mean a thing, you know. She had heavy makeup on, with silver on her eyelids and red lips, done up in a way she never would have dared here, a shiny dress, very short. I remember thinking, *So much money for such a short dress.* But her voice sounded like Layla's and she sang a Piaf song, which is funny because the others chose much more modern music, the kind you hear blasting on young people's car radios when they're stopped at a light with their windows rolled down, or when they don't shut their bedroom windows. I couldn't get a good look at her face, it went so fast, I yelled for Samir, hoping he could help me figure out if it really was her, but by the time he got there—he was helping another customer—it was already over.

The weeks after that I kept watching the show, but the girl—Layla—she never came back. I kept hoping for months, I told myself maybe it was just the first round and we were going to see her again at some point. But I never did.

A few months later there were the rumors. Somebody claimed they saw her in a bar, a nightclub really, then somebody else, and then somebody else again. They swore it really was Layla, said she was dancing every Saturday over there, near Pigalle, then they said the words *peep show.* I didn't know what that meant either, before. Around that time, her family moved out; they didn't even leave an address—I don't know if it was the shame of the neighborhood hearing that their daughter was dancing naked in front of men. Her mother just left a box in front of my door with the girl's things. They're still there, in my bedroom.

There isn't much left to my story. One day I went there. I don't know why, I think I was sure it wasn't Layla, just as I had been sure that I'd seen her on TV at the gates of fame with Piaf's song on her lips, but I needed to see her in person. The rumor had become more and more persistent and I basically knew where to look for her. I waited a few weeks, the time to get up my courage, and then I took the bus to Pigalle one evening around midnight. I didn't have to look far. There were photos of her at the entrance to one of the clubs. I looked at them for a long time, so long the guy watching the door got impatient and said, "Hey, Gramps, you coming in or you growing roots there?" In some pictures she was wearing dresses with slits at her thighs and between her breasts and in others she was almost naked. I had washed her when she was a baby and when she was a little girl; it didn't bother me to see her naked. But there wasn't one single photo where she was smiling. The lipstick was like a gash across her face, she'd lost her nice round cheeks, and her black eyes looked very big. When the guy at the entrance spoke to me I was caught unprepared, I couldn't stop looking at her face after not having seen her for months, and when he said, "Well, Gramps?" I asked, "How much is it?" and I fumbled around in my wallet to pay the admission.

Inside the peep show, as they call it, it was dark and it smelled of sweat, the music was too loud, you'd think you were in one of the worst bars in our neighborhood. I stayed standing near the door of the room they pointed me to, men kept coming in, pushing each other, I was hot, and then I realized I still had my cap on and I took it off. The first girl was a blonde in a shiny pink slip, she couldn't dance but the men were whistling and yelling, some of them tried to touch her but there was a strongman watching the edges of the stage. After that I didn't have to wait long, because the next one was Layla.

I won't tell you about how she was dancing under the eyes of those men, my poor ruined little girl. I didn't stay very long, just enough to see her pace back and forth on the stage two or three times on her high heels, with a sway-ing walk I'd never seen from her, and then just when I was putting my cap on to leave—maybe it was my motion that attracted her attention—she saw me. She didn't stop danc-ing but she dropped her arms, she'd been holding them over her head till then, and she twisted her ankle. I saw her mouth tighten in pain but nothing more because I'd already turned around, and I left without looking back.

I didn't tell anyone about what I saw. Nobody asked me anything but I think a lot of people understood, because I never went back to watch TV at Samir's. I just went out to walk the dog and shop for food. The rest of the time I stayed here sitting in the kitchen, and I tried not to think. I didn't even wonder anymore where I'd go when the building was torn down.

I didn't think she'd come. I didn't guess it in her look when she spotted me at the peep show, all I saw was boredom and that new toughness, and the jab of pain when she twisted her foot, but I didn't see joy or sorrow at the idea of what she'd lost, and I told myself she'd put all that behind her. Still, when there was a knock on the door one evening, very late, I knew right away it was her. I'd fallen asleep on the couch; since she left that's where I usually slept, as if giving myself the illusion she was in the room next door. I went to splash some water on my face before I opened the door.

She was pale, and I realized right away she'd knocked on the door across the hall first, the door of the apartment where her family used to live. It hadn't been rented again because of the plan to demolish the building, but two guys set up house there, with candles for light and a coal stove for heat. They drank all day and begged in front of the Monoprix supermarket on rue des Pyrénées, a little further up. She must have woken them up because the younger one, a guy with a beard, was standing in the half-open doorway looking at us. When she came in, I didn't hear him close the door and I'm sure he stayed there waiting for her to come out again.

Oh yes, I know what you're thinking. You're thinking he waited for her, followed her to the park, and then what happened, happened. But you're wrong.

She didn't cross the threshold until I told her to come in, and it was strange, that mix of humility and provocation in her face, like she was defying me to criticize her for anything. I found her taller, maybe it was her high heels, maybe her thinness, she was wearing a jacket I recognized and she floated in it like a little bird. She sat down on the couch and looked at me with a funny smile on her face. I could see immediately she'd taken something, something stronger than a couple of drinks, and that was new too: She looked at me and then seemed to look *through* me, she had to make an effort for her eyes to focus on my face again. She rubbed her nose with her forefinger and then she said: "So, they left."

Her voice was like her face, just as tough, like, grated—I know I should say *grating*, but it was something else, it was like they'd both been dragged over a hard surface and they'd lost all their softness. "Two months ago, yes," I said. "But your mother left your things, they're in my room, I can go get them if you like."

She shrugged indifferently, as if none of it had any importance. She stayed slumped on the couch with that half-smile on her lips and that floating look, twisting a strand of hair around her finger.

"Layla," I said, "come back. You can stay in the bedroom, you'll be fine there, I almost always sleep in the living room now. I can help you bring over your things, if you like. We can even go there right now."

She laughed, a joyless laugh, and I thought of the night before she left, that happy laugh I'd kept inside my ear like a good luck charm while she wasn't here. "And to do *what*, huh?" she answered.

I lowered my eyes, I never felt so old, so powerless, so silly too, but I made myself go on. "You can start singing again," I said. "Samir's looking for someone to take care of the cash register on weekends, it'd do me good to get out of here a little, and it could help pay for lessons. Maybe that's all you need to make it work."

She laughed again, rolling her head against the back of the couch, and then she said: "No, Grandfather, it's over, my voice is gone, can't you hear? It's not there anymore. It's gone, that's all there is to it."

It hurt when she called me *Grandfather* because there was no tenderness in her voice like when she called me *Grandpa*, it was more of an impatient tone of voice, kind of scornful, like the kids playing soccer in the little square in front of the park when they think I'm not getting out of the way fast enough. It hurt, and then it made me mad. It was also seeing her like that on the couch, sprawled out like a doll, occasionally scratching her knee or her nose, looking like she was bored, not giving a damn about anything. I went and sat down next to her. "You can't lose your voice just like that," I said, even if it's what I thought when I opened the door—that grated, worn-out voice, almost unrecognizable. "It's because you haven't worked on it for a long time. I'll make you herb tea, lemon and honey, and then those powders Samir sells for colds, you'll see, it'll come back."

But she just closed her eyes and shook her head with an angry expression, and when I held out my hand to push back a strand of hair that was falling over her cheek, she shoved it away impatiently. "No," she said. "My voice is gone. Don't you get it? It's all over. Oh, leave me alone."

She thought she was strong but she wasn't as strong as all that; she couldn't manage to brush away my hand and I left it there, near her cheek, even when she tried to push it away more impatiently, saying, "Stop it."

I slid my hand down and placed it on her throat. "Your voice isn't gone," I said. "I'm sure I'd feel it if you sang something—there, now, I can feel it vibrating under my fingers. Your neck's all cold, that's why too, but it's going to warm up."

"Come on, leave me alone," she repeated. "Leave me alone, I can't breathe." She could have screamed if she wanted to, there were neighbors, the two guys on the other side of the landing, and yet she whispered, and it was like a secret being born between us.

"Sing," I told her. "Sing something. Sing that song by Piaf you used to like so much. 'La Vie en Rose.' Sing."

Her throat vibrated under my hand when she murmured something, still softer, but I didn't hear it. We stayed like that for a long time. She hadn't opened her eyes again. She wasn't trying to push me away anymore, she had her hands on her knees, quietly waiting for something, and that smile that didn't look like hers was gone from her face. She didn't move. I thought she was asleep.

3.

Arnaud hadn't said a word while the old man was talking. He had opened his notebook and began mechanically taking notes after glancing over at the old man to make sure he didn't mind. But his notes were such a mess that later he would be unable to read them or understand what they meant, aside from the last words he'd written in the middle of one page: *La Vie en Rose*.

Now the old man was silent. Arnaud watched him. Big, fat tears were flowing from the old man's eyes, like a child's tears. He never would have thought such a deeply furrowed face could have so much emotion or so much water in it. At last the old man sighed, picked up his cup of coffee, and put it to his lips, then put it back down without drinking a drop.

"When her neck began to grow cold under my palms I understood," he said. "I took away my hands and her head slipped onto my shoulder. I didn't know what to do, so I laid her down gently on the couch and I got up. It's funny what goes through your head at moments like that, sir, because I wasn't really thinking and yet I went straight to the bedroom closet where I knew that long ago I'd put away the blanket we used to take for picnics in the park. I took it, I went back to the living room and wrapped Layla in it. All that time I was wondering what I was going to do, but I must have known already. I picked her up in my arms without any hesitation—it wasn't easy, since skinny as she was, she still weighed a lot, or maybe death just does that to you—and I walked to the door. The guy across the hall must've gotten tired or else he understood and didn't want any trouble, because his door was shut.

"I walked down the three flights with Layla in my arms, I went out into the street where it was still very dark, you couldn't hear a car, not even a moped, and I walked to the park gate that doesn't close very well. Everybody in the neighborhood knows there's a gate that doesn't close and all you have to do is jiggle it the right way to open it, any ten-year-old can show you how. I pushed the gate wide with my shoulder and I took the park path to the spot where we used to have picnics back then. It must have been close to dawn because a blackbird was singing in the trees, we must've stayed on the couch much longer than I thought, I may have fallen asleep with my hands on her throat. The smell of the flowers was very strong that night, I was surprised spring was in the air. I think I'd hardly been out of the house since the night I saw Layla in Pigalle.

"I stopped at a tree we used to sit under. I kneeled down and I put her down on the ground. I picked her up a little to tuck the blanket under her, I laid her out with her legs together and her arms straight down beside her body, I buttoned up her jacket to hide the bluish necklace around her throat, and then I got up. I looked at her for a moment. Oh, we were so happy under this tree, me and her. As I was walking back home, it started to rain and suddenly I couldn't stand to think of her staying out there in the rain. I went up to get a pink nylon windbreaker she'd left behind when she went away; her mother had put it in the box she'd left on my doormat. I took it out of its plastic bag, went back down, and put it on Layla; first I slipped it over her head, then I pulled her arms through the sleeves, and finally I drew the hood over her face. I could hear the sound of the raindrops falling on the plastic. Did she have her pink windbreaker on when they found her? She didn't get too wet?"

He was looking at Arnaud imploringly, and Arnaud lowered his eyes. "I don't know," he said in a low voice, "I couldn't cross the police barrier. But she was under another plastic thing, a kind of gray tarp. No, I don't think she was wet."

The old man shook his head with a pensive expression. He picked up the cap on the table next to his cup and wiped his face with it, then kept it in his hand.

"After that, I came back up here and waited for someone to arrive," he began again in a weary tone. "I waited for someone to come so I could tell my story. I will follow you to the police station. But the dog . . . I'd just like you to leave the dog at the grocery store on rue Piat."

Arnaud capped his pen and shut his notebook. The coffee must have been boiling for hours, it was much too strong; he felt as if it had ripped the skin off his mouth and his heart was beating very fast. He was thinking of all those newspapers he'd skimmed through since the fall, all those sordid crimes, stabbings, shootings, skulls cracked against walls, that search for evil he'd thrown himself into to find an ideal killer, and he remembered the incredibly gentle handshake of the old man. He was looking at them at that very moment, those two hands clenched on his cap, which he was stroking softly, the way you pet an animal. Then Arnaud glanced up again and forced himself to smile.

"I'm not the police, sir," he said. "I'm not going to put you in jail. Your story . . ." he went on hastily. "Don't say anything. Don't tell anyone anything. Layla did not come to see you. You were sleeping, you didn't hear her knock, you didn't open your door."

But the old man was staring at him as if he didn't understand. "Don't say anything," he repeated. "Why?" He had mechanically put his cap back on, he looked ready to go, to follow the police who'd come knock on his door in a few minutes or a few hours.

"I live outside Paris," Arnaud suddenly heard himself saying. "I can take you in for a while if you like. We can go there now. No one will know you were here last night. No one will suspect you."

But under the woolen cap, his face still reddened by tears,

the old man was looking at him with incomprehension, almost with mistrust.

"I don't understand what you're trying to do," he said at last. "What you're telling me there, that's not my story. I don't understand what you're trying to do." He continued to examine Arnaud's face as if he was seeing him for the first time, as if he didn't know how this stranger got into his kitchen, sitting in front of him with the coffeepot between them. He pushed back his chair and got up heavily. "Go away, sir," he said. "Go away, please."

Arnaud hesitated, then did as he was told. He stood up, slipped his notebook and pen into his pocket. The old man remained standing behind the table while Arnaud walked over to the door and went out. In the stairway he found the same stench of urine and soup; the door to the apartment across the hall was slightly open, but he was not tempted to take a look inside. He walked quickly down the three flights. Just as he was leaving through the doors of the building, he saw the police coming—three men who seemed to know where they were going—and he turned his face away so their eyes would not meet.

He headed back to the park. Most of the police cars had disappeared; so had most of the onlookers. When he passed through the gates, he saw that the yellow tape was still there but they'd taken the body away. He stopped on the path. He looked for a long time at the lawn, soaked by the downpour. In the grass under a tree, there was an oval in a softer green on the spot where the body had protected it from the rain. Suddenly he felt someone tap him on the shoulder. He turned around and saw his friend.

"Hey, you sure took your time," Legendre said. "I hope you came up with something, at least. Me, I drew a blank, nobody wanted to tell me a thing and then the cops threw me out. So tell me. What happened?"

But Arnaud was looking at the soft oval of grass again. He felt tears welling up in his eyes, tears that seemed to him as big and childish as the old man's. He didn't know where he got that absolute ignorance of the human psyche. All he knew, with absolute certainty, was that he would never write his book; but that wasn't what was causing this inconsolable sorrow. Legendre had lit a cigarette and was staring at him in amazement.

"For Chrissake, what's with you, man? What did you see in that building?"

Arnaud shook his head without answering. The last on-lookers were moving away, and couples, strollers, and children were coming in through the gates of the park. In a few weeks, a few months, no one would remember Layla M. except for the old man in his cell and me, he told himself. He thought of the pink nylon windbreaker the old man had taken down to cover the corpse with, and as his tears turned into sobs, he remembered the pink plastic hats the Japanese tourists were wearing a few hours earlier in front of the plaque for Edith Piaf. They had seemed so bright and cheery in the grayness of the morning.

PART III

SOCIETY OF THE SPECTACLE

RUE DES DEGRÉS

BY DIDIER DAENINCKX

Porte Saint-Denis

Translated by David Ball

Not very far from what used to be the cour des Miracles, rue de Cléry and rue Beauregard almost merge. They are separated only by a narrow series of old buildings, with sweatshops and showrooms in them. The clacking of sewing machines mingles with the noise of traffic, the shouts of men pushing hand trucks and carrying clothing, and the curses of drivers blocked on the street by the interminable deliveries. The eyes of women with plunging necklines glitter in the shadow of the doorways. Men look at them longingly, hesitating over their beers. Just before they meet the Grand's Boulevards at the Porte Saint-Denis, the twin streets are linked together thanks to the smallest street in Paris, six yards long at the most, in fact a set of stairs with fourteen steps that gives the street its name: rue des Degrés. A lamppost, steps framed by two walls, and a metal handrail in the middle shined to brilliance by the clothing of countless passersby rubbing against it.

That was where the cleaning lady of Chez Victoria found the corpse of Flavien Carvel while taking out the garbage cans at daybreak, below a red stencil of a punk girl's face with the caption, *What if I lowered my eyes?* He was lying on his belly across the flight of stairs, and his bloody head was resting on the pile of flattened cartons left there by the neighborhood storekeepers. Brown stains cut across the right-hand wall, under the flaking billboard for Artex Industries. When the policemen turned the body over, they saw that the blood had flowed from his belly, stab wounds no doubt, drenching the head of hair lying below it on the steps. As they were roping off the area, one of the men, Lieutenant Mattéo, followed other signs along the walls of rue Beauregard up to the café Le Mauvoisin. The owner was raising its iron curtain. Over the sign for the café, a candle was burning at the feet of a Madonna sheltered in a niche of the wall.

"You closed late, last night?"

"Shut down by midnight . . . Somebody complain?"

"No, the only one who could have has no way to do it anymore! Everything calm? Nothing special happen?"

He raised a hand to his mustache and stroked it a couple of times, spreading his thumb and index finger.

"No, almost nobody here because of the soccer game, since I never put in a TV . . . I run a café, not an entertainment center. Two customers at the little table, under the photo of the Voisin girl, the poisoner—she lived here, they say . . . I was waiting for them to finish their beers before I packed it up."

The police officer stepped forward to take a look inside. It smelled of dampness and cold tobacco.

"Was one of them blond, kind of long hair, wearing black jeans, white sneakers, and a reporter jacket . . . About twenty-five . . . ?"

"Yeah . . . the one facing me. He had a couple of beers—Leffes—but he couldn't hold his drink . . . unless he started before he got to my place. They walked out onto the sidewalk, toward where you are, they walked maybe fifteen yards away while I was locking up. I remember they stopped to keep talking. The young one you're talking about leaned against the wall while the other guy crossed the street toward rue de la Lune, a little lower down. He clearly didn't feel like dragging the other guy along. Not very nice, leaving a pal in such a bad state . . . The guy in jeans staggered away toward the Porte Saint-Denis, and I went home to bed."

Lieutenant Mattéo looked the owner of Le Mauvoisin up and down.

"Sorry, but I don't think you're opening this morning . . . You're going to have to come along with me. Your last customer of the night wasn't drunk: He'd just been stabbed in the belly a couple of times. We picked him up off the stairs of rue des Degrés. The bloodstains begin at the exact spot you just pointed out to me."

His interrogation revealed that the two men had come into the café one after the other, Carvel first, around 11:00, then his presumed murderer ten minutes later. They had talked quietly, in low voices; it was impossible to grasp the topic of their conversation. It was the victim who had paid for the drinks, with a fifty-euro bill. The second man was about thirty. The café owner didn't know him, any more than he knew the man he had been talking to. Elegantly dressed, shorter than average, brown hair, a round face, he talked with a slight Spanish accent.

"He had a little birthmark near his temple that he kept trying to hide by pulling a lock of hair forward. Kind of a nervous tic . . ."

They learned almost everything about Flavien Carvel from the passport and other ID they found in the pockets of his reporter jacket. He was born April 21, 1982 in Antony, listed his profession as "decorator," and lived on the impasse du Gaz in La Plaine-Saint-Denis. The visas and stamps decorating his passport showed that over the last eight months, Carvel had traveled to the United States, Australia, Japan, Vanuatu, and Lebanon for visits never longer than a week. Robbery was not the motive of the crime since the murderer had not taken his collection of credit cards or the eight hundred euros in cash that filled his pockets.

Mattéo discovered a piece of newspaper slipped between the plastic rectangles of the American Express Platinum and Visa Infinity cards; someone had penned on it:

> *Tom Cruise was seen last Monday on rue de la Paix in the second arrondissement of Paris in the company of the wife of a candidate in the French presidential election, while rumors of the American star's separation from Katie Holmes are making headlines in the celebrity magazines.*

He had gone to La Plaine-Saint-Denis early in the afternoon after grabbing a slice of Tuscan pizza at the Casa della Pasta on rue Montorgueil. He hadn't set foot in the northern suburbs for years. In his memory it was all gray, gas meters, oil-refinery walls, Coke plants, chimney stacks, ash-colored façades stained by constant rain, the open trench of the Autoroute du Nord and its constant flow of smoking carcasses . . . When they built the huge new soccer stadium—the Stade de France—it had completely transformed the geography of the area. The last remnants of the old industrial revolution had been razed to the ground. The buildings with the corporate main offices in them stood as if on parade along the huge flowered concrete slab that now covered the sewer of flowing cars. The rectilinear greenery and the erratic movements of clouds were reflected in the shining aluminum, the smoked glass, and the polished steel. The recipe had worked wonders in Paris: Thanks to the construction of the Pompidou Museum of Modern Art, the Forum des Halles, the Bastille Opera, the Arche de la Défense, and the Very Big Library, the city had been emptied of its lower strata. Now the recipe was being applied to the nearby districts outside the city. Nothing like a grand architectural gesture in the middle of the urban jungle to regain possession of a city.

Lieutenant Mattéo had always lived in the second arrondissement. He couldn't imagine the slightest exile from it, not even in a neighborhood next door. Montorgueil, Tiquetonne, Réaumur, Aboukir, Sentier, all these streets were like lifelines in the hollow of his palm. But for ten years now he'd really had to hang on, ever since the massive arrival of the bohemian yuppies: They spent way more every month at the sidewalk tables of the Rocher de Cancale, the Compas d'Or, and the Loup Blanc than he paid in rent. He walked along the canal, passed the camps of Romanian gypsies mixed with all the homeless displaced from the banks of the Seine, then took rue Cristino Garcia, moving into what remained of the old Spanish neighborhood. The impasse du Gaz was no more than four or five attached redbrick houses, like a mining town. It felt a little like England. Cranes were wheeling in the sky just behind this relic of the past. A mailbox had the name *Carvel* on it followed by the first name, *Mélanie*. He reflected that it was the same as his assistant's. He pulled the chain that hung next to the door with thick iron mesh over it.

A woman of about fifty came to open it, dragging her feet and grumbling. Yellow hair, tired waves of an old permanent, pallid face, bluish bags under her eyes, the corners of her lips sagging . . . and the same for the rest of her body: Flavien's mother was the very image of defeat, of abandonment. Contrary to what the lieutenant had feared, she absorbed the news of her son's death without collapsing. All she did was clench her jaw and suppress a tremor in her right hand before wiping away the tears welling in her eyes with the back of her sleeve.

"How'd it happen?"

As he entered, Mattéo glanced at the dining room where a low table in front of the TV, lit like a night-light, was buckling under empty bottles and ashtrays overflowing with cigarette butts.

"We don't know much yet. His murderer might be Spanish. There are plenty of them in the neighborhood: Your son must have known some of them . . ."

"Sure, dozens. Back in the day, he used to go next door to the Youth Center, to play cards, dance, eat tapas . . ."

"*Back in the day*, that means when?"

She had pushed open a sliding panel, revealing a messy bedroom with walls studded with posters. A smiling Bill Gates with pinched lips was like a stain in the middle of the rows of sparkling teeth of the stars of showbiz, movies, and sports.

"For the last two years he'd just drop by in a rush. We must've eaten together once or twice, with his current girlfriend . . . Last week he brought me flowers for my birthday . . ."

"You remember their names?"

She removed a pack of Lucky Strikes from the pocket of her cardigan, lit the end of a cigarette with a Zippo that stunk of gas.

"The names of the girls? No. He changed them even more often than he changed cars . . . I don't know the brands either."

Mattéo hadn't asked her permission to enter the room. He began to look through the collections of video games, photo albums, films, magazines. A few lines scrawled on a piece of notebook paper suddenly caught his eye:

Sunday, August 28th, New Orleans. The storm's getting nearer, stronger and stronger. The telephone never stops ringing. "You staying or leaving?" "Where're you living now?" "You have the cats with you?" "What should we do?" The governor is asking us to "pray for the hurricane to go down to Level 2" . . . Finally I give in. I'm going to move into a stronger building. An old cannery downtown made of brick and cement, five stories high. There are seven of us in the apartment, with four cats.

It was the same slanted, energetic handwriting as the message about Tom Cruise and the wife of the presidential candidate. He held out the paper under Flavien's mother's eyes.

"He's the one who wrote this?"

"Yes, that's his handwriting. He never stopped taking notes, scribbling . . . stuff he'd hear on the radio, on the phone, or things he found in the papers. It was like an obsession. I wore myself out telling him to stop, but he couldn't help himself."

"You know where he was living these last few months?"

She shook her head.

"All I know is, he bought a place in Paris . . . He never gave me his phone number. Just his e-mail address. What am I supposed to do with that? I don't even have a computer!"

The lieutenant's cell phone began vibrating in his pants pocket. He waited to get outside the house on the impasse du Gaz to call back. He quickly jerked the phone away as Burdin's shrill voice drilled through his ear.

"I wanted to tell you we've got a lead for the corpse on

rue des Degrés. He isn't in any of our files, a real ghost. I went through my usual stoolies with his photo on my chest. He's been hanging out for some time in the back room of the Singe Pèlerin, where the sex-shop customers of rue Saint-Denis leer at the two-legged meat . . . Seems he was interested in one of those places, but I don't know which one."

Mattéo knew the chatterbox of the Singe Pèlerin—a bartender—because he'd recruited him five years ago, when he caught the guy with his nose buried in white powder. The café used to be a ripening room for bananas; it was hidden in a little nook near the start of the Place du Caire, built over one of the entrances to the mythical cour des Miracles. For dozens of years he'd never even wondered about this name. Its probable meaning had been given to him the week before by an exhibitionist alcoholic they had to yank from rue Saint-Sauveur. It had taken him about an hour to give this explanation in the drunk tank of the police station, but it could be summed up in a few words. Every evening, when the beggars around the city returned to their dens with change jingling in their pockets, it was as if Christ had turned His face to them: The blind regained their sight, amputees stood up on their legs, the scrofulous lost their scrofula, the deaf became sensitive to noise, the mute began to sing, Siamese twins stood face to face; all they had to do was enter the perimeter of this refuge for miracles to happen!

The lieutenant pushed down on the handle and opened the glass-paned door where the old phone number was still displayed from the time when the numbers began with letters. Thirty girls or so were sitting on the imitation leather chairs, waiting to take their exams in the back room. Most of them were kids from Eastern Europe or Africa, along with an Asian girl and one from India. He walked straight to the bar. Leaning on his elbows in front of his debtor, he ordered almost without opening his mouth.

"Give me a strong coffee, real strong, then get out of here and make a little stop at the usual place . . ."

The bartender was about to protest, but Mattéo had already turned around to admire the slender legs of an Estonian girl who was passing the time by stretching out a pink piece of chewing gum in front of her silicone-enhanced lips. He made a face as he swallowed his coffee without putting sugar in it, crossed the room, walked about thirty yards up the sidewalk toward rue Saint-Denis, and entered the shop of the last strawhat maker in Paris.

Assaf, the master of the house, was born on the second floor of the shop. Rounded up by the French police like all the Jews of the neighborhood, he had survived the hell of Auschwitz before making a detour of almost ten years in the camps of his liberators. The lieutenant and the hat maker came together when Mattéo had chased out a gang hitting him up for protection money. Mattéo had then formed the habit of coming to play chess with the old man. He practically never brought up his past, except to reminisce about the games he'd played against a champion of the USSR suspected of Trotskyite sympathies. (Assaf had lost every one of them.) As tournaments were forbidden in the gulag, an inmate had someone tattoo a chessboard on his back. He would get down on all fours, naked from the waist up, until one player was checkmated.

Mattéo gave his old friend a hug. "A customer's going to come in for a visit. Don't waste your saliva, I can tell you he won't buy a thing . . ."

"You can go into the kitchen. I'll take him in to you as soon as he shows up."

When the bartender of the Singe Pèlerin arrived, the lieutenant saw that he had put on a raincoat over his working clothes. The bartender asked for some water to take a handful of pills, then refused the chair the lieutenant pointed him to.

"I can't stay, it's the noon rush. All the big boys are there. What do you want from me? Is it about the guy who got shot on rue des Degrés?"

"If you ask the questions and then answer them, it'll go a lot faster . . . His name was Flavien Carvel and he wasn't shot, he was stabbed . . . What can you tell me about him?"

The bartender raised his head with his mouth open, as if he was trying to get some fresh air. "All I know is, he was loaded. He began hanging around the neighborhood about six months ago. He bought some shares in The Sphinx as a way of getting in with the mob. Recently there was a rumor of his buying heavily into the peep show on the corner of rue Greneta . . . a first-class business. They were talking about his coming in with 200,000 euros."

"I took care of them two years ago; a real rough place. You sure you're not giving me the wrong club?"

Mattéo got up to fill a pot of water and put it on the gas stove.

"No, everything's back on track again. It's one of the joints that brings in the most. All the bread in cash, tax-free. From what I know, there were lots of extras too . . ."

"What kind?"

"They opened up little trapdoors so the customer could stick his hands through 'em and feel up the dancers' tits and stick dildos or vibrators up their asses or pussies. Stuff they bought exclusively at the shop, for the highest price imaginable. It went both ways—if the customer asked for it, the dancers screwed them with the same utensils."

"You have any idea where he lived?"

The bartender stuck his hand into the pocket of his rain-coat and took out a business card he then handed to the police officer. "I did him a favor by telling him what I heard . . . He told me I could reach him through this real estate agency if it was urgent."

Mattéo took the card. It was from Luximmo, a business on rue Marie-Stuart. He memorized the name of the person printed under the company name: *Tristanne Dupré*. Then he turned the paper rectangle over, mechanically. The other side was covered with Carvel's tense writing:

December 26 could have been the happiest day in Rafiq's life if the tsunami hadn't struck, because he was supposed to get married that day. The time of the wedding was set for noon, but the waves came in the morning. Rafiq was in the village of Patangipettai, near the other villages that were hit. Immediately, all the men in the community swung into action with Jamaat, their local organization. They took away the food for the wedding and gave it to the disaster victims. Up to the day we met them, one week after the tsunami, the organization provided breakfast and lunch to the victims, cooking lemon rice or veg. biryani.

The lieutenant drank a mint tea sweetened with acacia honey before saying goodbye to old Assaf.

All you had to do was walk a hundred yards and you left the sex and garment district behind; you were entering the area reserved for the winners in the new economic order. All the pretty little faces in the world of finance, advertising, top civil service jobs, TV and movies would be walking around on these harmless decorative cobblestones. They crowded into sidewalk cafés, their cell phones glued to their ears, connected to vitamin cocktails by means of fluorescent straws. Mattéo liked the place, despite everything: the façades, the smell of eternal Paris. But he had lived here too long to forget how fake it all was. Going beyond rue Saint-Denis into Montorgueil was like crossing a border. He felt almost as if he were at a show, or a tourist: Sometimes he was sorry he hadn't slung a camera across his chest.

He quickened his pace. Street people were sorting through the garbage cans lined in front of Suguisa, La Fermette, and Furusato, the Japanese restaurant. They were looking for edible garbage in the form of organic food. He cut onto rue Marie-Stuart, which used to be a fierce competitor of rue Brisemiche in the old days, when they were more prosaically called Passage Tire-Vit and Tire-Boudin.* The realtor was on the ground floor of an old house with exposed oak beams and stone. Tristanne Dupré looked like one of the girls who waited on customers in the Singe Pèlerin. The bodywork was identical, but the license plate was quite different. Everything she was wearing, from her stockings to the cut of her hair, from her pumps to her perfume, came straight out of the pages of *Vogue*. Badgley Mischka skirt, Alexander McQueen shoes, Carolina Herrara glasses . . . With one look, you save the price of buying a copy. Mattéo slid the card along the desk.

"According to what I've been told, you're the one who acted as a go-between for Flavien Carvel . . ."

She stared at him with eyes wide open behind her lightly smoked glasses before looking over the inspector from head to foot, scornfully. "I don't understand."

"Mattéo, Criminal Investigation. Carvel's in the morgue, and I'm trying to nail the guy who bought him a one-way

*"Prick-Pull" and "Sausage-Pull."

ticket there. The sooner the better. You teamed up to buy the peep show on rue Greneta, right?"

The theory had come out of his mouth without even thinking about it. From the panic-stricken fluttering of her eyelashes, he realized he'd hit a bull's-eye. Now he had to proceed with caution.

"Flavien is dead? No, he can't be!"

She threw herself back in her chair, her chest under the silk shaken by spasmodic breathing. Her distress was not affected. He wondered if she was one of those interchangeable girls who waited for the prodigal son in the car when he made a visit to his mother on the impasse du Gaz. Mattéo pushed away a pile of interior design magazines and sat down on the couch.

"Forgive me, I didn't realize you were that close . . . He was found this morning near the Porte Saint-Denis, stabbed . . . I'd like to learn how you met him . . ."

She stuck a Camel into a cigarette holder with a python emblem and lit it with a matching lighter.

"In the simplest possible way. He opened that door and sat down in the exact same spot you're in now . . . He wanted to buy an apartment in the no-car area, preferably Tiquetonne . . . After ten visits or so, he decided on a big four-room in a historical landmark building on rue Léopold Bellan . . ."

"It's not cheap, in that sector. You gave him a good deal?"

She shrugged.

"Seven thousand euros a square meter. He had about a hundred and twenty square meters . . . You can do the math . . . Flavien had a third of the money and he was sure he'd have no problem getting the rest from what the peep show brought in. He was supposed to move in next month."

"Where was he living in the meantime?"

"Upstairs, fourth floor, a studio apartment that belongs to the agency . . . I have a copy of the keys."

Mattéo learned that the real estate agency owned the building with the rooms for voyeurs, that Tristanne had tipped off her rich client, and that his bank was on the Place de la Bourse, near the editorial offices of the *Nouvel Observateur*. The lieutenant then brandished the notes Flavien had taken.

"Do you know why he wrote down these bits of human interest stories on paper scraps?"

"No. He used to copy them onto his computer in the evening, to post them on a website, that's all he told me . . . I held onto a few of them. I also remember he backed up all his work on his flash drive."

The young woman opened her bag—a Vuitton—and fumbled around in it.

"Here, this is something he wrote."

The police officer took the paper:

The police have been heating up since the start of the riots, they're provoking us more and more. The brother of one of the electrocuted children was hanging out with us as usual, in front of his building, when the police got there. They started to look us up and down and finally they said to him: "You, go home to your mother." He walked three steps toward the cops to talk to them and one of them said: "Stop or you'll regret it." We ran away to the eleventh floor, they started firing gas cartridges into the lobby. They smoked out the family in mourning.

He had just finished reading it when she gave him another one:

Cotonou Airport, December 25. I had a very bad premonition and I really felt ill at ease. Every time something bad is going to happen to me, I can feel it. And this time my sixth sense was telling me we weren't going to take off. I was really expecting something to happen. I even told one of my coworkers what I felt. A few seconds later, the plane was in the water. The people who were still alive were screaming. I wasn't afraid because I'd sensed something terrible was going to happen. Everything happened very fast. I'd say there were two minutes between takeoff and the accident. When I got out of the plane, I wasn't far from the shore. So I swam back to the land and survived.

The lieutenant put them away in his wallet with the others, then walked to the stairs. He didn't need to use the keys the real estate agent had given him. The door had been forced open and every nook and cranny of the studio had been searched. He looked at the disaster—the drawers thrown over, the bed upside down, the slashed mattress. He picked up the furniture, looking for the computer or the flash drive Tristanne had mentioned. Apparently the visitor had taken everything away. Mattéo found one more enigmatic message in a trash can in the bathroom:

December 26. Rababa and his son Hamed were sleeping when the earthquake hit the little town of Bam, in Iran. Before they had time to run outside, their house had collapsed around them. They remained trapped for four days until a neighbor came to the rescue, digging into the wreckage with his bare hands.

He walked back to rue de la Lune, near the old postern of la Poissonnerie, the fish-market gate: They used to bring the day's catch into Paris through it at dawn. A tiny, almost provincial enclave, with its small public garden, its church, and its little bands of children. Just a step away from the noisy Grands Boulevards, the excitement of rue Saint-Denis, and the sector reserved for bohemian yuppies. From the kitchen he could make out the ceramic advertisement for Castrique, promising *Total dust removal when you vacuum*. He had kept the apartment after his divorce, when Annabelle left with the kids, spending almost half his income on rent for a place where he used only two rooms out of four. Everything was ready for their return. Moving out would have meant admitting defeat. He heated up a tajine, lemon chicken with carrots, cooked by the Moroccan woman who took care of the building as well as his laundry and cleaning. Later he watched a gangster film on TV the way you look at the passing landscape from the window of a train, unable to follow the plot, his mind fixated on the murder of Flavien Carvel.

The next morning, after stopping by the offices of the Criminal Investigation Department, Mattéo went to the bank that managed Carvel's accounts, the Financière des Victoires. No one seemed to be aware they had lost an important client the day before on rue des Degrés. The dead man's financial adviser very grudgingly agreed to enter the password to access information in his computer about Carvel's financial transactions.

"Monsieur Carvel's net holdings amount to nearly 400,000 euros. We have also approved transactions for double that amount. Real estate projects. I can give you a statement to the last centime."

"Thank you very much, but what would really help would

be to know where Flavien Carvel got his money from . . . If I understand correctly, he made his fortune rather suddenly. One might wonder . . . Everything was legal, in your opinion?"

The banker tensed up at the mere suggestion of money-laundering.

"I don't see why you would have any doubt . . ."

"No reason . . . Experience, maybe . . . I'm just asking you to reassure me. Where did those 400,000 euros come from?"

"From all over . . . Europe, the United States, Japan, Russia, South Africa. Close to a hundred countries in all . . . Last month, he received nearly 10,000 transfers via the Internet at an average of three euros per transaction. He sold connection time, access to information . . ."

Mattéo took out his wallet and unfolded the scrap of paper found on the corpse.

"This kind of information?"

The banker pinched it between his fingertips to read the message:

Tom Cruise was seen last Monday on rue de la Paix in the second arrondissement of Paris in the company of the wife of a candidate in the French presidential election, while rumors of the American star's separation from Katie Holmes are making headlines in the celebrity magazines.

"Our role is limited to making sure that all transactions are legal and managing the flow of money in the best interest of both the bank and its clients. We would never intervene in our clients' activities in any way. All I can tell you is that Monsieur Carvel got his income from selling information on the web. Nothing more. I am putting these lists at the disposal of the examining magistrate."

"We'll wait."

When he got outside, a gathering had formed on rue Notre-Dame-des-Victoires. A rainbow-colored banner attached to the iron fence around the stock exchange proclaimed the construction of the *Marker of Evil*. Mattéo mingled with the onlookers to watch the inauguration of some kind of monument in the form of a coffin with the names of all of today's dictators and warmongers printed on it. He walked away when he heard the police sirens.

His steps carried him toward the garment district. As he walked up rue Beauregard, he saw the mustached owner of the Mauvoisin polishing his coffee machine in the shadowy light of his café, then he retraced the last path of Flavien Carvel up to the fourteen steps of rue des Degrés. The sanitation workers had erased all traces of the murder. All that remained was a memory of the bloodied body rubbing against the wall under the peeling billboard for Artex. The lieutenant pressed himself up against the wall, into the exact spot where the victim had been found. He raised his eyes and then noticed a few drops of blood a foot or so above his head. He stood on tiptoe and saw that there were some more drops a bit higher, at the edge of the plaque where it said, *ARTEX distributes CHAL-DÉE creations, manufacturer*. He slipped a fingertip under the inside right corner, which was slightly raised, and wiggled it around. A small object, freed from behind the metal, fell to his feet. He bent down to pick up the small flash drive that Flavien had managed to hide before he died.

Ten minutes later, Mattéo was loading the contents of the drive onto his office computer. Two icons indicating videos popped up in the middle of a dozen other files. The first was titled *09-11-01*, the other one *Tom-Cécilia*. He double-clicked on the second one. The scientologist actor and the flighty wife were walking near the Opéra de Paris and laughing as they stepped into Café de la Paix arm in arm. Insignificant pictures that only a tendentious commentary managed to turn into a secret idyll. The content of the second sequence, also a minute long, was totally different. It was clearly filmed from a surveillance camera with a zoom lens at the top of a building with a roof terrace; Mattéo could make out a corner of the façade when the camera swept around. He began to recognize the massive architecture of the Pentagon, with gardens, parking lots, and entrances sprinkled with sentry boxes at checkpoints. After about fifteen seconds of the webcam's slow scanning, a white object came into its field of vision, from the right, and smashed into one of the sections of the large concrete wall, sinking into it with a huge burst of flame. A digital clock gave the date and time of the crash: *09-11-01, 9:43 a.m.* The slow motion that followed allowed Mattéo to recognize the fuselage of a Boeing 757 with the colors of American Airlines. It was as obvious—and as horrifying—as the newsreels showing the two planes moments before slamming into the Twin Towers. Mattéo could not recall seeing a film as precise as this about the attack on the Pentagon. Everything the Bush administration had made public to refute the conspiracy theories failed to stand up to scrutiny, whereas here, before his eyes, the reality of the explosion of AA Flight 77 was indisputable.

He opened the other files to find several dozen messages similar to the ones he'd already found in his investigation of Flavien Carvel: testimony from all the disasters that had struck the planet in the course of recent history—tsunamis, earthquakes, environmental disasters, suicide bombings, tornados, volcanic eruptions . . . Every message corresponded to visual imagery and was labeled with its source—last name, first name, and a telephone number or an e-mail address—

followed by a sum in euros. A group of tourists in the Philippines running wildly from an incandescent cloud was 300 euros; the confession of a Hezbollah martyr child wearing an explosive belt was valued at 200 euros; while the pictures of an old man swept away by a gigantic wave in Thailand was worth 1,000. Just one paragraph had no price tag on it: the one relating exactly how the Pentagon's outer rings had been destroyed. Yet the alleged source of this document was listed: *Fidel Hernandez.* The lieutenant figured this might be the elegant guy with the Spanish accent who had been with Flavien Carvel in the Mauvoisin café shortly before his death. It took his assistant less than two hours to locate the address Hernandez had given for his cell phone bill: a hotel near the stock exchange.

"It doesn't seem fake. I was able to check calls from his cell over the last three days; a number of them were traced to that neighborhood."

"Thanks, Mélanie."

Mattéo walked around the Opéra building and headed toward the old library, the Bibliothêque Nationale. The Royal Richelieu, wedged between two banks, displayed its gilded, intertwined initials under the windows of all six stories of this Haussmannian building. The police officer set his forearms on the reception desk.

"Good morning. I would like to talk to Monsieur Fidel Hernandez. I don't have his room number . . ."

The receptionist looked at her reservation screen.

"I'm sorry, I don't have anybody with that name."

"I was told he was still here yesterday."

She typed on her keyboard, consulted several pages of listings. "No, no Hernandez over the past few weeks . . . None."

Mattéo slid his police card over the varnished wood. "I

can't explain, but it's very important . . . This Hernandez may have registered here under another name. Very elegant, fairly short, round face, a slight Spanish accent . . ."

"That doesn't ring a bell."

Mattéo pointed his forefinger at his temple. "He has a birthmark right there, which he tries to hide by pulling his hair over it . . ."

Her face lit up with a smile.

"That's not Monsieur Hernandez, it's Monsieur Herrera! You have the wrong name. He's been a guest here for a week. Room 227, third floor. Do you want me to call him?"

He stopped the hand about to pick up the phone.

"Absolutely not. Hand me the duplicate keys for his room, I'm going to give him a little surprise."

When the lieutenant reached the floor, he drew his revolver before opening the lock. Hernandez was stretched out naked on his bed watching TV; he jumped when he heard the click. To Mattéo's surprise, instead of trying to grab a weapon, he clapped his two hands over his penis.

When the manager opened the safe under the name Herrera in the hotel strong room, Mattéo recovered Carvel's computer and palm pilot stolen from his temporary apartment above the offices of Tristanne Dupré. Fidel Hernandez wasn't really named Herrera either, but Miguel Cordez. Originally from Mexico, he had been in France for about ten years, living lavishly through a series of swindles, each one more clever than the last. The development of sites like Flickr, Dailymotion, Starbucks, and YouTube, with pay-per-view amateur videos on them, had attracted his attention. Too big for him. He had then set his sights on a little upstart, NewsCoop, created a few months back by Flavien Carvel.

"I knew a lot of guys who worked in planes. As soon as

there was a disaster somewhere, I'd run off to Roissy or New York to get the photos or video tapes from the first people coming back from the place. I was able to buy exclusive coverage of the tsunami and Katrina for next to nothing . . ."

"Where does the one filmed by the surveillance camera of the Pentagon come from?"

"A cousin who works for a security company in Washington . . . He pirated it before the FBI picked up every piece of material and embargoed it. He was asking a hundred thousand dollars for it. Carvel agreed right away, except I later found out that he was secretly negotiating to resell it for six times that much."

"Is that what you were talking about in the Mauvoisin? He didn't want to back off, or return the tape . . . ?"

"Correct."

At the end of the day, a special adviser from the State Department came to pick up the video showing the impact of AA Flight 77 on the Pentagon and return it to the American authorities. The only thing Lieutenant Mattéo was still wondering about was what the wino on rue du Gaz was going to do with all the loot she inherited from her son.

DEAD MEMORY

BY PATRICK PÉCHEROT

Les Batignolles

Translated by Carol Cosman

I 'm going to kill him and I don't know why. Wait—"know" isn't the right word. I certainly *know* what led me to hold a pistol to his chest. You don't just do things like that accidentally. To anyone at all. At least that's what I think. Unless you weren't brought up right. Which is not the case with me. Or you're a serial killer. That's what they're called now, right? Whatever. I'm not a serial killer. Being like that must leave traces in you—an aftertaste of blood, a smell of death.

The smell comes up without warning, like bile rising after you've been on a binge. It's morning. These moments are always mornings. Dawns, to be precise. Precision is important. So it's dawn. You wake up out of a troubled sleep, all nauseous. Opening your eyes is sometimes like a sudden need to throw up. In the half-light, the shape lies on the floor. A heap. Soft, of course. Soft? The idea came to you because you thought of a pile of laundry. Each time, you think of a pile of laundry. There; you took that from a bad book and you kept it. Otherwise, why? The body curled up at the foot of the bed is completely rigid, and you know it. And cold. Its muscles hardened, its tendons petrified. Its veins too. Blue under the ivory skin, they're like ink cartridges in a pen with the ink dried out.

You murdered him before you went to bed. You'd never seen him before, but some nights you have to do it just to get some sleep. There's nothing to be done about it. At least you know why you've killed him. In order to sleep. That's a reason, right? And a good one too. When you've watched the clock going around for days without getting any sleep, it's understandable.

But him—I don't even remember why I'm going to kill him.

A memory! That's the word. There is a reason why he has to die, but I no longer remember what it is. His death is a necessity. Still, it's embarrassing—his being there at one end of my pistol with me at the other. All the same, I can't decently ask him why I'm killing him.

"You want to kill me, Monsieur Robert? And why?"

There, you can't count on anyone. It's not like I'm asking him for the moon. He's going to die, so a little piece of information just in passing wouldn't cost him much.

"No big deal, really."

"Excuse me?"

"Oh, don't make it worse."

"Make *what* worse, Monsieur Robert?"

"Everything. The situation, your dazed expression, your idiotic questions . . ."

"Ah, I understand . . ."

"You sure took your time . . ."

"He's tired, isn't he?"

"What?"

"He's not his best today . . ."

"Who?"

"It happens to everyone. Does he want to rest a little?"

"For God's sake, who are you talking about?"

"Take my arm, I'll help you over to the armchair. And give me that revolver—"

"Pistol!"

"That pistol. It must be very heavy."

"Not at all. Eight hundred and fifty grams. It's clear you don't know anything about weapons."

"Right."

"Obviously, you have to add the bullets, which takes us—with eight grams per bullet, at twelve per clip—to around a kilo."

"Bravo!"

"Good! I can still carry that."

"No, I was saying 'bravo' because of your memory . . ."

Maybe I have to kill him because he's so irritating. It's astonishing how irritating he is. Look at him, he's happy with himself now. The guy is a moron. That's another reason!

"You see, Monsieur Robert, when you concentrate, your memory works. It's important to exercise it. Do you want us to do some exercises?"

He really is very dumb.

"Shooting exercises?"

"Ah! I like you better like that. When he jokes, it's because he's feeling good."

"But who the hell are you talking about? There's only you and me in this room!"

"Come close to the window. And your revolver—"

"Pistol!"

"Sorry. I'm not very sharp on this subject."

"That's an understatement."

"Okay, fine. Your pistol, then, weighs more than eight hundred grams . . ."

"One kilo plus ten grams. Don't forget, it's loaded."

"Can you point it in a different direction? . . . Thank you. What make is it?"

"The make? It's a Luger. Parabellum P-08."

"Perfect!"

"Yes, it's a fine weapon. A little capricious, but it passed the test."

"A collector's piece . . ."

"The Americans would give a truckload of chewing gum for one."

"The Americans?"

"The guys who didn't have the luck to get one off a dead Kraut."

"A Kr— Are you talking about the war?"

"I have to spoon-feed you everything. Of course, the war. You haven't noticed?"

"The . . . *last* war?"

"How should I know? They say that every time!"

"Thirty-nine to forty-five?"

"Another one of your lame games? You want me to add? Subtract? Three plus nine equals twelve. Four plus five equals nine . . . What do we have here? A logical equation?"

"Are you serious?"

"Young man, I can assure you that a Luger Parabellum P-08 gives you many urges, but rarely the urge to joke."

"I'm talking about the war that involved a good part of the world from 1939 to 1945."

"Hold your horses! Germany's taking some serious hits, but really, nothing's over. At least nothing you can put a date on. You might as well say '46, it seems to me. Besides, open the window."

"The window?"

"Go over there, what do you see?"

"Nothing. Well, rue des Dames . . ."

"Yet, the street! But what else?"

"Um, okay, pedestrians, cars, the line at the bakery—"

"The eternal problem of bread rations . . ."

"Rations? Monsieur Robert, we're in 2007, it's 4:30 p.m., it's the end of the school day, and the bakery is selling cakes to the kids like . . . like hot cakes, precisely!"

I'll kill him tomorrow. By then I'll remember why. And I will be rested. He's tired me out. People who are going to die are exhausting. Most people are no picnic. But with one foot in the grave, they become impossible. To the point of making you want to murder them, if you didn't already feel like doing it. This one's hit the jackpot. Fifteen minutes, and he's worn me out! It's the world upside down. Now I don't even know what he came for. Or what he was telling me. A chatterbox, words coming out of his mouth like oatmeal. Mush. A swill of words that leave you parched.

Pip, or in French *pépie*, from the Latin *pituita*, a bird sickness characterized by the presence of a thick coating on the tongue. Makes them terribly thirsty. Isn't my memory impressive? Its whatchamacallits and what's-his-names, crammed like junk into a wicker trunk. Open it! Rummage around! Find stuff you like! A real treasure hunt.

Parched. Or thirsty. Thirst, human sickness characterized by the presence of words you couldn't swallow. Gets cured at the bar.

The Renaissance Bar is just as good as any other. With its crooked façade like a down-turned mouth, it owes its name to Pétain. The owner saw the Maréchal and his National Revolution as a sign of recovery, rebirth. The return of values, of black coffee and white sauvignon. Yellow, too, the color of anisette. Yellow mainly leaked on the stars. As for the rest, cheap, adulterated wine and sawdust calvados. Finally, when he saw that nothing was changing and his big nose felt the wind turn, he removed Pétain's mug from the wall. Everyone forgot the reason for the Renaissance. I didn't. Dead memory . . . memories are the shreds of life that stick to you. They burst out of the depths of time when morning itself evaporates like water. Why this one? The Renaissance at the corner of rue des Dames. And the "dames" you see passing by are no spring chickens. But hell, streetwalker isn't a profession that makes for eternal youth.

"A Cinzano!"

"I'm sorry, monsieur, we don't have any."

"A dry day?"

"Excuse me?"

"Is it an alcohol-free day?"

"I'm not sure I understand you. Martini, cognac, Suze, I can bring you whatever you want. Except for drinks that are no longer sold."

"They've banned Cinzano?"

"That's funny. We don't serve Cinzano because no one buys it anymore."

"Since when?"

"I think I served the last one . . . let's see. Twenty-five years ago?

"Twenty-five years?"

"And that was an old bottle and a very old client."

"A mandarin citron, then."

"I see . . . Monsieur wouldn't prefer an absinthe? Or a Gallic beer? A good Gallic cervoise?"

With his cloth over his shoulder, he's as boring as the other one. The future dead man. You'd think they'd passed the word around to each other. If that's the case, perhaps he knows why I have to kill him. But it's not the kind of question you ask a man thrown off by the idea of a mandarin citron. He needs something basic. Counter level, you might say.

"Garçon!"

"Monsieur . . ."

"Where have the girls gone?"

"What girls?"

There's a confab at the espresso machine.

"Are you the gentleman on the fourth floor?"

"I haven't counted floors, but that must be right."

"You went out alone?"

"Yes. Well, it's not exactly an exploit, it's something that happens often, you know. Besides, I'm going to do it again right this minute. You're really irritating, acting like you've just landed here from outer space."

A café without Cinzano, rue des Dames without dames—aren't you surprised that memory has no memories? That's not quite right, actually. I do have memories. And that's the strangest thing. The neighborhood, for instance. I could tell you a lot about it. Like rue des Dames. The bars, the furnished rooms, the ankle-twisting pavement, and the sky you glimpse above the lopsided buildings. The street and the street girls—you might think they're connected. Wrong, it owes its name to the nuns. They followed it to go up to their convent up there in Montmartre. That must have been in the time of musketeers and sedan chairs. Because I don't recall meeting any nuns here. No musketeers either. Streetwalkers, yes. Fishnet stockings and slit skirts, with their weary saunter, exhausted from too much soliciting. Lips like embers that don't want to die, and eyes that have seen everything. The laundresses, too, that was their spot. Rosy skin, hair wild in the steam of the workshops, their blouses opening to the movement of their naked arms. And those smells, making you hungry as a wolf, with a ferocious yen to bite hard. To howl like a tomcat. Blood boiling in your veins. Hot, red, and very thick. Blood . . .

I shouldn't forget to kill him. But who? That's what escapes me. That man on the bicycle riding down from Place de Clichy, his briefcase strapped to the rack? I don't think so. The pizza deliveryman, perhaps. I don't much like pizza. Or that one walking along rue Darcet . . . He came out of the Hotel Bertha, at the corner of les Batignolles. Rue des Batignolles, les Epinettes Park. Names that sing like music boxes. You wind them up, and off you go up the boulevard. "*C'est la java bleue, la java la plus belle . . .*"

It's a summer evening. The paving stones are still warm from the heat of the day. The air carries the scents of linden blossoms and white wine. That comes from Sainte Marie. The trees from the square and the outdoor cafés all around it, like garlands. They've set out the tables and chairs, and barrels when there are no tables left. We passed the bottles around, the nice fine wine with the stony taste—house reserve—and the sparkling wine that makes you sing. "*C'est la java bleue, la java la plus belle . . .*" The grocer donned a fireman's helmet, big Marcel found himself a rusty old gun, and the postman is proudly showing off two grenades in his mailbag. "Express parcel," he says. And that makes him laugh. That was just before he fell. *Bam! Bam!* A flight of pigeons hid the sky. Someone cried, "Sniper!" and people threw themselves on the ground. Now we hear the whistle of a train rolling toward the Gare Saint-Lazare. Crouched behind a barrel, I'm watching life seeping out of the little postman. Blood is escaping from his chest. It runs onto his white armband, soaked like a sponge, the Lorraine cross becoming invisible little by little.

That's today. Or yesterday. It's August 1944.

"We're in 2007, Monsieur Robert . . ." Tall tales. I know what I see. A great silence has covered the square. It's Liberation Day, and a nice boy just got himself killed.

Bam! Bam! It's starting again. A bullet has shattered the window of the bookstore. The owner had displayed a fine copy of *Poèmes saturniens.*

"Les sanglots longs des violons de l'automne blessent mon coeur d'une langueur monotone . . ."

(*"The long sobs / Of autumn / violins / Wound my heart / With a monotonous languor . . ."*)

—They're landing! He was laughing. They're landing. The Americans will soon be in Paris.

In the window, Verlaine was shining like a sun.

Bam! A bullet for the poet!

Bam! Bam!

"Oh, I'm sorry. I frightened you, monsieur. Nothing to be afraid of, I'm not going to murder you. Not you. I've never even seen you before. Killing people you don't know is something that happens only in novels . . . Novels! It's coming back to me. It's because of novels that I have to eliminate him . . . Excuse me? Oh no, I'm not crazy! Don't be rude, monsieur. After all, I might kill you too. It's taking the first step that's difficult. And looking at you now, I think you'd be a first step that wouldn't cost much . . . Shut up! You're worthless . . ."

What an idiot! Listen . . . if you had to waste a bullet every time you met one . . . Eight grams of lead per fool; frankly, the joke would cost too much . . . No, I must stick to basics. And the basic thing here is that this guy has to die because of books.

A writer? The bad ones bore you to death. Eliminating one from time to time is a case of self-defense. But I have trouble imagining he's a writer. He'd be more convincing as a critic. The way he has of imposing his opinion. "Good. A little tired. Poor form." Does one kill a critic? Authors must feel like it, but I'm not one of them. If I ever was one, I forget what I might have written, thus I'm not imperishable. And we're not talking about my death but his. A bookstore owner? A librarian? It seems to me he's lent me some books. I didn't even ask him to.

Here I am at Brochant. To the left, along the beltway where the no-man's-land used to be, is the cemetery. To the right, Porte de Saint-Ouen, the field, and the flea market. I come here often. Should I say I used to come here? A second-hand clothes dealer. All sorts of old clothes, worn shoes, and for those in the know, coal, jerricans picked up at railway warehouses. You can find everything at Riton's in Clignancourt. Including, for those who know how to ask for them, parachute silk and weapons—Lugers?

I got nabbed near his shop.

"Papers, *bitte!*"

As they pushed me in the car, I had time to glimpse the ticket office of the stadium, the guy inside, his cap and his embarrassment at having seen this. No more soccer match, I thought. At that moment, nothing could have been more important.

They took boulevard Berthier. Outside, life was going on. At the red light, a woman on a bicycle looked at me with infinite tenderness. Green. The driver turned off toward Malesherbes to reach avenue de Wagram. Classy part of town. Rich-looking façades, broad sidewalks. People walk there, relaxed, important, between two business meetings handled with broad, elegant gestures. There are charming, rousing encounters from 5 to 7, and pleasant memories. The car stopped in front of Hotel Mercedes, number 128. *Geheimfeldpolizei.*

I remember everything.

The room with chipped porcelain tiles. The bloodstains on the floor. The metal chair, the naked lightbulb dangling from its wire. The hideous bathtub, its obscene pipes.

They talked about Riton, the weapons, and the forged papers.

"Who gives the orders?"

A guy turned on the faucets in the bathtub. He was completely ordinary. I heard the water gushing from the faucet.

"We're going to refresh your memory!"

I don't remember anything.

When I came to, they were smoking and chatting like three buddies sharing a good story. A really great dinner. A good place to go. The girl they had the night before in a very comfortable house. Two steps from Parc Monceau. The girls of the house were very clean. Hygiene—that's the main thing . . . So many guys got the clap in sleazy whorehouses. They were no longer concerned with the bathtub, nor with the metal chair, nor with the basement with the foul smell of death. They were no longer concerned with me. They went into the next room. They headed out into the scent of chestnuts, on the beautiful, straight, pleasantly shaded avenues. With the perfume of women still lingering in the early-morning hours after they've left such a comfortable whorehouse, so typically Parisian.

They were three good friends chatting.

You had to convince yourself of the unbelievable, go through the corridor, reach the laundry room with its door

230 // <small>PARIS NOIR</small>

open to the street. The piles of sheets and soiled towels, like lifeless bodies. Outside, the air had never been sharper. And yet so soft and sweet in the summer evening.

You had to go down the avenue, strolling like a regular customer, despite your heart jumping in your chest. At the end, Place des Ternes, florists, white tablecloths at the café Lorraine. And the steps to the metro hurtled down four at a time, because you're about to make it now.

I remember everything.

Look, the newspaper stand over there, at the corner of rue Balagny, I remember it too. The paper seller in his box looks like a puppet in its little theater. His nose of gnarled wood like a vine.

Ah . . . today it's someone else selling the papers.

"*Paris Soir*, please . . ."

"Is that a paper?"

"What a question!"

"A new one?"

"After twenty years its novelty has worn off."

"Twenty years . . . it's been around since 1987?"

"What are you talking about? Since 1923, of course! Okay, I've rounded off one year. Let's not quibble. It's been around for twenty-one years, are you happy now?"

"You're not confusing it with *Paris-Turf*?"

"What would I want with horse racing?"

"If you don't know, it's not for me to say . . ."

"You're not very helpful."

"I don't have to be. Don't get on your high horse, now."

"Do you sell newspapers or don't you?"

"For thirty years, monsieur, and I've never heard of *Paris Soir*. Wouldn't it be *France Soir*? Or *Le Parisien*?"

"Of course, the name may have changed with the Liberation. It wasn't very respectable anymore."

"The liberation . . . ?"

"Of Paris. For someone who sells information, you seem ill informed. Goodbye, monsieur."

One thing's for sure, he's not the one I have to kill. He doesn't open his papers, he couldn't have lent me books. Paper sellers should never change. Nor avenues. Avenue de Clichy has its usual look. Dusty from all the humanity beating the pavement, the same worn-out hope in their pockets. And the bargain display windows, the cheap items, the fake-jewelry stores, the greasy spoons . . . Nothing's missing. Yet I have trouble recognizing it.

"*Ni tout à fait la même ni tout à fait une autre.*" ("*Neither completely the same nor completely other.*") Verlaine again. Did he go to Cité des Fleurs? The poets all go there, I suppose. As for me, rarely. Why don't they ever want me to go out alone? Getting lost in the streets is dizzying. They don't like me to get lost. It's stupid. They end up finding you. They always do. The worst thing is getting lost inside. They call that wandering. But they often say all sorts of nonsense. That we are in 2007, for instance. Who told me that crap? The one I have to kill? He'll get what he deserves. All I have to do is take the right street. Through Cité des Fleurs, since time has stopped there. A long and peaceful path, wisteria on the walls, small gardens and bourgeois houses. Nothing disrupts its peace. Neither the flow of cars on the avenue nor life swarming at the intersections. Nor the overflowing sidewalks. Right near there people walk, eat, slave away, and die too. But no echo of that ever penetrates here. Can one die in Cité des Fleurs?

A cat stretches out in the sun. Was it stretching out when the soldiers came? The pavement echoed with the noise of their boots. The gray-green trucks were barring the path. The door of the house broken open, the screams. Inside, they're caught in a trap. There were only three of them. Two and her. Did they try to escape? Did they resist or did they tell each other goodbye? Now the soldiers turn their guns on them. Everything is sacked, books trampled on, furniture overturned. Paintings thrown to the ground. And the shouts, like barking. Why do soldiers always bark? They immediately found the printing press hidden in the cellar. They were well-informed. To show them they were nothing anymore, the soldiers hit them. The three of them, one after the other. What happened when they led them away? They shot her in the courtyard. A burst of gunfire. Clacking. She fell into the fuchsias. She was twenty-five years old.

No one ever saw the other two again.

Who remembers?

My God . . .

"Mademoiselle!"

" . . ."

"Mademoiselle . . . please . . ."

"Are you ill, monsieur?"

"I would like to go home."

"Are you lost? Do you live far from here?"

"I don't know."

"Monsieur Robert, do you still want to kill me?"

"Don't wear me out with your questions. Tell me, instead, whether you've lent me any books . . ."

"Ah! You remember . . ."

"Where are they?"

"On the cupboard. Have you read them?"

"*The Old Man from Batignolles* . . . I suppose you had me in mind . . ."

"Where do you get that from? It's because of the location. The story takes place near your home. Do you know that Émile Gaboriau's novel may have started the detective thriller genre?"

"Nothing to be proud of. And that one, *The Man Who Got Away*. Albert Londres . . ."

"A fabulous journalist."

"A lot of good that did him! He got away from the 17th arrondissement? It's not hard, all you need to do is cross the avenue . . . Unless . . ."

"Unless what?"

"You're hinting at something again . . ."

"Who knows?"

"My getaway from the *Kommandantur* this time . . ."

"You got away from the *Kommandantur*? You never told me about that . . ."

"You didn't need me to find out about that."

"I swear I didn't know anything."

"Really? Then why this book?"

"The escapee here is a prisoner that Londres met during one of his reporting stints at the penal colony in Guyana. Eugène Dieudonné."

"Don't know him!"

"A typesetter accused of belonging to the Bonnot gang. Those anarchists they nicknamed the Tragic Bandits back during the Gay Nineties. An innocent man, condemned to a life of forced labor. His workshop was right next door, rue Nollet."

"And this book . . . *The Suspect* . . . you're going to claim he has no connection with me . . ."

"None. Why would he? I brought it to you because Georges

Simenon lived here when he came to Paris. At the Hotel Bertha. It's still there, you surely know it . . ."

"What bull! Why did you lend me these books?"

"But . . . To refresh your memory: so you could remember the places here, the neighborhood, its history . . ."

"To refresh my memory."

"Monsieur Robert, can you put down that revolver?"

"Pistol, for God's sake! *Pistol!* Luger Parabellum P-08. You're a speech therapist; instead of making me do your stupid exercises, do them yourself. You need them."

"Monsieur Robert, please, your pistol . . ."

"Speech therapist . . . Are you the speech therapist?"

"Of course . . . I come every week . . . Lower that weapon."

"The man I have to kill . . . it's not you . . . You haven't talked, have you?"

"Talked?"

"You're too young. How old are you?"

"Twenty-six."

"I was that age when they arrested me. The identity cards at Riton's . . . It would have only taken an hour. I got out of their clutches two days later . . . A miracle. It seemed suspect to our network. But should I have croaked down there because some torturers got distracted for a moment? Because a laundress left a door open that should have been closed? Because fate did me a favor? I was cleared, right?"

"Calm down . . ."

"My God . . ."

"Monsieur Robert!"

"I remember everything . . . They didn't need to touch me. The bathtub . . . I fainted before they threw me in . . . When I came to, I talked . . . I told them everything I knew . . . And I would have told even more if I could have."

". . ."

"Twenty-six. I was twenty-six years old. Have *you* already smelled the scent of death at the bottom of a filthy cellar?"

"No . . . I . . . No one—"

"They let me go . . . I was supposed to give them more information . . . A few days later the Americans landed . . ."

"The war's over, Monsieur Robert."

"Not yet . . . Leave me alone. I'm tired."

"Can you give me your revolver?"

"Pistol . . . Think of the exercises, young man, memory is a strange machine."

"Monsieur Robert . . . what are you doing?"

"Now I know who I have to kill. He's a twenty-six-year-old boy . . . No, not you; you can relax now. The one I'm talking about never leaves me. He hasn't left in more than sixty years. Time has no grip on him."

"Please . . ."

"Do you see him? He's in front of you. Every morning I've seen him in my mirror. He's haunted me every night, leaving me sleepless. He eventually dozed off, but you've awakened him with your books and your good intentions."

"I didn't know . . . I swear . . ."

"I have to finish him off now . . ."

"Please . . . Your death won't change anything . . . It was such a long time ago."

"'*Je me souviens / Des jours anciens . . . I can recall / The days of yore . . .*' Do you know Verlaine? It was yesterday. It's today. Get out."

"I won't let you do something stupid."

"Go to hell . . ."

"Monsieur Robert!"

"I'll be waiting for you down there."

БЕСЦЕННЫЙ
(PRECIOUS)
BY **DOA**

Bastille

Translated by Carol Cosman

The office where I was sitting was on the top floor of the building, right under the roof. "Rear window," a police officer with a weary, ironic tone of voice had said when we arrived. He was part of a group of three who had come with me from the crime scene to the hospital for the required medical visit. A nurse had cleaned the dried blood off my face and turned me over to an intern. After taking an X-ray of my spinal column and sewing some painful stitches on me, he pronounced my state *compatible with police custody.* I had a long gash on my left eyebrow, with a hematoma under the eye, another to the right of my mouth, and one on the back of my head, at the base of the skull. "Nothing too bad," the doctor had said.

That was half an hour ago and the day was rising behind the window of the examination room. After going through these procedures and taking some blood samples, they'd brought me to police headquarters at the Quai des Orfèvres. Now I was watching the sky turn blue through a fan-light with iron crossbars.

"They installed them because of Durn." The cynic the two others called *Sydney* and treated like their boss must have followed the meanderings of my puzzled, not yet altogether sober gaze.

I turned toward him. "Who?"

"Durn, the crazy gunman in 2002."

"I wasn't living in France then."

"Oh . . . A demented man we arrested . . ."

He went on with the conversation but I had lost interest.

". . . who killed himself by jumping through a window like this one, but in another office, across the hall . . ."

My eyes drifted around the gray bureaucratic surroundings. Two little rooms leading into one another that opened onto a neon-lit corridor. A different world from mine, shabby and hostile.

"He'd just made a full confession . . ."

The walls, whose neutral paint had seen better days, were covered with administrative documents, maps, and war trophies. A few elegant watercolors too, but only behind *Sydney.* Probably painted by him.

"The bars were put there right after."

There was a light-starved green plant in a corner, a rack of walkie-talkies charging, several metal cabinets topped by boxes of whiskey, exclusively single malt—the denizens of the place were clearly connoisseurs—and six cluttered desks, each with its aging PC that had replaced the typewriter of yesteryear.

"How long have you been living abroad?"

Not forgetting the three cops. The one facing me, *Sydney,* a little guy with a double-breasted suit too large for him and a pipe; the one on my right, at the keyboard, whose first name was apparently *Yves,* tall and thin, slightly bent, wearing jeans; and the last one behind me, still silent. I hadn't heard his name, but since he was wearing a purple shirt with the logo of a polo player, I mentally dubbed him *Ralph* from the start.

"Seven years." And finally, me. I was there too. At least physically, because otherwise I felt unconcerned. I was experiencing all this remotely, with the feeling of not being fully there in the stale back rooms of the famous 36, Quai des Orfèvres, headquarters of the Paris Robbery and Homicide Division, trying to unscramble what had happened that night.

"In London?" *Sydney* motioned with his chin to *Yves*, signaling him to be prepared, while I answered him with a silent nod. "Monsieur Henrion . . . Valère, right?"

Another nod. *Valère Henrion.* A strangely familiar name. Mine. In the mouth of a stranger, a police officer to boot. *Reality check.* I looked at my shackled hands. The gravity of my situation suddenly struck me, and I nearly choked. This was not a friendly interview. These guys were treating me like a suspect. I swallowed. "Don't I have the right to a counsel?" Pitiful.

Sydney flipped through my passport. "You sure do a lot of traveling."

It wasn't a question, and his voice had lost all of its weary warmth. He pointed his nose at me. "The lawyer comes later, first we talk between us. This loft, Place de la Bastille, the place where we found you, who owns . . . ?" He didn't finish his sentence.

"It belongs to a friend, Marc Dustang. He let me borrow it for a few days.

"Very nice of him. Doubt if he'll do it again soon." Smile.

For a moment I flashed on Marc's room and its light walls splattered with red.

"And where is this Marc Dustang?"

"In New York for two weeks."

"For?"

"Business, I guess."

"And you, you've come to Paris for what?"

I sighed, feeling tension mounting inside of me, annoyed at the idea of what was about to follow. I wanted only one thing: to shut myself up in the dark and get my ideas straight. "To work. I just came back from Fashion Week in Milan and I cover the one in Paris right after. September through October is a pretty busy season for me. All the fashion capitals are buzzing, I work a lot."

"You're what . . . ? Oh yes, *sound . . . designer?*" *Sydney* waited, looking at my nervous right leg, which was jumping uncontrollably.

Again I conceded. "That's right. I create the sound tapes for the runway shows. Sometimes I do set mixes for designers' private parties."

"And the money's good?"

"Not bad, yes."

"That's how you met Mademoiselle Ilona . . ." he consulted his notes, "Vladimirova? She was also part of that crowd, right? And not just that one."

"I don't understand."

"Come on, Monsieur Henrion, you want me to believe that you didn't know how your girlfriend made her living? Even *we* know it. I see here"—he pointed to his PC monitor with his index finger—"that she's already met some of our colleagues a few times."

"She was not my girlfriend, and no, I didn't know it." I was having difficulty talking about her in the past tense. "We didn't know each other . . ."

At my back, *Ralph* snickered.

"Really."

Sydney gave me a condescending smile. "The two of you

were kind of intimate for people who didn't really know each other. Unless you paid to screw her, which would mean that you knew perfectly well who you were dealing with. What am I supposed to think?"

I looked for words to answer him but only managed to spit out the banal truth. "Listen, I met this young woman last night for the first time in my life. I'd heard about her, but I'd never seen her before."

"Ah, and who told you about her?"

"Her best friend, one of my exes."

"Her name?"

"Yelena Vodianova."

"You've got a thing for Russian babes, Valère." *Ralph* invited himself into the discussion. "Model too, I suppose?"

I nodded without turning around or rising to the taunt.

"Where does she live?" *Sydney* took things in hand again.

"Yelena? In Milan. She's married with a kid. She still works the catwalk and sometimes we meet in the fashion show season. I told her that I had to spend a few days in Paris, so she asked me to make contact with Ilona."

"Why?"

"To give her a gift. Missed her birthday, I guess, or something like that."

"What sort of gift?"

"I don't know. It was wrapped and I don't like poking into other people's business. I can only tell you that it wasn't very large. Or very heavy." With both hands I indicated the shape of the box, about twenty centimeters long, ten across, and ten thick.

"And you didn't ask your Yelena what kind of gift it was?"

"No."

"You're not very curious."

"I'm not a cop."

"Or very careful." *Ralph* again, aggressive. "She could have had you smuggling dope on the sly. Sure you don't know anything about the contents of this package? It's not too late to—"

"Yes. I'm sure. And I have no reason to mistrust my ex-girlfriends." This answer, a stupid and gratuitous challenge, sounded hollow even to me. If I ever got out of this hornet's nest, there wasn't a chance I'd trust anyone ever again.

"You have this girl's number?"

"In my cell phone, under *Yelena*."

Sydney located the phone among my personal effects on his desk. He tossed it to *Ralph*, who went into the next room.

"So you made contact with Ilona, and then . . . ?"

"We met in the 11th arrondissement." I saw myself entering that bar near the Cirque d'Hiver, where Ilona had said she'd meet me at 11 o'clock, the Pop'in. It was full of noise and smoke, a young crowd, very hip, in the midst of a pop rock revival. As background music The Von Blondies were singing "Pawn Shoppe Heart," a piece I'd used to close a show two years earlier. And there she was at the counter, perched on her Jimmy Choo high-heeled sandals, the latest black leggings, a denim miniskirt, a white blouse open over a sequined tank top, under the de rigueur military jacket. She was talking with the bartender without really paying attention to him, her elbow resting on a pink motor scooter helmet, with her pale blue gaze outlined in black towering over the room. Not difficult to recognize; Yelena had shown me a photo of her.

She'd spotted me too, an older guy not in sync with the rest of the clientele. I walked toward her, she greeted me quickly, in French but rolling her r's, no warmth, scarcely polite; she accepted another glass, then abruptly took her gift and buried it in her purse. Without opening it.

"Strange, don't you think, that she didn't want to see what it was?" *Yves* looked up from his keyboard for a few seconds.

I shrugged. This had intrigued me at the time. But the girl's haughty manners had hardly made me want to try and understand or linger in the bar. I was tired after my week in Milan, and the idea of a peaceful evening was rather attractive. Besides, very early on she'd given me hints that she wanted to leave, and she got up from her stool without waiting for me to finish my beer. With a half-hearted goodbye, she took her helmet, headed for the door at the entrance of rue Amelot, then froze abruptly, her hand on the doorknob. After turning around, she came back toward me, all smiles. She was really beautiful when she smiled.

A bit surprised, I'd taken a look outside, seen a few passersby, particularly a hefty guy a little older than me, kind of tough looking in a black three-piece suit. But he had turned his head away when he caught me looking at him, and by the time I asked Ilona about it, he'd disappeared. She herself had chosen to play the guilty party, so I could forgive her for her behavior.

"She came back just like that and apologized?"

"Yes. She was a strange girl."

"And what about the guy in the suit? Did you ask her if she knew him?"

Nod. "She claimed she didn't. At that point I had no reason to doubt her."

Sydney didn't seem convinced but went on: "And then what did you do?"

"She suggested dinner. We left the Pop'in and went to Oberkampf." But, in fact, things didn't happen that simply. After talking for another half hour inside, Ilona had made me climb up to the second floor and then back down again into the bar's concert hall. There we zigzagged between full tables so as to leave through an emergency exit that led to an inner courtyard, and then into Beaumarchais.

"And her bike?"

"Her bike?"

"Yes, you said that she had a helmet, was it just for decoration?"

"No, she had a scooter, but she wanted to go on foot." Because she'd parked it in front of the bar. And that was when I understood the reason behind this and the paranoia Ilona was showing. She kept looking behind her on the way. I had attributed her behavior to her eccentricity. All the Russian girls I've met in my work have been a bit eccentric. In fact, she had obviously wanted to avoid rue Amelot—and the people who were waiting there for her. "We walked for about thirty minutes, around Place de la République, up Faubourg du Temple as far as Saint-Maur, then turned right to get to Oberkampf and the restaurant. Café Charbon, know it?"

Sydney didn't react but I felt *Yves* nodding on my right and heard him commenting on my lack of judgment, strolling around like that on a Saturday night in such a neighborhood with *that kind of girl.*

I heard a noise behind me—*Ralph* was back in the room: "No answer to the number you gave us, Valère." His voice was first very close, controlled, then I had the impression that he was straightening up to talk to his boss. "I got our colleagues there. One guy speaks English so I asked him to check a couple of IDs. He's going to call back."

"Go on, Monsieur Henrion."

"We ate, talked a little, there was a crowd. It wasn't very good."

"Still didn't open the present?"

"No."

"So, this Ilona girl wasn't as bad as all that."

"I did it for Yelena, because she was her best friend." And perhaps a little for myself, I thought.

"Very nice of you."

Ilona had insisted that we sit in the rear, near a big mirror. She sat down so she could have her back to the restaurant window. In order to see what was behind her without the risk of being recognized from the outside. During the meal, she'd called a number on her cell several times but no one answered. At every aborted call, she'd seemed more tense. As for me, I was learning a little more about her because she was lowering her guard. I was only guessing really, catching signs. I'd already heard other stories like this and had no trouble filling in the blanks.

Like Yelena, she had arrived in Paris around the age of fifteen, leaving behind a crappy life with no future in a ruined, corrupt country. Ready to do anything to have her place in the sun. A pretty kid like so many others. Unscrupulous agencies relying on older former models from the same background who had actually become pimps had dragged her from capital to capital. Never forgetting to pump as much bread as they could out of her. Agencies that didn't hesitate to put her on lousy jobs once she'd started to age, which meant turning a lot less tricks.

Of course I suspected what Ilona was doing to pay the rent. I had one foot in the scene, and even if I wasn't into those things myself, I knew them well. I'd cross paths with many girls of her type. For a while I'd thought that Yelena was working as a high-class whore too. She talked so little about her life at the time that in the end I didn't trust her. She hadn't understood my attitude, and our affair fell apart.

By the time I realized that her discretion was only modesty and shame, she'd already gone elsewhere to work with others and start over. That was six years ago, just after my arrival in London. Since then we'd stayed in touch anyway, and this at least had given me the chance to apologize, to try and be a better friend.

It was probably because of that, because of an old, unresolved guilt, that I had agreed to do something for Ilona at the end of the meal.

"So really, she asked you to go to her place alone, and you said yes without hesitating, without asking for an explanation?"

"Of course I did!"

"And so?"

"I can't remember what she told me anymore, I . . . I'm tired."

"With all the junk you took?" *Ralph* didn't want to be forgotten.

I couldn't reply. No point trying to justify the coke, I'd taken it willingly, like an idiot. They'd made me swallow the rest by force. But my three interrogators didn't seem ready to believe me.

"So you agreed, and . . . ?"

"And I went out of the Charbon . . ." Into the Saturday-night zoo, a little nervous and not very uplifted by the local crowd. I'd known the Oberkampf neighborhood a few years earlier when it was trendier, sleeker, newly revitalized. Now it was like anyplace else again, with even more bars and restaurants.

The building where Ilona and her housemate had their apartment was located in a private, gated alley not far from the restaurant. What used to be called a cité (housing block) in the 11th, a kind of narrow alley where artisans had their workshops before. These had disappeared a long time ago, replaced by very expensive, slightly bohemian apartments for models, photographers, and artists of all kinds. Or by public housing. Social diversity in the making.

"There wasn't much light in the courtyard and no one in sight." I stood a moment outside, listening to the sounds of a party several floors up and watching people in the street on the other side of the gate. "I climbed up to the third floor, I found the entrance Ilona had mentioned on the landing, and I was going to knock when I heard the cry." I had never been confronted with such suffering. A terrible scream, interrupted by deep gurgles and sobs. "It was a girl, I think. I thought it must be Ilona's housemate, and I almost tried to enter, but . . ."

"But?" *Sydney* leaned toward me.

"Two men began talking to each other inside, in Russian. There were heavy punches, more moaning from someone in pain. Even through the . . . I . . . I could practically feel the punches."

"The address! Quick!"

I gave it to *Ralph* from memory, this time turning around. Impossible to forget it after what I'd heard behind that door. *Ralph* went to make phone calls in the next room.

"What did you do afterward?"

"I left."

Yves shook his head behind his computer screen.

"I . . . I wanted to tell Ilona, ask her for her key, warn someone, get people . . ." I tried to explain but it was useless. "And what would you have done in my place? I had no weapon, I don't know how to fight." I lowered my head. "I got scared."

The office was silent for a few seconds. They let me stew in my shame. I felt their mocking eyes on me.

"You left, and then?" *Sydney,* the humiliation had lasted long enough.

"I was going back down when I met the guy I'd seen in front of the Pop'in. He was carrying a McDonald's bag. We were both surprised but he didn't recognize me, at least not right away. He just checked me out from head to toe as I casually passed him, trying to stay calm. I was already running along the alley when I heard shouting in the stairway. Names, I think, at least one: *Victor.*"

"His sidekicks in the apartment?"

"I didn't try to find out. I rushed to find Ilona at the Charbon. She understood there was a problem as soon as she saw me come in."

"Not stupid, that babe. Then?"

"Then she refused to follow me outside."

"Why?"

"Instinct, I guess. The threat was behind me. She dragged me into the bathroom, and from there we stepped into the nightclub next door, the Nouveau Casino." Barely through the door, she'd done something that puzzled me. She'd gone to the cloakroom and checked her purse. But not her helmet. Then she gave me the ticket she'd gotten from the girl in charge. I didn't tell them this, though.

"What did you do once you got inside?"

"She led me toward the bar at the back. We lost ourselves in the crowd and we waited. She refused to listen to me. I could see she was scared stiff, and this began to make me panic too. I wanted to call someone."

"Who?"

"You, the police. Who else?"

"Why didn't you?"

Behind me, other cops were filing into the second office.

Ralph started to talk to them, and I understood that these were the guys who had stayed at Marc's while we'd gone to the hospital. They exchanged information in low voices.

Sydney returned to the job at hand. "Why didn't you call us, Monsieur Henrion?"

"She stopped me. She didn't want me to go out to make a call, and my cell wasn't working inside. Plus, I couldn't hear above the music."

"A little too easy."

"For you, maybe. Anyhow, I wouldn't have had time."

"Why not?"

"The thug from the stairway showed up in the club with another guy, same type only older. Ilona saw them first, me just after. They were quick to spot us and elbowed through the crowd to catch up with us."

"That's where they cornered you?"

"No." I closed my eyes and rubbed a hand over my face to ward off the memories. Suddenly I snickered.

"What?"

"There was a concert later that evening at the Nouveau Casino, and they were spinning the British band Franz Ferdinand to keep people from getting impatient. 'Auf Achse,' you know it?"

Sydney shook his head.

"Okay, forget it. There were three black guys sitting next to us at the bar. They'd been checking out Ilona since we'd arrived, so she went to ask them for a smoke. The two Russians turned up, and the first grabbed her by the wrist to yank her around. She slapped him."

After that, everything went very fast. The thug had wanted to slap her back, but one of the black guys gave him a violent shove. They all started fighting, and Ilona and I slipped out, taking advantage of the confusion.

Outside, there was a black Mercedes waiting with a third man. Fortunately, it was parked on the other side of the street, pointing in the wrong direction. He'd seen us, but by the time he reacted and got out of his car, we were already far away, hurtling down Oberkampf in the middle of the Saturday-night partygoers. I remembered that Ilona had taken off her Jimmy Choos to run and we had gone through side streets, then down toward the Cirque d'Hiver to get the scooter. A mistake. In the meantime, the Russians had regrouped and, without a hitch, seeing the direction we'd taken, had made a quick return to the Pop'in.

The Mercedes had shot up rue Amelot just as Ilona was starting her scooter. Without missing a beat, she'd jumped it up on the sidewalk to try to shake off the car.

"Then I got really scared. I had no helmet and we were taking lots of small one-way streets in the wrong direction. We almost hit several people." I shook my head. "I think we broke the speed record for crossing the 11th· but we couldn't shake them, and they were going to catch us any minute. At some point, on one of the boulevards, I can't remember which . . ." I stopped in the middle of my story to search my memory, in vain. "Well, I can certainly find it on a map. Anyhow, I saw a public works van parked near one of those huge metro air vents planted in the sidewalks. It was wide open, with several cables and pipes running from it into the ground."

Then I told Ilona to go around the block the wrong way. This time we got lucky, a car heading toward us from the other end of the street forced the Russians to slow down. We went back to the van and I told her to get off the scooter. I dumped it into the vent opening, and we jumped right after it onto a large conduit. The scooter was wrecked, but we were invisible. No one saw our maneuver, not even the poor guy doing the maintenance on the vent. He only saw us climb back up thirty minutes later, a little dirty, once we were sure the coast was clear.

Sydney stared at me in disbelief.

"Go check it out, the scooter's probably still in the hole. We caught a taxi back to Marc's place. I thought we'd gotten out of the jam we were in. I was wrong."

The phone started ringing in the next room. *Ralph* picked up. I sighed. This didn't escape *Sydney*. A second call, a few seconds later. They were asking for *Ralph* again. I closed my eyes. The second conversation, in English, was more laborious. Italy. When *Ralph* hung up and joined us, his voice was less assured, more concerned. "I have bad news."

I lowered my head, sniffled. "Yelena's dead."

"How did you know?" The cop in the polo shirt wasn't so condescending anymore.

I knew it because of what had happened afterwards. Ilona and I had arrived at Marc's very annoyed with each other. Especially me with her. The adrenaline was subsiding, giving way to a more muted tension.

"What time was it?"

"Two-thirty in the morning, maybe three."

I remember yelling at her while pacing in front of the bay window of the loft. At my feet was the Place de la Bastille, with its July column and its little golden Genie of Liberty at the top of it all lit up. But I didn't care about the view, I couldn't stop yelling.

Ilona backed into a corner of the living room, near a low table, far from my outbursts. After a long moment without her reacting, she removed a packet of powder from her jacket pocket and traced some lines on the table. I jumped on her, beside myself, grabbing her by the shoulders and shaking her. I stopped when I saw her sad, beaten look. The look of a girl who knew she'd lost everything. She put a finger on my mouth, snorted a line with a rolled-up bill before passing it to me. "I hesitated and then did the same. Believe it or not, it has been a long time since I've done coke. We finished the lines and stared at each other."

Then everything got pretty hazy. She stroked my cheek, kissed me on the mouth, and bit my upper lip. Until it bled. First we made love there, on that low table. I could see myself again, lifting her skirt and pulling down her tights. She's the one who had wanted me to take her like that, urgently, from behind. A violent, desperate ass fuck that went on for a long time, everywhere, until we both ended up passing out in the bedroom. "When I came to my senses, the three Russians were standing around the bed."

"How did they find out where—"

"Yelena. She was the only one who knew where I was staying in Paris. I'd told her and she also knows . . . *knew* Marc." I swallowed to avoid crying. "Did she suffer?"

Ralph nodded yes.

"And her kid?"

"All of them, the husband too. The thugs took their time." *Ralph* looked at his boss. "Same for the housemate in Oberkampf."

"Jesus! Who are these assholes, for God's sake? Tell us if you know!" *Sydney* banged his palm on his desk.

I shook my head. "They spoke Russian the whole time. One of them dragged me off the bed and punched me in the face. I ended up in the paws of the older one, the famous Victor. That much I understood. I think he was the boss. He pushed me onto my knees, threatening me with a gun. Then he made me drink vodka from the bottle. To put me out, I think. He kept poking me with the barrel to make me swallow faster."

I would have preferred to forget what happened next. The two other Russians had set to work on Ilona. One was holding her by the arms, the other was straddling her thighs to prevent her from moving. This guy started to cut up her face with a knife while he questioned her. "They never spoke French. Between every cut, he'd pour alcohol on her wounds. She was screaming." A tear ran down my cheek. "She was struggling, and the more she screamed, the more the thugs enjoyed themselves."

"You did nothing?"

I pointed to my cut eyebrow. "After a long time, she stopped moving. I thought they'd killed her. There was blood everywhere, on the sheets, on the walls. The torturer turned to Victor to speak to him. He got a reply and stuck his face close to Ilona's. That jerk was holding his knife just under her chin, like this . . ." I mimicked his posture, "the blade facing up. And then . . ."

Then, Ilona shoved his hand with her head. The point of the blade sunk into the guy's neck and he fell back holding his throat. His pal, the one with Ilona's wrists, stood up, surprised, before reacting and hitting her with all his strength. Victor had forgotten me. His piece pointed to the bed, he was too busy trying to understand what was happening.

"In a burst of despair, I stood up and lunged at the gun. We fought, shots were fired toward the bed. I heard a thump and I knew his pal was hit."

"A good hit, all right."

I ignored *Yves's* lame irony. "The weapon passed between us, we fought some more. There was another blast and Victor fell on top of me. I hit my head on the ground and lost consciousness. When I woke up under his corpse, the police were there. All the others were dead. Then you came."

"That's all?"

No, obviously. I looked at my interrogators one by one. "You don't think it's enough?" Probably not, but they would have to make do.

As he was aiming his gun at me, Victor had told me—in broken French—what he and his henchmen were looking for. He owned a special kind of airline that dealt in illegal freight. *I even work with CIA, I transport prisoners terrorist*, he'd slipped in, laughing, between two swigs of vodka, in Marc's living room. At the end of the '90s he had a *business partner*, Leonid, a Ukrainian Jew who had acquired Israeli nationality. Victor thought that was hilarious. They were selling weapons to the rebels in Angola and Liberia and the rebels were peddling some of them to al Qaeda for diamonds. Down there everything was paid for in local precious stones, conflict diamonds, war diamonds.

Six years earlier, Victor and Leonid had met in London to seal a pact with a rival. They'd ordered some girls—Ilona and Yelena—to celebrate. The evening had gone well, but in the early hours of the morning they'd noticed that the payment for their last African shipment, five million dollars in rough stones, had disappeared. They'd blamed the other criminal, of course, and settled the score with him. Neither of the two would have suspected *those little whores*, as Victor called them, of pulling off the theft. And as for the girls, they waited.

Not long enough, apparently.

A month ago, Ilona had traveled to Antwerp with Polaroids of the uncut set of stones, to find out their market value from some diamond merchants. A rumor had swept through

254 // Paris Noir

the diaspora before reaching Leonid, who started to watch her. He quickly understood that Yelena had also been in on the job, and his plan was to send some of his men to Italy to get the diamonds back.

Without suspecting anything, Yelena had gotten ahead of everybody by entrusting me with the gift to Ilona. Then her luck turned, and I nearly got myself killed. Bitch. "I'm tired."

"You'll be able to rest soon."

The cops released me the next day. The DA told me to stay in France a few more days for final verifications and then told me that the case would probably be taken to court, and that I would have to come back. I was able to go back to Marc's place to collect my things, particularly the jacket I'd been wearing that evening, which I'd intentionally left there. Inside was Ilona's cloakroom ticket.

I'm a really, really patient guy.

NO COMPRENDO
THE STRANGER
BY HERVÉ PRUDON
Rue de la Santé

Translated by David Ball

Diary

Paris is a full city. Every morning I empty out my head: It's like in the country—last day of November—a new blue sky improves—upon acquaintance—with a bare sky—advancing openly emptiness—on a glass tray—sea without spray—sea of ice—and the city disappeared—like in the fields—when time passes—the wind dies down and pain disappears—you take a chair—you sit there—you feel like painting that—nothing oppresses—caresses from beyond . . .

I'm not going out but I'm not the only one: cocoons, tribes, parties, cells—family cells or others—ghettoes, armored doors, double-paned, triple-locked, padlocked, barricades, everybody standing firm. Nobody moves. To go from my place to the chic neighborhoods, you have to climb on trees, go from branch to branch like the baron in the trees. I'm too acrophobic. Also too claustro to crawl through catacombs. So walk along the asylum, the big prison, the convents and hospitals. Closed spaces. What they call maximum-security areas. Maximum tension. That's rue de la Santé, from one end to the other. Health Street. The sickest street in Paris.

Iron

It was a fine end of November, abnormally mild. People were swimming in Nice and Biarritz. In some Parisian neighborhoods a vacation mood must have been in the air, the kind of spontaneous fragrance that floods you with pleasure, makes you fall in love, and fills you with bliss in front of a store window or behind a behind. No fragrance like this in other neighborhoods. It wasn't a good idea to go out today. Outside it was too empty in spots. Real black holes of antimatter. Elsewhere dripping with picturesque. There are days where this city is borderline bipolar. I had zero grams of iron in my blood and I should have known that one way or another this deficiency was going to be turned around—and dangerously so.

In detective novels, demons or buddies always catch up with the guy who has served time: He goes down again, falls again, and dives back into the life again. But like I said, that's in books. In reality there's less reality; more things happen inside your head than on the street. Dead things, for example, or old ideas—they don't have a grave but keep on dying in bits of brain in the unsafe area. All this to say that there are very threatening days when I don't feel right inside and my life is like an old tape you can't rewind or even decipher because of the hieroglyphics, belches, obsolete sonnets, postmodern jargon, and intensity levels of collective or individual memory. I needed a technician who could stick his fingers into the softened hard drive of my decomputerized neurons and the visceral tar of my decorticated cortex—not an oncologist. But the vagaries of the medical calendar are such that I had an appointment here, not there, and I couldn't avoid having to walk the whole length of rue de la Santé. For some it's a quarantine line, a humanitarian corridor, Social Protection, for others it's death row. This street stretches out under an infinitely high wall of millstones full of holes like sponges; it's a street buried alive inside its walls. There I go from jolt to decay.

Health

"A man can live on emotion, doctor, you can't live on fatigue, you live under it. You can surf on emotion, you're a flying fish, a land-air missile, but fatigue torpedoes you, it drowns you."

"Go back home and get some rest."

"Rest on who, on what?"

"Get out and see people."

"People? Where am I supposed to go? Into a store window, as a mummy? Sit in a heated sidewalk café between two coat hangers? This city is a frustrating mirage. I never go out, doctor, unless you hand me a summons for medical tests. Outside, on street level, you're closed in, locked up, walled up. You really want me to go out on the street, this street? In the jolted, ultra-vulnerable state you put me in? This street is a black sword, it goes through me backwards, it tears out my guts and my head, it's a brutal street, it's sick and crazy and dangerous. You saw the wall? Fifteen yards high, hundreds of yards long, nothing but big millstones and every single one of them wants to get out of the wall and jump on you. Behind the sticky wall a fucking ferocious neighborhood, a human zoo. An Indian reservation, no reservations necessary. A concentration camp universe. The back room, the rubbish, the unsold items, all the ugliness of the most beautiful city in the world. A secret, private collection where you can find everything that's wrong. It jumps out at you through the walls. I wasn't educated in violence, and I still don't know what side I'm on. There are two sides on rue de la Santé, a wall side and a house side. The two sides clash. Those who have almost everything and those

258 // PARIS NOIR

who've lost everything. This isn't a Parisian street and I don't think it ever goes anywhere."

I don't remember what he answered. Move along, there's nothing to see.

"Rue de la Santé is a slit, a geological fault in the exhibitionist system, the opposite of the Operation Open Doors that the City of Lights is putting on right now. It cuts through the eastern part of the 14th arrondissement from north to south, a neighborhood they call residential, in contrast to commercial. In actual fact a neighborhood of nothing. A place dismissed, like a case dismissed. In the game of Monopoly it does not exist."

"You're fixating."

This street, merry as an exhaust pipe, begins at Val de Grâce (military hospital) and ends on rue D'Alésia (defeat of the Gallic chieftain Vercingetorix against the Roman general Julius Caesar) at the intersection with Glacière, rebaptized Place Coluche (French comedian, died on a motorcycle at forty-two, founder of the Restos du Coeur soup kitchens); on the even-numbered side it passes by Cochin (civilian hospital), La Santé (only prison inside Paris), and Sainte-Anne (psychiatric hospital). The blind walls of these institutions, confined there until further notice, face deaf buildings anyone is entitled to find ugly, especially after the elevated line on boulevard Saint Jacques, as you get nearer to the outlying neighborhoods where they've built modest and low-income housing. Further up, between Arago and Port-Royal, more historical places—convents and religious or monastic institutions; they conceal their rich, permanent heritage behind cleaned-up walls and clumps of trees.

"I'm not fixating, doctor, life put me in the fix I'm in, I have to stay in my room at one end of the street, it shut me up, it hammered me down, and you're at the other end, one foot in my grave and the other among the fortunate of the earth. I'm stuck with the whole length of this street that's locked away behind surrounding walls oozing with misery and pain. Only cemetery walls look that much like the walls of asylums and prisons. You don't know who these walls separate from whom, the living from the dead, the normal from the abnormal, honest people from criminals, the sick from the healthy, animals from human beings—they separate some from others, that's all you have to know. All you have to do is imagine that behind the walls it's more than a zoo, it's a jungle, Africa, hell, and the ghetto of living. Nobody walks on rue de la Santé, and car traffic is rare. People who live here are invisible, protected by their anonymity. Their children don't play on the sidewalk. Nobody would get the idea of moving here, facing the walls, except for Samuel Beckett who chose to live right across from the prison. He used to say he'd always be on the prisoners' side, but most of the prisoners never read Beckett; he lived on the other side of the street, the other side of the walls. The walls have the thickness of reality, but on both sides of the walls life has the consistency of a fantasy. On rue de la Santé you can't see anything but you can hear voices, groans, and shouts, moans, calls, frenzies, revolts, and death throes. You're never sure. It's like being at the edge of a deep forest. It's like a no-man's-land, the Mexican border or the Berlin wall. Good happy honest normal people never go near asylums, prisons, or hospitals. They have no idea the centuries-old convents even exist. They don't know what kind of life is lived there, what vices are practiced, or what types of surprises they're cooking up for us there.

"Life here is not Parisian, no sidewalk cafés, no shops, no strolling around in the sun. It's a life of shadows. The banks of the Seine and the Champs-Élysées are elsewhere, but the Seine is a bland sauce and the Champs-Élysées is paved with soft stones. The History of France is declaimed out there, under l'Arc de Triomphe. Paris is a grandiloquent city; it shines but leaves everyone in the dark, and the featherless Gallic Rooster is disguised as a phosphorescent peacock. The history of the French people is no longer written in newspapers or books, it went to sleep somewhere between long ago and formerly, between elsewhere and further away, but rue de la Santé is the bottom you hit before you bounce up again. De Gaulle and Mitterrand were treated in Cochin, all the great criminals made a stay in the prison, and in Sainte-Anne the pathways are called Maupassant, Baudelaire, or Antonin Artaud. Rue de la Santé is a black knife, a cut-throat alley, a cold trench, a fault, a slit, a scar, a short silence, and a draft of cold air. Every particle of air is a piece of shrapnel slashing through your brain. Far from the crowd, the passerby you encounter is an escapee, a survivor on suspended sentence, a jailbird, an abnormal person, or even an anchorite. At any rate a foreigner, not a citizen. He can't be a tourist, an employee, or a storekeeper. A neighbor, perhaps, but from what side? He can't ignore you, there's nowhere he can look, he wants to hug you—or bump you off. He seems to know you, or recognize you. He already saw you in good company when he was in the padded cell, or solitary, or on a gurney, in prayer or in sorrow. It's not the clash of civilizations, it's the drift of continents. The guy in front of you is an iceberg in a thick fog. You're ready to fight to the death, because this is where it's happening, on rue de la Santé, at last you're going to battle, after wandering around this fucking snail-shaped city for years without finding your niche—or the exit."

Camus

"Mom died today. Or maybe yesterday, I don't know. But I know she died today. Or maybe yesterday, I didn't know. What does it matter? Yesterday, today, dead or not, her or me? Last night I reread Camus's *The Stranger* to fall asleep. Result: I didn't sleep at all. I dreamed that a dog who was allowed to go anywhere was dragging me by the sleeve through the sleaziest places you could think of, dungeons of passing time, the bottoms of which you could never get out of since the social elevator's broken and the competition is international, I was in a nine-square-yard cell with two other inmates, I was on a hospital bed next to a cancer of the liver, I was like an overmedicated zombie in a cafeteria in Sainte-Anne and the dog was telling me to hurry up, we still had to visit the Catacombs and the Montparnasse cemetery. That dog finally left me alone but I began thinking about our appointment. I really shouldn't have done that, because I hold you completely responsible for making me come here and then leave without getting anything. It would have been better not to come and not to think about it.

"At 9:30 a.m. I left the house at the last minute to see if I had any mail. There was that letter from the eviction officer about my unpaid rent and the eviction notice. My father died penniless and my mother worse, all alone, she'd even lost her mind. Paris was off limits for her, because of her blood pressure and the high rents. For her, Paris was no way to live. For me, that's all there was. In the '60s I'd already burned down all the projects outside Paris with napalm the way cobalt can get rid of your cancer."

General-in-Chief of the Middle Class

"When I was a kid I always dreamed of the Champs-Élysées, the banks of the Seine, and the Quartier Latin. I lived twenty miles from Paris in low-income housing. My father was general-in-chief of the middle class and a representative of smalltown France. That just shows you he didn't exist. He used to bike back from the station and into the parking lot in front of the neighbors' cars and their wives' windows. Of course he had battle plans and naval maps in his pockets but he wouldn't spread them out in front of his family who had homework to do or dinner to make. In the '50s and '60s the son of a modest wage earner in the southern suburbs could consider a career as a teacher in Paris. Paris was a conquerable citadel. The kind of target you could hit. It seemed to me the right spot for a young man with some French culture to have the firm illusion he'd be living in the center of the world. But it wasn't a target made of concentric circles, it was more like a spiral with a constantly moving center. The more Parisian I was, the more of a stranger I was. An immigrant. I didn't even give myself the right to vote, or a work permit. I would settle into apartments without paying the rent until I got evicted. I could always manage to melt into the city, I looked like seaweed, the spitting image of the crowd. I lived by writing and lying; in other words I lived on nothing. Most of the time I lived underwater, in the fog, but with the technique of the flying fish, I had flashes of scintillating lucidity that lead me to say I actually did live. Or at least I think so."

Impoverishment

"It seemed to me that in the '70s, as I emerged in Paris, I was reproducing the fate of all humanity, I was like that fish with legs coming out of the ocean and becoming a monkey in a few million years, then a man; I was on dry ground, the promised land. I came from the southern suburbs, I didn't realize I was leaving that impalpable, infinite, slimy old-people's home to its economic stagnation and unemployment, hopelessness and mindlessness. I landed at the Porte d'Orléans, and I stuck there, all around Denfert, Montparnasse, and Port-Royal, without ever crossing the Seine. At least back then, the people of the 14th looked middle class and not yet like a bunch of chickenshits sliding into impoverishment. But I didn't want to be prosperous. I wanted to be Verlaine or François Villon. Verlaine ended his life here, in the hospital neighborhood, going from sleazy hotel to hospice, from the arms of Eugénie Krantz and Philomène Boudin, well-known prostitutes, to the less tender arms of the hospital sisters in their habits."

Esophagus

"I ended up at Cochin Hospital. Not really ended. Not really continued. I stopped there. The Achard wing is a huge blue thing that would bring anybody down, but from the ninth floor you can look out over all of Paris. At night it looks like the scintillating sea. I had become the ghost of a big crow and I had a rotten egg in my esophagus. A bodyguard never left my side: It was a kind of giraffe or gibbet from which a goiter was hanging, a bladder, a belly heavy from chemotherapy. I also had a syringe on my lap, and in my chest a tube between a vein and pipes through which substances were flowing. Every morning a stretcher bearer would come get me and take me to an ambulance that crossed the city toward the Place Gambetta. In a sci-fi setting I was bombarded by X-rays to the music of Keith Jarrett. In the big waiting room where a horde of frightened paupers were waiting, I would smoke Craven "A"s while waiting for the ambulance drivers to come back. I no longer thought about downing large quantities of alcohol, I was much calmer. I had no desire to get out of there and into a café, didn't feel like picking up girls either. I had all I needed, because on the one hand I could see my life like a real thing and not a beautiful piece of fruit, and on the other my life was an object of care for all the people who surrounded me, and that gave it a certain reinforced substance. I was naked in my life but that life was an air cushion. The weight I'd lost was the weight of guilt, bad fat. I felt unbelievably forgiven. Of course I was wrong, but as long as I was in the hospital or even in the ambulance listening to the drivers' bullshit, I was untouchable—admirably lucid, but only relevant on one side of the wall, nine stories higher than other peoples' lives."

Adoration

"I looked out over rue de la Santé—I think I've said the main things about it already—and the square courtyard of a little Ursuline convent. At 10 in the morning a window in the building would open and a woman would appear in smiling majesty, and the memory of her majestic smile would accompany me all day through the obedient time at the hospital, for I rediscovered in her slow, secluded life the secret impatience of childhood time, when there is a century from one Christmas to another and two hundred thousand palpitations of the heart between two kisses.

"'She's not smiling, she's making a face,' my roommate would say. He was really nasty in his unhappiness, and his company was a nasty face behind my back.

"I knew that once I fell out of my observatory down there, driven out of the asylum parenthesis, everything would move very quickly between two fatal accidents and from sequels to metastases, from personal bankruptcy to planetary cataclysm, everything would go bust, irremediably, from day to day for centuries and centuries, with no ritual to consecrate the moment or drunkenness ever again to sublimate it, no surprise would shake up the exhaustion of living when the memory and consolation I had found was erased, not near that Ursuline nun I couldn't see very well with my own eyes from so far away, my eyes fucked up by the drugs, but I could have walked at least once barefoot into emptiness halfway to the sky to meet her, barefoot, in pajamas, light, on the invisible tightrope of my desire, even after her arms get tired of opening and sorry that my late lamented desire is worn out and dangles down, defeated by medication and other things in my mental constitution, this being noted well before I was freed from the cancer wards.

"But who was she smiling at twelve months out of twelve all the goddamn day between her four walls and the arcades of her little convent? Was she cloistered there forever? Was she really as I saw her when she stood against the wall in her window frame, Ava Gardner and the *Mona Lisa,* and if not, then who?

"'A slut,' my roommate would say. 'She's doing a mouth striptease with her smile.'

"It's true she'd fucking contaminated me with her smile. All I had to do was think of her crowned with light, her breasts raised and her arms open in a sweeping gesture inaugurating the glorious day, and a smile would spread over my beaming face, remaining between my lips like a sigh of the greatest beatitude. The guy who shared my room was a bad-tempered paranoiac with bipolar tendencies; it made him nervous that I never stopped thinking about her, all mischievous and generous, hence the smile. He didn't like the idea of me smiling behind his back.

"Not so long ago, when I was nervous too, I felt that time spent doing nothing is blood you're losing, blood leaving your body. My blood was over there, in the veins of that little nun. Little or big, I don't know. That's where life was. Behind the walls. Between four walls and in a bed, in the conversation she has with the world at the intersection of morning and eternity, a certain way of turning the courtyard of a convent on rue de la Santé into the Sahara of Charles de Foucault, and praying there without saying anything and without wasting her time. As for my time, my time for living or not, other people could spend it, think about it, put it to good use. My use of life had been disappointing, especially my own life I mean, I never really managed to live, but if you've tried yourself you know it isn't easy, but I was beginning to hear, in the breathing of the tangible, invisible, and in a word discreet universe—quite unknown, like that Patuyan territory where Lord Jim carved out his fate—something livelier than life, the radar echo of infinitely gentle matter that might welcome me for a while. Things and people we look at stealthily—we steal something from them, as the root word shows, probably a bit of their image, as if we're surveillance cameras, but why not benevolence cameras? We trust them to lead us, to walk us about, and they embody us, as if that fucking metempsychosis didn't wait for us to die. We become the dog in the street, the tree waiting for its leaves, the baby bawling in its stroller, and the nun in her room who can't see you but is probably praying for you, for you to be saved.

"I saved a greeting for her every morning, she would smile her smile, and it all fused together and remained hanging in the air.

"The first days at my window it was passionately sexual, I was lying in wait, feverish and predatory, a generous sperm donor, but what with habit and laziness and a whole lenitive chemistry, it turned into something else: murmuring a sweet song, not breaking crackers anymore, taming a titmouse, leaving the night nurses alone, giving a bit of oneself little by little, day after day—I moved all my hope into the nun's place across the courtyard, making my nest in her flowerpots and my faith in her catechism, whereas my roommate slit his throat in the communal showers.

"I would not regret our conversations, not because he called me Monsieur Schmaltz or Sister Smiley, but because I had no idea what he was talking about. One day, before opening his mouth, he wrote out a draft of his declaration:

Unless seeing what never seen nor possible to know unimaginable to this day of which one would have to in order to say other words than always the same ones and thus today senseless and outdated tomorrow by audiovisual without a printer, I do not know what to say, Smiley—in French in the original.

"'No,' I would say. 'You don't always know what to say.'

"'You don't always say what you see either, because what you see is unspeakable, in French in the original, right? Schopenhauer can say that the true existence of man is what takes place inside himself, and that in the same environment each man lives in another world, we're still in the same room, right? So do me a favor, stop smiling. Or you're gonna get it from me too.'

"'According to Swami Prajnanpad, one must say yes to everything and when we accept something willingly there is no suffering, and fear must be banished from our lives.'

"'If I didn't run a schizophrenic support group in regular life, I wouldn't feel like I was talking to the wall of an autistic crap-house covered with graffiti smelling sickeningly and sweetly of shit. You put smiles all over this goddamn room, what the hell do you like here?'

"'Me.'

"'You remind me of that fucking young mother who smothered her baby and threw him into a pond. The same night she was smiling into the TV cameras claiming someone had stolen her kid. Why was she smiling, huh? Why're you smiling too? Fuck off, get the hell out of here, you asshole. Dickhead.'"

Monkeyfish

"Well, he died, that's life. So everything would have been okay in the hospital if they'd kept me inside their walls; they'd even confiscated my prick so I couldn't injure myself, so that my temporary impotence was perfectly interlocked with the votive chastity of my Ursuline across the way. I felt more and more like I was sitting inside myself, like a stone in the sand. There was nothing else I had to do. I was born to be there. I was legitimate, like Verlaine.

"Then they gave me a Turk for a neighbor. Or maybe a Kurd. He was no poet. I didn't understand a thing he said, but when he didn't say anything he looked dead.

"And when he died he had a smile that looked like me. I wondered why this Turk or Kurd had come to die in the 14th.

"I told you about the fish with legs who became a monkey and then man, but I didn't tell you about his dismay when he understood, with his great intelligence, that the dry or promised land was not the center of the world. The center of the world had changed places in the meantime. From then on it was submerged, or Chinese, or somewhere in the suburbs of the world, in the anonymity of forgotten, tiny, unconscious lives, protozoan small fry. So all the monkeyfish could do was go back to the ocean, wherever the currents carried it, but it no longer knew how to swim or breathe in the water. That's why we can see it on the strand, that strip of wet sand between the beach and the ocean, it talks to seashells and hears Apollinaire's line: *And the single string of the sea trumpets . . .* It paces around without knowing if it's time to get wet or dry. You really don't want to keep me here, doctor, the way you've seen me, do you?"

"I'm a gastroenterologist, not a psychiatrist. I can see you're a depressive, but you're not the only one and beds are hard to come by. Your colon looks okay, your stomach has definitively found its spot in the mediastinum, and aside from the problem of anemia, you're in perfect health. I don't want to see you here anymore. Next time, go see your primary caregiver. You had an operation ten years ago, that's old news, and you still keep coming to see us. You live next door? You're just dropping by like a neighbor? You moved into a boarding house across the street?"

"Across the street there's a convent. And your nearest neighbors are jailbirds and insane people. I live further away in a new neighborhood where the lower middle class lives. I feel like I'm my father, but unlike me he didn't have debts and he paid his rent."

"Good. What did your father do?"

"He biked every morning and evening to the station and back, but I'm walking back."

"Don't get caught in the demo with your dickhead and your wobbly legs. It's the firemen against the CRS riot police; things are going to heat up. And call me this evening for the results of the biopsy."

Farewell

I went back up to see my room. It had no smell anymore. The moron who'd slit his throat ten years back was there, he'd come back again, all sewed up, in bed, in bad shape. He didn't want my compassion, and he didn't even recognize me. I went up to the window to take a look at the convent. Veiled Ursulines were walking around the courtyard, I didn't know which one was mine. They never went outside, or very rarely. A little like me. We were not fated to meet. On the other side over the rooftops you could see the Eiffel Tower as if it were brand new.

Genocide

Once I was outside I backed up. I crossed the boulevard and I went and sat down in a garden of the Observatory. From there I could see Sacré-Cœur, but between the big hill of Montmartre and that part of Montparnasse, there sits all of Paris: In the mist, it wasn't much. And to think I'd wanted to stick something up the ass of this fucking city. Walls, houses, and behind the walls of the houses, heads, and in each head other walls, dollhouses, makeup, and monkey-dreams—that's all there was.

I was mad at myself for not being in good shape. I'd been afraid of a relapse and my body had become an irresponsible mechanism.

I say eternal words to myself with no substance, fine day, bare sky, the blue transparent skin of emptiness, the trembling of the air, the border of absence, rue de la Santé, Health Street, the health of the street. So everything is in everything else? But I am in nothing. Isolating, escaping, thinking against the grain, alone, thinking Tao, sparrow and Tao, not acting, no longer moving, until the reality test.

That's when that first corpse came into the picture. I heard myself saying: *He's dead, that's life.* There was no border between him and me. I had already thought all that about someone I loved, or maybe not, or else someone with wings, or crawling, or an inanimate object. A household robot? No doubt FN, French Norms, I have always been faithful to French Norms, even to my smallest whim.

I am a man of quality, I said aloud, French quality, a creation of national craftsmanship. Not a top-of-the-line product, but not supermarket junk. I am a "cultural exception" in the French sense, except for the fact that there's nothing exceptional about me. Perfectly average. It seems to me the corpse is sitting on the bench and I'm sitting on my ass. I have no other spiritual base but my own bottom, bottomless anyway, ever since I got sick, but that's the base I'm talking from, right? To the walls, to the dead.

I stir thoughts with the pins and needles in my legs. Maybe they're the pins that stir my thoughts. They think in German, like strategists, they hold me very straight in my boots, like Bismarck. But I'm going to take French leave, like the Invisible Man. I may think like a strategist but I still act like a wanderer. I wander standing still. I have this corpse on my hands, it's hard to get away from it. He's a young man and I find him touching. What should I do? Administer first aid? Aid yourself first. Wait for help, some clarification, after which I could kiss this episode goodbye and enjoy the benefits of resilience? This city is dead and inhabited by corpses. Even the leaves of the chestnut trees are dead. The wind growls at the big trees and the rain's teeth are chattering on the surface of the Fontaine des Quatre-Mondes. A leaf falls on my nose, soft and wet, dead. An actual slug coming out of my nose. I'm more or less in the same state of dismayed stupor as the day I was excluded from the Great Competition of Floral Poetry because I shat in my pants before the official jury.

At present, through a shining rain, I am distressed to see a young man next to me on the bench all slumped down with his shoulders hacked to pieces by a machete, and just five minutes ago he was telling me with a smile and flawless teeth about his reasoned ambition to live here in France, the land of welcome—a young, practically French-speaking friendly Rwandan who lived, from what I could glean from his damned gobbledygook, in the dorms of the Cité Universitaire and wanted to give up his studies in Paris. He had met a girl he liked, someone of the same culture and status, and his temporary job as an interpreter for tourists on the Bateaux-Mouches was enough for him to begin integrating into society, while he waited. Waited for what? I said to him. Waited to get old? He had Camus's *The Stranger* in his pocket, that asshole. It's funny. When you read *The Stranger*, you always think you're Meursault, the one who kills, the one who thinks, and never the Arab who dies like an asshole. If I were the general-in-chief of smalltown France I wouldn't have been very proud of myself. A guy asks someone for a cigarette, the other guy's a nonsmoker, so the first guy persists, walks away and comes back with a machete, and hacks the guy to pieces. No comprendo. I hadn't seen the danger coming, I didn't sense that the enemy offensive was coming around the Maginot Line either. But after all, we don't have eyes on our backs. On our backs we have wings, right?

"Yes," she said.

"You're still acting in shitty films?"

"I write books," she said. "I'm the new Virginia Woolf."

I shouldn't have been there in the Closerie des Lilas, a stone's throw from Cochin and the Observatory. Famous writers had come to this brasserie, then their ghosts, finally plaques on the tables in memoriam and finally fat men smoking cigars and skeleton women coughing away.

The last time I saw the woman facing me was twenty years ago and the shitty film was a time in my life, not a masterpiece they show in the cinematheque. I should go back home along rue de la Santé with my eyes closed and lock myself up at my place. Last time, I'd managed to make her laugh with Parisian gossip, that red-haired slut in leopard tights. Maybe I had intrigued her, maybe not. I gave her a hard-on, what else can I say. I had a furious beast between my legs, a famished tiger. She looked like an elegant scarecrow at the time and now like an epileptic mummy. She was always smoking little foul-smelling cigars and she used to laugh loudly but without gaiety or any reason to laugh, aside from me. She drank large quantities of beer. Ten or twenty years ago—the last time—she was already a former dancer, or a former model, and a former American too. She already had an impressive length of service in a whole bunch of fields. She didn't speak French very well and wasn't listening to what I was saying. She didn't want to listen to just anything. She was in a rush to live and now in even more of a rush, in a state of emergency really, except with me. It was as if for ten or twenty years she'd been recharging her battery and I'd emptied mine. I had absolutely no desire to be sitting across the table from her. If I could have chosen a female companion I would rather have chosen a dead woman, or one with Alzheimer's, a mischievous little madwoman, inoffensive, hesitant, stammering, out of it, with gestures and signs of affection from another era. I was not unhappy to have left my cock in the cloakroom. I had nothing under the table that could have given me a hard time; under the table there were only cigarette butts that nobody would have thought of lighting.

I had set foot in a place I shouldn't have, onto the other side of the boulevard. In the space of a hundred yards I'd gone through the 5th and 6th arrondissements, whereas that night I had dreamed that I belonged to the middle middle class, you know, the one people say is neither more nor less. So in that dream I was walking my dog, a ghost dog, without hurrying, and the dog starts pulling on his leash, he crosses through Sainte-Anne from rue d'Alésia to the elevated subway, then he scratches at the little metal door of the prison and he goes sniffing out sickness in the crowded ER of Cochin, as if he's looking for something or someone. Not at all. He's just trying to get rid of me among the crazies, the jailbirds, and the dying. He makes me go through the revolving door of the Closerie des Lilas, pulls me up to a lady with bright red hair and leopard tights, then leaves through the same revolving door and makes me wander out onto rue Campagne-Première, a street Godard used in *Breathless*. He bites the ass of the stone lion on Place Denfert, plunges into the catacombs, and to finish things off, to finish *me* off, he raises his leg on me. I wake up all pissy, sticky, sweaty, in a lukewarm smell that makes your stomach heave and breaks your heart, and makes you cry pissy, sticky floods of tears, it's the smell of chemotherapy embalming you and profaning you while you're still alive, I'm stretched out on a bed in a white room and the dog's not there anymore, he must be sniffing around the Montparnasse cemetery behind the high gray walls, looking for a concession. That's the kind of polytraumatising dream I came in for. But the worst is still to come: A doctor throws me out of the room saying I'm a simulator. Go figure Parisian life!

Sure thing. Everybody's more Parisian than I am. The whole world is Parisian. The Chinese woman who makes little Eiffel Towers in the depths of Shanxi and the illegal Malian who sells them on the sidewalks of Quai Branly, the interpreter of Albert Camus or Jacques Derrida, and the French cancan dancer who raises her leg around Hamburg. Nothing is more Parisian than the *Mona Lisa* and yet she's Italian, that Mona Lisa. My Parisianism isn't worth a damn. I haven't left the 14th arrondissement for ten years, the only one on the Left Bank through which the Seine does not flow.

"You are absurd," the woman writer said to me.

"I am a stranger, a foreigner. I'll never make it back home. Besides, I got an eviction notice."

"So you're not paying for my drink?"

"Not paying for your glass, not screwing your ass, we got no class."

"Fuck off, you asshole, you dickhead, get the hell out of here."

Honorable Exit

Reread this in *Lord Jim* in the bookstore next door:

> *We are only on sufferance here and got to pick our way in cross lights, watching every precious minute and every irremediable step, trusting we shall manage yet to go out decently in the end—but not so sure of it after all—and with dashed little help to expect from those we touch elbows with right and left.*

Less courage than indifference. Does all that really concern me?

"What?" asked the bookseller.

"Me, the eviction officer, the biopsy. What's the use? When my mother died she wasn't in her right mind anymore, but if she had been, what could I have done with her mind?

And my children . . . what the hell do they care about the biopsy, the eviction officer, and me? When China opened its economy to the free market, it led to the biggest exodus from the provinces human history has ever known. Young Indian women work sixteen hours a day in export industries for a salary of fifteen euros a month. In the same month a model or a soccer player makes a million euros."

"Are you buying the book?"

"No, I don't buy anything anymore."

Rue de la Santé

I humbly returned to the 14th arrondissement. As long as I was on boulevard de Port-Royal I was in the sun, broad-shouldered, with my head held high despite the humiliations of my constitution, but the end of rue de la Santé came down on me like a notch in a tomahawk, I turned off into that gorge, Little Big Horn. On my left the good guys, on my right the bad. So it was kind of hard for me not to zigzag, stagger, and go bumping from a wall to a gate, from a sentry to an intercom. Good thing I don't walk by the prison every day, because I can't help going inside to see my son who happens to be housed there through the fortunes of life, and he doesn't like me to come see him all the time in the visiting room looking as if I want to get him out of there. When he sees me he always has that dismayed look he had when he opened his Christmas present under the tree—a nice book, when he was counting on a PlayStation, latest generation.

He knows very well that I don't like knowing he's in there, but he also knows very well I don't like knowing he's somewhere else. In short, I've never known what to do with the big guy since the day he was born. He's a boy who has no problem telling good from evil, but claims that the former is more harmful than the latter, and the promoters of universal good have created more victims than the devotees of dirty tricks. In other words, he says the Crusades, the Inquisition, Communism, and colonialism have been more generously murderous in good faith and in the name of God's law or man's than a handful of rascals fearing neither God nor man.

"Why'd you come here, Dad?"

"I was in the neighborhood, passing by, son."

"You're sick? It's your cancer?"

"Don't worry, boy."

"I'm not worrying, Dad. I'm inquiring, that's all—you're hanging in there."

"I'm holding up, big guy."

"I don't see what hold-up you're talking about, Dad."

"We're talking man to man, son, it does you good."

"The trouble with you, Dad, is that you talk when there's nothing to say, and you don't say anything when I ask questions."

"I don't have all the answers, big guy, you don't get answers just like that."

"You never saw the sunny side of life."

"And you did?"

"I'm going my way, and you've always been in the street. You're the man in the street, Dad, a nobody. Nobody pays any attention to you."

"How do you like it here? Good food?"

"I'm fine here, Dad, nobody can kick me out and nobody wants to take my place."

"You're pretty smart, the way things are now. People lose their jobs, can't pay the rent anymore, their wife cuts out on them, their boys sell drugs and their girls sell their ass, all of them end up homeless, young, old—forty-eight percent of the French are afraid of becoming homeless. You got a cushy place here, don't screw around with me."

"Life isn't rosy every day, Dad. The National Committee on Ethics reports that prison is a place of regression, despair, violence done to oneself, and suicide. The suicide rate is seven times higher than in the general population."

"You know, boy, like I say, it's not exactly all brotherly outside either. Here, at least you're with people of your own kind. It's like in Cochin or Sainte-Anne, or the Ursuline Convent. You see your mother?"

"No."

"Well, I saw her on TV, on a literary show. It seemed to be going good for her: She had nice bright red hair and panther-skin tights. She was testifying about her orgasms, but nothing that could have incriminated me."

"Hey, while you've got your mouth open, you're gonna do me a favor. Not that I want to boss you around, but . . . you know the yellow café further down, right next to the boulevard, at the metro stop?"

"I know it without knowing it, it's not my hangout."

"The waiter there, his name is Willy, ask him for the package I gave him, and stash it away for the time being."

"The time being of what?"

"That's all, Dad, stop your bullshit."

It's amazing how much self-confidence this boy has now. A guy who used to give up his turn on the slide to other kids, I see him walking away, towering over the guards by a head. A kind of sun king. Well, a sun locked away in the shade. But with global warming, maybe that's not such a bad place for it to be for the time being.

"For the time being of what?"

"You can do time without being, dickhead," the guard answered me. "Get the hell out of here, asshole."

Once I'm outside, I stare life in the face and I don't see myself in it and a kind of perplexity takes hold of me, in fact a feeling of melancholy like that twinge of sorrow I used to feel when I dropped off my son, or was it his sister, with the woman who took care of them, a fine woman no doubt, often very easy-going, but certainly perverse.

Come to think of it, I've always abandoned my children. I left them with an inheritance of insecurity; insecurity isn't bad, for someone who likes surprises. One day he'll have his PlayStation. If I had the money I'd buy him one right away, I'd send him a package. But I don't have any money, I don't want any, I don't deserve any. If I wanted money it wouldn't be around here. Here, people not only have everything, they know how to use it too. They even know how to use you. They would even use my boy, if he was of any use whatsoever.

Packing Tape

The prison wall seemed even higher and longer than it had on the way there, or else the sky seemed lower.

It was 1 o'clock when I walked back under the elevated train. The café was crowded, Africans eating pink spaghetti twisted in a heap on their plate like handfuls of complicated neurons. People often think Africans are cheerful, but these were sad. It was only the owner who was merry—a red-haired white woman, with zebra-striped tights—she danced behind the counter. I think she was missing half her teeth but I could only see with one eye because of the smoke. I asked for Willy in a low voice, as if I were coming on to him.

I laboriously explained my business to this Willy, who didn't answer because, as the boss confided to me, he'd had his vocal cords slit in Kigali, in 1994. Willy listened to me, staring straight into my eyes as if I were finally confessing that I was responsible for the massacre of his family and his whole people, as the commander-in-chief of the French army that protected the Hutu militia who murdered 800,000 Tutsis with machetes and screwdrivers. The manager seemed to agree, she wasn't laughing anymore either. Willy disappeared and came back with a package wrapped up with tape. He put the package in a plastic envelope and then in a Nicolas wine-bottle bag. He put it on the bar and again I thought of my boy unwrapping his presents under the Christmas tree. It seemed polite to order a beer and buy one for Willy, but the manager said fuck off, asshole, we've had enough of you.

"Yeah, we had enough of you," Willy echoed. "Fuck off or I'll gut you like a chicken."

I thought my guts had been emptied out already but I didn't get into an argument.

Episode

I went back by crossing through Sainte-Anne. It's a shortcut, and a peaceful walk. You'd think it was a big convent with its tennis courts, archways, statues of men on horseback (or not), a romantic garden, and a decent cafeteria with reasonable prices. My daughter is a performer there sometimes. It took her a long time to find her way. When she was thirteen she became introverted and anorexic and I really thought she would become a nun, but that's when she came back to us with bright red hair and a black mouth, fishnet tights and parachute boots. She was inseparable from her girlfriend Fred who had the same deadly pale gargoyle face tattooed with aggressive devils and pierced from eyebrows to lips with square-headed nails. Which is why, when Fred jumped out of the fourteenth floor across from our apartment, first I thought I saw the two of them together, but I was seeing double at that time anyway. Now I see clearly, I see simply, I see things the way they are. I think my daughter was the one who pushed Fred, the way you push away your evil genius. So my daughter wasn't so crazy, but she was crazy enough to be locked up in an asylum with a room kept for her here for the last five years.

"No such thing as crazy," she said to me last time. "I'm paranoid because of you. I was unable to sublimate my homosexual desire, which you never recognized, into a social drive. You never accepted Frederique as my sister because then your attraction to her would have been incestuous."

"I wasn't her father."

So we sort of had an interesting discussion, I mean it went way beyond the disgusted faces and monosyllabic yells our father-daughter dialogue had been reduced to. At the time she was part of a theater group in her psychiatric hospital. If there had been an audience she would have turned her back on it, and if she'd had a script to recite she would have watched out for spying ears. But there was no script, no audience, just a director, who in fact didn't have a stage. Nonetheless, my daughter had found her way and if some might say it was a dead-end street, what could they say about their own way? I really felt like consoling my daughter and telling her that her little dead-end was finer than the widest highways. I knew where I could find her, she usually hid behind big trees to throw stones at the birds. I don't look anything like a bird and yet when she saw me she screamed and threw a handful of big pebbles. I think she recognized me. At least she recognized a man. A potential rapist: She hates that. That's the way she's been, especially since her nonpsychiatric episode a year ago. She was doing better, she'd gone back to school and even found a temp job as a cashier to pay for it since I was unemployed at the time, but the boss kept telling her she was a dumb jerk and a fat bitch and a fat jerk, all day, behind his mustache, so she quit that job to become a temp prostitute and that disgusted her, that masculine promiscuity, the disrespect for the human person and the assault on feminine dignity.

As for me, I wasn't so brave. I retreated, and when I turned around I couldn't see her anymore, but the tree was shaken and trembling. The tree was going into convulsions and howling dickhead, asshole, get the fuck out of here, go roll in your shit. A psychiatrist took me by the arm, dislocating my shoulder, and I asked him if there were any rooms free. That cracked him up, because they were emptying the mental hospitals to fill the prisons. I thought of the policy of family entry and settlement and I felt like going back home.

I left the walls of the hospital thinking about my father, the general-in-chief of the middle class, who never knew his grandchildren, but always had faith in social progress and the great chain of being. He also used to say you had to get a good education, be equipped for life without killing yourself, and find a nice cushy job in the public sector.

Others

I hadn't done anything to improve my anemia. I didn't even know if I'd had a biopsy in Cochin or a bio-psych in Sainte-Anne. This kind of word problem could torment me, unsettle me to the max. I never should have walked on my head. A bunch of young hoods saw my weakness right away: "You sick, or you dead already? What were you doing with the crazies? Why're you hanging out in front of the prison? Why don't you go home?" They called me a dirty Frenchman; they must have been Arabs or blacks, I have a problem with colors. I said I had indeed passed by the hospital, the convent, the asylum, and the prison, and I'd heard the walls crying, but I hadn't seen anything. There's nothing to see on rue de la Santé. No-where. I could have walked by shop windows, brasseries, and cafés, I still wouldn't have seen anything. There might've been bright lights, they might've been laughing in there, oh yes, but I would've walked on. I'm broke, nothing to sell nothing to give. I'm tired. When I go out I get claustrophobic. Outside not at home. At home's bigger than outside. This city is a dead city the way a language is a dead language. Obsolete. Nothing is alive. People are thinner and thinner. They have the thickness of a light jacket, of spandex tights, jeans with holes in them, or a DVD. I tell these young assholes I can't hear them, I can't see them, I don't even know if they're there every day, dealing, hassling people, waiting while waiting for life to wait for them. Life doesn't wait for anyone. They don't exist. They're sub-shits.

I tell them that because Hassan, the gardner, is behind me with a big pitchfork and he's strict about the rules. He doesn't like to see pre-delinquents smoking in his garden, sleeping on his lawns, or challenging honest passersby.

"You okay?" he asks me.

I don't tell him I'm just out of the hospital, he doesn't give a shit. I tell him I'm okay. He tells me about the garden. I don't give a shit. I wonder what the teenagers are thinking. They're not thinking, they're waiting, they push things out of their way. I don't know what Arabs think either, you never know what they're thinking, they don't think, they pray. Hassan gardens while he prays, maybe he prays while he's gardening. Who knows. I don't know what women think either—they talk, but do they think what they're saying or say what they're thinking? And when they think they don't think about me but about Brad Pitt or George Clooney, I can tell. I don't call that thinking. Anyway, my aggressors aren't black or Arab or young, just morons. You have no idea what morons are thinking. A wild boar, a tiger or a snake, even a mosquito, you can imagine, but a moron? He thinks about himself. He doesn't think of others. I don't think of others either, but at least I try to think for others. I hear the walls crying. I don't piss on prison walls, I don't tag the walls of hospitals. Suddenly I realize I'm in Hassan's arms, like an old fag crying his eyes out. It's the anemia. Seems it dilates the tear ducts. Hassan is extremely embarrassed because he's a modest, reserved man.

"You should go home."

I tell him the kids are blocking my way. He drives them away with the back of his hand, like flies. You'd think he'd done that all his life, driving young assholes away like flies. I know them, he says, they're not really bad. I blurt out that's exactly what I tell my children about wild boars, snakes, and tigers, they're not bad, but that being said, it is not unpleasant to see a fence, a wall, an ocean, and a few virgin forests between them and you.

The teenagers are threatening me behind Hassan's back, they're cursing me out, they're cursing my mother and my children to the seventh generation, they're saying they're going to whip my ass. In their pants they have either fat dicks or huge knives, but it's the same humiliation of my human person.

"Leave him alone, he's crazy in the head," one of them says. "Go finish yourself off," he says to me. "We don't play with dead people."

"Don't listen to them," says Hassan. "They'll play with anything."

Elevator

In the elevator a neighbor, blocked breathing, impenetrable face. He looks at me while looking somewhere else. It's almost like we're turning our backs on each other while forcing ourselves into a merciless face-to-face confrontation. He looks around thirty, with a fresh, pink complexion. Each new generation is an invasion, a recent wave of immigration trying not so much to integrate into society as to disintegrate me. We have nothing to say to each other and we don't say it. Well well, he has a little pimple on his lip, that's normal. One, two, three, four, the floors go by without saying what they're hiding like the walls on rue de la Santé. The neighbor doesn't bat an eyelash. Me neither. I look at the pimple on his lip. Our bodies are close. There is nothing between us. As I say that, I don't know if I mean that nothing separates us or that we have nothing in common between us. I can see his face as if he were an enormous sphinx, or the *Mona Lisa*, every detail, but a huge mystery. I don't particularly believe in the existence of God but the existence of man remains to be proven. A lot of absence in all that. I have an urge to poke his pimple to verify its material existence. The elevator stops at the sixth floor and the neighbor gets out, says goodbye. No smile. Fuck him, that asshole.

Waiting for What?

Home. It's on the last floor; above that, there's the sky. I feel like I'm on vacation here, in transit—away from the world and life. I'm closer to the sky than to the street. The world is locked out. I see the world on TV, it has the consistency of a plasma screen, nice colors, and often there's background music to muddle up the commentary.

I was wrong to go out. Without the French medical-social

system that provides access to free care, I never would have left home, given the price of the scan, the fibro test, the colon test, the ultrasound, and a friendly word of advice.

"You sure took your time," says Sarah. "What'd you do?"

"When? Nothing."

(It's true almost nothing you might as well say little and badly done but after all far away means almost and in a bad way but after all hidden elsewhere or else hidden here crouching inside but disaffected like totally devitalized so this evening nothing more, no thanks, I'm full, a few more steps yes preferably in town without the seasons coming down with the noise and the back of the crowd and the back of the walls and already come back to sleep no doubt or eat to talk a little alone or not watch television and then turn it off and say something always the same thing about finally going to sleep before getting a cold from a window that's not closed well or shade from a tree there outside night pain and fear of giants first then dwarfs and all kinds of flying and crawling insects in great numbers and a foreign language but not more than a hasty translation than the idea you have of it now furtive with cloud and whirlwind so to be grabbed with a certain precaution before making honey from it on the contrary from your surroundings shapes and noise in the house maybe joyfully but still sort of always the same thing joyful toothless that is pretty little might as well say almost nothing next to two bumblebees in the left ear and the right ear and a sty on your eye first and then deafness and glaucoma the next day and stiffness of the hands and feet and the mouth and lights out of love to the disgust with moving and saying the essential minimum not to mention vain naïve pain and fatigue because well all that why again what can you say if not to warn once again about what whoever didn't already happen every day and before days of a

necessary or optional absence or presence for the proper func-
tioning of the troops or the end of hostilities how to know
without foreseeing the ability to worry or despair generating
reactions of joy explosions of hatred but I should be asleep
already gone to or remained asleep here or there in the same
state of a dead or ignorant ignored thing.)

"Nothing? No news is good news. Did you buy some wine
at the Nicolas store?"

"Meursault."

"What's that package wrapped up with tape?"

"It was in my mailbox this morning. It must be the iPod
you ordered on eBay for Chloe's birthday."

"Cool! Did you see my leopardskin tights?"

"You dyed your hair again?"

"Yes, to relax a little. I went to the bank because of that
business of unpaid rent, it's a crazy story."

"It's always a crazy story."

"*We've never been so alone, fused together in the same madness, lost in a world that has the consistency of a fantasy, it worries
us to death.* I read that in a book by Dardenne, I'm going to
write something about it."

"You're lucky you can still write."

(As for me, all I'm good at is waiting for the results of the
biopsy. It's like waiting for a verdict. Ten years, twenty years?
A few weeks? And at the same time I don't give a damn. Nothing I can do about it. The die is cast.)

"Where are the kids?"

"Julien's at his PlayStation and Chloe's sleeping over at
her girlfriend's."

(I have no power over their lives. Here or not here, same
thing. I floundered around all day whereas the street was
straight. I screwed around, I nearly, I don't know what I nearly

did, I nearly did something I didn't do I didn't smile enough, I looked pissed off all day, not what you call an honorable exit.)

"When do you get the results?"

"I don't give a shit."

"Talk louder, I'm in the shower."

Nobody pays attention to me with my dickhead and my asshole. The world turns. Women blossom. China is catching up with the rest of the world. I go out without waiting. Waiting for what?

Closing Time

It's cold, night. Rue d'Alésia, deserted. Shutters closed. Bar-tabac shop lit up. I'm in the café at the very bottom of rue Glacière and rue de la Santé, the light in the jailhouse is diffuse at night, it isn't lit. Walls eat up the blackness of the sky. Anemic streetlights shining very weakly on the barbed wire. The street is full of murders, fits of madness, creeping illnesses, and a whole planned contagion. The threat of an epidemic, gangrene. Dirty tricks. Everything is maintained there, a shadow zone, like a nuclear power plant. You have the feeling something's going to happen, finally.

I'm reading a crime book by Albert Camus. Reading and writing for oneself and not counting on other people is a way of being French, being a zero from A to Z. So I'm reading *The Stranger*. I am that stranger. It's a way of being out of it, being here by chance, in transit.

"Get out of here," the manager says. "We're closing up. You've read enough, dickhead."

"I'm finishing the page, boss."

I took a step, one step, forward. And this time, without

getting up, the Arab drew his knife and held it up to me in the sun. The light shot off the steel and it was like a long flashing blade cutting at my forehead . . . My whole being tensed and I squeezed my hand around the revolver. The trigger gave; I felt the smooth underside of the butt; and there . . . is where it all started.

The light went out, the café closed. Everything closed. I finished living for the day. I'll never know what began.

ABOUT THE CONTRIBUTORS

SALIM BACHI is the Algerian author of *Le Chien d'Ulysse*, *La Kahéna*, and *Tuez-les tous*. *Le Chien d'Ulysse* won the Prix Goncourt for best first novel and *La Kahéna* won the Prix Tropiques in 2004. He has been living in France since 1996.

DIDIER DAENINCKX was born in Saint-Denis, France in 1949. After working for ten years in a printing office, he began to write and created his series hero, Inspector Cadin. He has won many literary awards, including Le Grand Prix de Littérature Policière in 1985 for *Meurtres pour mémoire* and the Paul Féval prize for lifetime accomplishment.

DOA was born in Lyon and worked as a creator of video games in France and London before finally settling into the dark side of literature. He is the author of several highly acclaimed novels, including *Les Fous d'avril*, which won the Prix Agostino in 2005, *La Ligne de sang*, and *Citoyens clandestins*, which won Le Grand Prix de Littérature Policière in 2007.

JÉRÔME LEROY was born in the north of France. Whether writing short stories that are primarily poetic (*La grâce efficace*) or a science-fiction novel (*Big Sister*), Leroy's work is always adventurous, dark, and visionary.

DOMINIQUE MAINARD is the author of the novels *Le grand fakir* (2001) and *Leur histoire*, which won the Prix du Roman FNAC in 2002, the Prix Alain-Fournier in 2003, and was adapted into a film by Alain Corneau in 2005 under the name *Les Mots bleus*.

LAURENT MARTIN was born in Djibouti in 1966. He is an art historian and archeologist. His first novel, *L'Ivresse des dieux*, based on a Greek tragedy, won Le Grand Prix de Littérature Policière in 2003. His subsequent novels include *La tribu des morts*, *Or noir peur blanche*, and *Des rives lointaines*.

AURÉLIEN MASSON was born in 1975 and became an editorial assistant for la Série Noire at Gallimard, one of France's premier publishing houses, in 2002 ; he was promoted to director of the series in 2005.

CHRISTOPHE MERCIER was born in 1960 and has worked as an editor, literary critic, and translator. He published his first book, *Les singes hurleurs sur l'autre rive*, in 2003, then *La cantatrice* in 2005.

PATRICK PÉCHEROT wrote his first novel, *Tiuraï*, at the age of forty-six. He is the author of eight novels, including *Soleil noir*, recently published by la Série Noire, an imprint of Gallimard. He won Le Grand Prix de Littérature Policière in 2002 for *Les brouillards de la butte*.

CHANTAL PELLETIER wrote for theater and film before publishing her first novel, *Eros et Thalasso*, featuring Inspector Maurice Laice. Her subsequent novels include *Le chant du Bouc* and *More Is Less*.

JEAN-BERNARD POUY is a celebrated figure in the French literary landscape and the author of many groundbreaking works of fiction. Born in 1946, Pouy is the creator of the highly acclaimed *Poulpe* series featuring protagonist Gabriel Lecouvreur. His novel *La Belle de Fontenay* won the Trophée 813 and Prix Mystère de la Critique; and *La Clef des mensonges* won the Prix Polar in 1989. He also writes for film and radio.

HERVÉ PRUDON was born in 1950. His novels include *Mardi-gris*, *Le Bourdon*, and *Nadine Mouque*, which won the Prix Louis Guilloux in 1995.

MARC VILLARD has written books revolving around a wide variety of subjects, including dead jazz musicians (*La dame est une traînée*) and redemption for junkies (*La vie d'artiste*). But his talent shines brightest, according to Villard, in his short stories.

Also available from the Akashic Books Noir Series

ROME NOIR
edited by Chiara Stangalino & Maxim Jakubowski
300 pages, trade paperback original, $15.95

Groundbreaking collection of original stories, all translated from Italian.

Brand new stories by: Antonio Scurati, Carlo Lucarelli, Gianrico Carofiglio, Diego De Silva, Giuseppe Genna, Marcello Fois, Cristiana Danila Formetta, Enrico Franceschini, Boosta, and others.

From Stazione Termini, immortalized by Roberto Rossellini's films, to Pier Paolo Pasolini's desolate beach of Ostia, and encompassing famous landmarks and streets, this is the sinister side of the Dolce Vita come to life, a stunning gallery of dark characters, grotesques, and lost souls seeking revenge or redemption in the shadow of the Colosseum, the Spanish Steps, the Vatican, Trastevere, the quiet waters of the Tiber, and Piazza Navona. Rome will never be the same.

ISTANBUL NOIR
edited by Mustafa Ziyalan & Amy Spangler
300 pages, trade paperback original, $15.95

Brand new stories by: Müge İplikçi, Behçet Çelik, İsmail Güzelsoy, Lydia Lunch, Hikmet Hükümenoğlu, Rıza Kıraç, Sadık Yemni, Barış Müstecaplıoğlu, Yasemin Aydınoğlu, Feryal Tilmaç, and others.

Comprised of entirely new stories by some of Turkey's most exciting authors—some still up-and-coming, others well-established and critically acclaimed in their homeland, as well as by a couple of "outsiders" temporarily held hostage in the city's vice—*Istanbul Noir* introduces a whole new breed of talent.

BROOKLYN NOIR
edited by Tim McLoughlin
350 pages, trade paperback original, $15.95
*Winner of Shamus Award, Anthony Award, Robert L. Fish Memorial Award; finalist for Edgar Award, Pushcart Prize.

Brand new stories by: Pete Hamill, Arthur Nersesian, Ellen Miller, Nelson George, Nicole Blackman, Sidney Offit, Ken Bruen, and others.

"*Brooklyn Noir* is such a stunningly perfect combination that you can't believe you haven't read an anthology like this before. But trust me— you haven't. Story after story is a revelation, filled with the requisite sense of place, but also the perfect twists that crime stories demand. The writing is flat-out superb, filled with lines that will sing in your head for a long time to come."
—Laura Lippman, winner of the Edgar, Agatha, and Shamus awards

LOS ANGELES NOIR
edited by Denise Hamilton
360 pages, trade paperback original, $15.95
*A *Los Angeles Times* best seller and winner of an Edgar Award.

Brand new stories by: Michael Connelly, Janet Fitch, Susan Straight, Héctor Tobar, Patt Morrison, Robert Ferrigno, Neal Pollack, Gary Phillips, Christopher Rice, Naomi Hirahara, Jim Pascoe, and others.

"Akashic is making an argument about the universality of noir; it's sort of flattering, really, and *Los Angeles Noir,* arriving at last, is a kaleidoscopic collection filled with the ethos of noir pioneers Raymond Chandler and James M. Cain."
—*Los Angeles Times Book Review*

HAVANA NOIR
edited by Achy Obejas
360 pages, trade paperback original, $15.95

Brand new stories by: Leonardo Padura, Pablo Medina, Carolina García-Aguilera, Ena Lucía Portela, Miguel Mejides, Arnaldo Correa, Alex Abella, Moisés Asís, Lea Aschkenas, and others.

"A remarkable collection . . . Throughout these 18 stories, current and former residents of Havana—some well-known, some previously undiscovered—deliver gritty tales of depravation, depravity, heroic perseverance, revolution, and longing in a city mythical and widely misunderstood." —*Miami Herald*

TRINIDAD NOIR
edited by Lisa Allen-Agostini & Jeanne Mason
340 pages, trade paperback original, $15.95

Brand new stories by: Robert Antoni, Elizabeth Nunez, Lawrence Scott, Oonya Kempadoo, Ramabai Espinet, Shani Mootoo, Kevin Baldeosingh, elisha efua bartels, Tiphanie Yanique, Willi Chen, and others.

"For sheer volume, few—anywhere—can beat [V.S.] Naipaul's prodigious output. But on style, the writers in the Trinidadian canon can meet him eye to eye . . . Trinidad is no one-trick pony, literarily speaking."
—Coeditor Lisa Allen-Agostini in the *New York Times*